Trails of LOVE

The Bradens & Montgomerys
(Pleasant Hill – Oak Falls)

Love in Bloom Series

Melissa Foster

ISBN-10: 1948868032
ISBN-13: 978-1-948868-03-7

Print Edition
V1.0

Cover Design: Elizabeth Mackey Designs

WORLD LITERARY PRESS
PRINTED IN THE UNITED STATES OF AMERICA

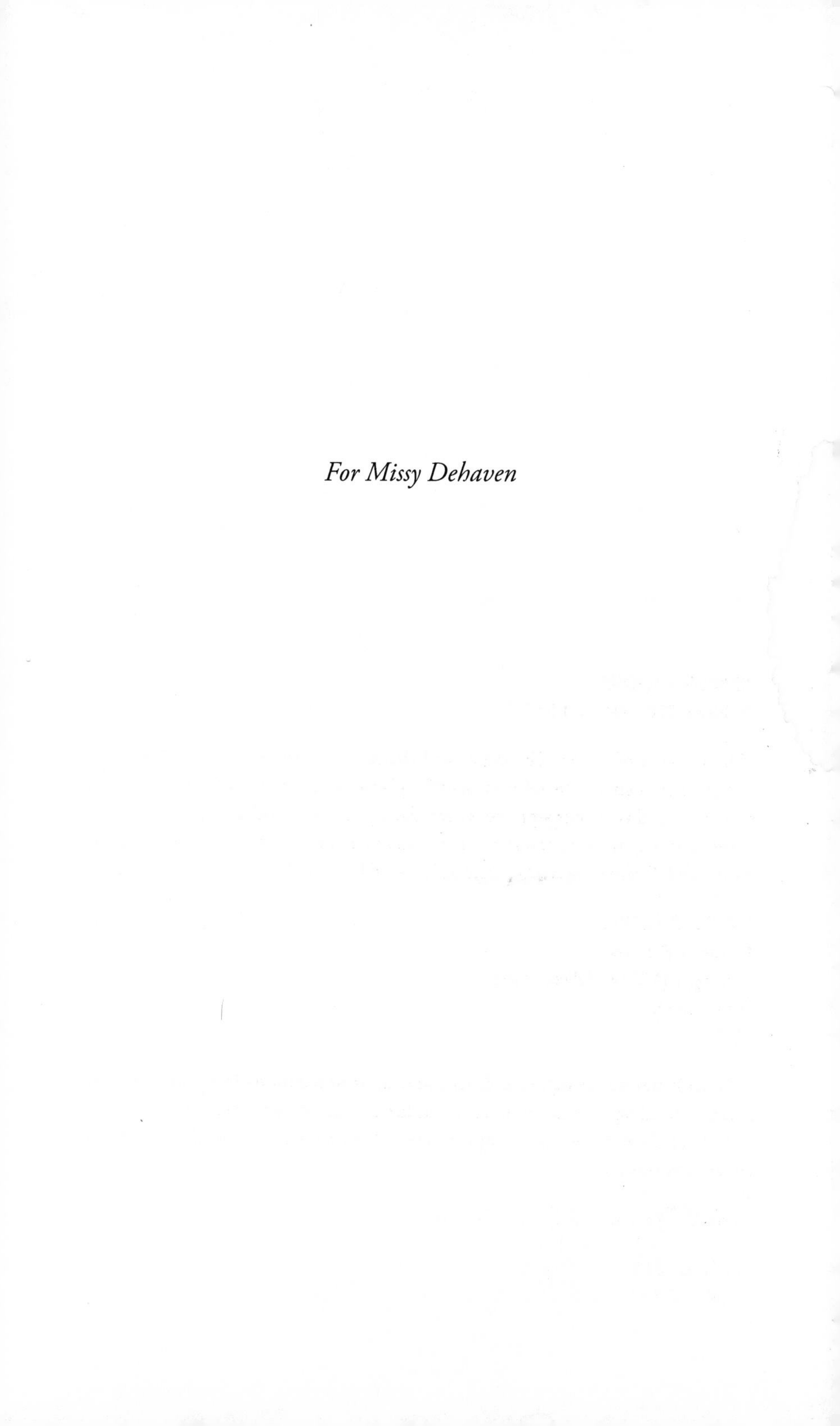

For Missy Dehaven

A Note to Readers

What a joy it is to bring two of my favorite families together! Graham and Morgyn are two truly happy people, and their love story is a hot, hilariously fun ride all the way to their happily ever after. I hope you love them as much as I do. If this is your first Love in Bloom book, all of my love stories are written to stand alone, so dive right in and enjoy the fun, sexy adventure!

The best way to keep up to date with new releases, sales, and exclusive content is to sign up for my newsletter or to download my free app.

www.MelissaFoster.com/news
www.MelissaFoster.com/app

About the Love in Bloom Big-Family Romance Collection

The Bradens & Montgomerys is just one of the series in the Love in Bloom big-family romance collection. Each Love in Bloom book is written to be enjoyed as a stand-alone novel or as part of the larger series, and characters from each series make appearances in future books, so you never miss an engagement, wedding, or birth. A complete list of all series titles is included at the end of this book, along with previews of upcoming publications.

Visit the Love in Bloom Reader Goodies page for free downloadable checklists, family trees, and more!

www.MelissaFoster.com/RG

Chapter One

MUSIC BLARED FROM the enormous amphitheater at the far end of the festival grounds. Musicians had been playing all afternoon despite the rain and wind pummeling the small town—and Morgyn Montgomery's makeshift tent. The summer music festival was one of her favorite overnight events, and it was only about an hour away from her hometown of Oak Falls, Virginia. With five sisters and one brother, there was usually someone willing to camp out with her. But her oldest sister, Grace, was getting married in two days and couldn't see past veils and flowers, and her sister Sable and their younger brother, Axsel, both played in bands that were being featured at the event and would be hanging out with their bandmates. Two of her other sisters hated loud music, so that left her with Brindle, the sister with whom she was closest. Brindle was always up for fun. Unfortunately, she was also about as reliable as a flame in the wind, and at the moment her ass was hanging out of her Daisy Dukes as she collected her things to leave.

"I cannot believe you're ditching me for Trace. *Again.*"

Brindle tossed her wet blond hair over her shoulder and set her hand on her hip with an amused expression. "We're in *Romance*, Virginia, Morg. Don't you think I deserve a little romance?"

"Oh, so now Trace is *romancing* you?" Morgyn laughed. "You might want to grab a shovel on your way out to clear a path through all that bullshit."

Brindle looked across the sea of tents littering the muddy field at her tall, dark, and arrogant on-again off-again boyfriend for the last bazillion years and sighed. "I know, but *look* at him. That cowboy is a walking orgasm, and after delaying my trip to Paris, I think I'm due many rounds of earth-shattering sex."

Shoot. Now Morgyn felt bad.

Brindle was supposed to leave for Paris two weeks ago for a well-deserved vacation, but Grace and her fiancé, Reed, had postponed their wedding because Axsel's schedule had gotten messed up. "Then say that, Brin. Don't give me some crap about romance when we both know you and Trace will never find your way past hot sex to something more meaningful. You're worth so much more than being Trace's fuck buddy."

A wave of emotions passed over Brindle's face too quickly for Morgyn to read, but just as quickly, a smirk settled in. "He's *my* fuck buddy, and trust me, a man like Trace Jericho doesn't need romance..."

She hoisted her backpack over her shoulders as their sister Sable's band, Surge, took the stage, blasting one of Brindle and Morgyn's favorite songs. Brindle took Morgyn's hand and ran out of the tent. The sky opened, and they turned their faces and palms up, catching the rain in their mouths as they danced. They spun and shimmied, splashing in the puddles and laughing like fools. Morgyn was going to miss the heck out of Brindle when she was away.

"You know you love me!" Brindle yelled as the sudden shower turned to spitting rain.

A deep, infectious laugh drew Morgyn's attention. She quickly found the source of it—a shirtless guy strutting across the field with his arm around a long-haired guy. An MIT baseball cap shaded the shirtless guy's dark eyes, and his big, plucky smile did something wicked to her insides. He turned that gorgeous smile on the guy he was walking with and winked. Okay, so maybe he was gay, but *sweet baby Jesus*, who cared? She was allowed to look. It wasn't like she could turn away if she'd wanted to. Her heart thudded hard and fast as she greedily drank in his athletic body. Planes of toned and tanned flesh and a treasure trail that disappeared beneath wet denim, clinging to thick thighs. Oh, how she loved thick-legged men! An army-green duffel was slung crosswise over his broad chest, and he had leather and beaded bracelets around one wrist. Morgyn had a thing for men who wore jewelry, confident men who were comfortable in their own skin.

"Hey! Who are you—" Brindle followed her gaze. "Holy smokes, look at those arms."

"Look at his *legs*." She grabbed Brindle's arm and said, "And that smile…"

Hot MIT Guy turned, and for the briefest of seconds their eyes caught with the impact of metal to magnet. He lifted his brows, and that toe-curling smile widened, lighting up the gray afternoon and causing a flurry of flutters in Morgyn's stomach.

"Wow. Look at you all weak-kneed over a stranger," Brindle said as the crowd swallowed him and Morgyn lost sight of him.

"A possibly *gay* stranger," she mumbled as Trace sauntered over.

Mischief glimmered in her sister's eyes as she whispered, "You could always watch."

Brindle threw her arms around Trace's neck and kissed him.

"Hey, babe." He looked at Morgyn and said, "Nice hat."

She absently touched the umbrella hat she'd bought off some girl earlier. No wonder Hot MIT Guy had been laughing. Hot guys didn't wear umbrella hats. They were too cool for that. She kind of hated *cool*. She had the worst luck with guys. Brindle might not have forever with Trace, but at least she'd found a guy who liked her and accepted her for who she was. Their mother always said Morgyn needed a real man. *A man who's not jealous, doesn't need neat, organized, or conventional, and appreciates your beautiful free spirit.* Morgyn was pretty sure that man didn't exist.

"Hi, Trace. I thought you weren't coming," Morgyn said as he crushed Brindle against him.

"JJ and Beckett dragged me against my will," Trace said.

Morgyn and Brindle had grown up with JJ, one of Trace's brothers, and Beckett Wheeler. Morgyn and Beckett had dated for a while, but they made better friends than significant others.

"Then I saw your sister's fine ass hanging out of those Daisy Dukes, and…" Trace pressed his lips to Brindle's. "She made it all worthwhile."

Brindle gazed longingly up at him.

Her sister was kidding herself if she thought she didn't want more than sex with the cocky cowboy. But Morgyn knew better than to say that. Her sister would deny it until the cows came home. Brindle liked to do what she wanted, with whomever she wanted, and if anyone tried to tell her otherwise, she'd rebel out of the sheer need to prove everyone wrong. She and Sable had that in common, whereas Morgyn might do things her own way, but not out of rebellion. She did what made her happy, which had the odd effect of usually pissing guys off.

"I'll see you back home tomorrow." Brindle looked over her

shoulder as they walked away and yelled, "Try to find some romance! Or at least a good f—"

Trace smothered her words with another kiss, and they stumbled off, smooching like new lovers, when they'd been all over each other for a decade. Their kisses went on and on, and a streak of jealousy zipped through Morgyn. Hot no-strings-attached sex wasn't something Morgyn had ever sought out, but it wasn't looking too bad right now.

She dipped under the canopy and grabbed a beer from her cooler, and then she made her way toward the stage to find her friends. She took the long way, hoping to catch sight of the hot gay guy again, because they didn't make guys like him in her small town. She weaved through masses of poncho-wearing festivalgoers, looking for a gray baseball cap.

"Hey, Morgyn!"

She spun around, catching sight of Gavin Wheeler, Beckett's brother. Last she'd heard, he'd left the big design firm he'd worked for in Boston and had moved to Cape Cod to partner in a smaller company. He was dirty dancing with a blonde she didn't recognize, though he sure looked like he knew her intimately. Or was about to.

"Hey, Gav! I had no idea you were coming!"

"Well, I'm here." He tugged the blonde against him with a dark look in his eyes and said, "And I hope to be *coming* later."

Was everyone going to have sex tonight except her? Morgyn continued making her way through the crowd, dodging dancing bodies and skirting tents and puddles. Her boots were full of rainwater, sloshing with every step. She hadn't checked the weather before leaving for the festival. Luckily, she had a pair of gently used bright red rain boots she'd embellished with colorful jewels and silver bangles and bells to sell in her eclectic clothing store. They were two sizes too big, but they were better than the sandals she'd worn, even if her feet were currently swimming in an ocean of water.

She squeezed between a painfully skinny woman and two heavyset guys, stopped to pet a curly haired black puppy who got muddy paw prints all over her while giving her sloppy kisses, and joined a group of people dancing to country songs, before making her way to a storage container that backed up to a fence. She set her beer on the top and hoisted herself up to empty the water from her boots. She plopped down on her butt, watching her sister strut across the stage. Even trapped by her ever-present cowgirl hat, Sable's dark hair billowed wild and thick over her shoulders as she played her guitar and belted out the lyrics. Morgyn swayed to the beat as people traipsed by. She tugged off one boot, then dumped the water over the fence behind her.

"What the…?"

Morgyn scrambled up on her knees and peered over the fence, meeting the angry, and insanely sexy, eyes of Hot MIT Guy, standing with his pants unbuttoned and his cock in his hand. "Oh gosh! I'm so sorry!" She tried to look away, but her eyes were glued to him—or rather, to his eye-poppingly thick male body part.

"Sunshine…" He laughed, but it wasn't the loud, infectious laughter that had first caught her attention. This laugh was a low rumble that made her insides grow hot.

"Um…" *Look away. God, look away already. Sunshine?* She forced her eyes up to his, and he arched a brow, amusement replacing his initial annoyance. "I'm sorry! I didn't mean to…"

"I can hold it out as long as you'd like, blondie."

Her jaw dropped, which earned the infectious laughter she remembered. His long-haired boyfriend, who was also quite stunning, appeared out of nowhere, giving the other guy a curious glance.

"I'm sorry!" she said to the long-haired dude as Hot MIT Guy tucked himself back into his jeans. "I just dumped water all over your boyfriend."

Silence fell between them, and then they both burst into hysterics.

"I'm not sure how that explains his massive cock in his hand," the long-haired guy said as he draped an arm around Hot MIT Guy, pulling him closer and waggling his brows. "But damn, dude. Now I'm going to have to get you out of those wet pants, aren't I?"

"Lucky" slipped out before she could stop it. She slapped her hand over her mouth and spun around, scrambling to tug on her boot. She tried not to listen to the muffled whispers but was unable to help herself. *From behind...hard...wet...Brace your foot here.*

Festival sex was everywhere, but she did *not* want to listen to those two hot guys going at it! She stilled. *Or maybe...*

No! Geez! Brindle must be getting to me.

She dumped the water from her other boot *beside* the storage container and heard a *grunt*. The fence shook, and her pulse sprinted. She slammed her eyes shut, as if it would block out the noise, and tugged on her boot. In the next second Hot MIT Guy was scaling the fence. She snagged her beer as he plopped down beside her—*God, he is gorgeous. And fast.* His boyfriend landed with a *thud* on her other side.

"WHY SO SHY, sunshine?" *Damn,* she was even more radiant up close. Graham had wanted to stop and talk to the gorgeous blonde when he'd first seen her dancing in those funky boots, with that silly hat on her head, like she couldn't care less about what anyone thought. She was so beautiful, she took his breath away. But his goddamn brother had wanted to chase down a friend, who, it turned out, had already left the festival.

"I'm not shy, but I didn't mean to interrupt your..." Her blue eyes flickered curiously between Graham and Zev. "Time together."

Zev put an arm over her shoulder, speaking loudly to be heard over the band. "Nonsense, three is always better than two."

Graham glowered at him and swatted his arm from around her shoulder. "I was taking a piss," he explained. "I'm Graham. This is my jackass brother, Zev. Both straight, and if I *were* gay, I'd have better taste than this guy."

"Brothers?" Her eyes moved between them again, and she laughed. The melodic sound carried in the air. "Okay, that's *totally* hilarious, because it sounded like you two were um...I mean, I heard a grunt, and I thought..."

"You thought I was taking him to town?" Zev waggled his brows.

"Who says you'd be taking *me* anywhere?" Graham cleared his throat and said, "I'd be the dominant one—"

"Are you two seriously arguing over this? Boy, you're definitely brothers. I've got a pack of sisters, and you sound just like us."

Zev had that look in his eyes. "Any of them single and hot?"

"*Jesus.*" Graham shook his head. "Real smooth, Zev."

She laughed. "It's okay. You have no idea how often I'm

asked that. Yes, I have several single, *hot* sisters, and you'd scare the hell out of all of them except Sable, who's rockin' out onstage right now. She's the lead guitarist and singer in Surge."

"No shit?" Zev glanced up at the stage. "Man, not only is she hot, but she's got strong, talented hands," he said lasciviously. Then he looked at Morgyn, who was laughing, and said, "No, seriously, I love their music. She's awesome."

"That she is," she said. "And my brother, Axsel, is the lead guitarist for Inferno. Too bad you're not gay. Axsel would dig your long hair."

The no-thank-you look on Zev's face was almost comical.

She slid a darker look to Graham and said, "And Sable would be all over you."

"Hey, what does he have that I don't?" Zev asked.

Graham stared down his brother and said, "*Class*, bro."

"I've got class," Zev said. "Chicks dig me."

"I'm sure they do. You're fun and you're definitely hot," she said. "And you've got this playboy vibe going on that my sister Brindle would go apeshit over."

Zev lifted his chin proudly in Graham's direction; then he took the beer from the blond beauty's hand and said, "You mind?"

"Go for it," she said, and he lifted it to his lips. "You're what my sisters and I call *foreplay*."

Zev spit out his beer, and Graham cracked up. *This chick is wild.*

"Foreplay? What the hell? Just for that I'm finishing your beer." He guzzled the rest, then said, "What does that even mean?"

"You know, the guy girls hook up with but don't really want anything long-term from. Foreplay for real boyfriends."

Graham couldn't suppress his laughter. "*Foreplay.* Great nickname for you, bro."

"Fuck that. What does that make *him*?" Zev thrust the bottle in Graham's direction. "He hasn't had any longer relationships than I have."

She studied Graham for so long, he wondered what was going on in that beautiful head of hers. She pushed to her feet and said, "I'm not sure, but maybe *mine for tonight.*"

He wasn't a one-night stand kind of guy, but this carefree beauty who smelled like sweet summer rain and wasn't afraid to bust his brother's balls just might change that.

She grabbed their hands, pulling them both up beside her on top of the container. "Dance with me."

"Not my thing, sweetheart." Zev leapt to the ground.

She glanced at Graham and said, "Looks like you're the dominant one after all."

"Damn right I am." *Beautiful and sassy.* Man, he loved that. Women usually went crazy for Zev with his long hair and wily personality. He was glad *she* wasn't one of those women.

Zev scoffed. "Good luck getting this guy to dance on that thing without first doing a complete risk assessment."

Graham ground his teeth together. *Jackass.* "You going somewhere?"

"Making my way to the stage to prove my sexual powers." Zev winked and said, "Nice to meet you, sunshine. I'm sure your sister will tell you how incredible I was tomorrow."

"Good luck," she said.

"Find me before you take off for the airport," Graham hollered after him. Zev waved, making a beeline toward the stage.

"He's leaving town?" she asked.

"Yeah. He travels a lot. All kidding aside, he's a great guy.

Bigmouthed and cocky as hell, but a good man. And you, sunshine, you're something else."

"*Hard to define.* I know. I hear it all the time. But I'm not going to apologize for who I am."

"Apologize?" Was she kidding? She had a great personality and she was gorgeous, from her golden hair and tanned shoulders—which begged to be kissed—to her sexy figure, funky boots, and crazy hat. "I think you're fantastic."

Curiosity rose in her eyes. She wrinkled her nose, which made her even cuter. "You're just trying to distract me because you don't dance, right? Just for the record, I'm not a sure thing. I only said that because I couldn't think of a better comeback."

"You want to dance?" He swept an arm around her waist, drawing her closer, and said, "There's nothing I won't do, *after* you tell me your name."

She smiled, brightening everything around them as she said, "Morgyn."

"Morgyn. *Beautiful.*" He loved the way her name rolled off his tongue. "How about if we dance on the grass so you don't slip and hurt yourself?"

She stepped from his grasp and twirled in a circle, giving him a gorgeous view of all her curves, and then she grinned as if she'd proven her point.

He looked down at her boots, unconvinced.

"Zev was right. You are totally assessing the risk of dancing up here, aren't you?"

"Maybe," he admitted, because he was a lousy liar. "But only because the idea of you getting hurt and us missing out on spending the next few hours together sucks—and because those boots look about three sizes too big."

"Two sizes." She grabbed his arm, steadying herself as she

tugged off her boots. "I forgot to check the weather, so I came in sandals." She set her boots on the edge of the storage container.

"You didn't check the weather? Are you staying overnight? Do you have a tent?"

"Of course! And no, Mr. Prepared, I did not check the weather. Where's the fun in that? I had those boots in my van, and they work fine other than filling with water when it poured." She peeled off her umbrella hat and shook out her hair. Long blond tendrils tumbled around her face, making her blue eyes stand out even more. She shouted to a woman walking by, "Hey! Need a rain hat?"

The woman shrugged. "Sure!"

Morgyn clutched Graham's hand and leaned over the edge to give it to her. Her dress crept up the backs of her legs, barely covering her ass. She didn't seem to notice or care as she popped upright, looking sexy as sin and carefree as the wind.

"You might need that hat later," he pointed out.

"And you *think* too much." She waved her hand dismissively. "I'll just borrow yours."

"I'd build you a shelter before I'd part with my lucky hat, sunshine."

She made a pouty face that was freaking adorable, and then her eyes narrowed and she crossed her arms, studying him. "What's so special about that hat?"

"You want my secrets? You've got to give me some of yours." The hat had been his father's, and it had always brought Graham luck. He wasn't about to tell her that he'd never met a woman he wanted a long-term relationship with, and until that happened, his lucky hat would remain solely in his possession.

"I don't have secrets, so you can keep yours." She leaned

closer and, lifting the strap of his green duffel bag over his head, said, "Ready to live dangerously, Mr. Risk Assessor?"

He tossed his duffel to the ground as she began shimmying and swaying to the beat of the country song, her eyes locked on him, and in that moment, he didn't give a rat's ass about his hat. When the beat quickened, she kept pace, dancing with seductive confidence, like she was born with rhythm in her blood. Her allure was too strong to resist, and he began moving without thought. As an engineer and an investor, he did careful research, planning, and execution for everything he did, and that carried over to the extreme sports he took part in. Doing anything without thought was a first for him, but he wasn't about to fight it because *Sunshine* was watching him like she wanted to disappear into him, and he sure as hell wanted to disappear into her.

He swept an arm around her, drawing her against him again, and her eyes flamed, but there was no hint of a blush on her cheeks. A bolt of heat shot through him. There was nothing sexier than a confident woman.

He put his mouth beside her ear as he said, "For your information, I *thrive* on danger."

Chapter Two

"DAMN, CRACKER, YOU *do* have moves," Morgyn said as Graham's powerful hips swung and thrust in perfect sync with hers. They'd danced to several songs, and even though there were gorgeous, half-dressed women everywhere, his attention never wavered.

He flashed that addicting smile that made her stomach summersault. "*Cracker?*"

"Graham cracker...?"

He laughed, and as she'd noticed earlier, the sexiest dimples appeared, softening the inherent strength in his face. The guy had a serious *presence*, the kind that made a person want to hear what he had to say. He wasn't authoritative, because he didn't come across demanding or commanding, but the confidence he exuded was made even stronger by the cut of his jaw, his broad shoulders, and eyes that didn't just see her, but seemed to *read* her.

"You're a trip, sunshine. I haven't heard *cracker* since about grade school. You haven't even seen my best moves yet."

His gaze rolled over her face as they danced, like the answers to whatever questions he had were written in her skin.

"Just ask," she said as the sun broke through the late-afternoon clouds. She tipped her face up to soak in its warmth and felt his arms come around her.

"I'm just wondering why a beautiful, outgoing woman like you is here alone."

"You think I'm beautiful?" she said just to make him laugh, which he did. "What makes you think I'm here alone?"

The song ended, but they didn't stop dancing. She liked being in his arms, watching the gears of his mind churning behind that devilish grin.

"You didn't run off when you caught me behind the fence, or when Zev propositioned you with a threesome." He held her tighter, and she felt that particular body part she'd spied earlier pressing against her. "And you're still dancing with me. Usually women have friends who save them from guys like me."

Honesty. She liked that. "I came with my sister, but she blew me off for a guy. I have other friends here somewhere, but I'm a big girl. I don't need saving. Although now I'm curious about just what kind of guy you are that you think I might need rescuing. Because I have to tell you, your aura tells me you're safe, while Zev's told me to tread carefully."

His brow wrinkled. "You believe in that stuff?"

"Absolutely, but I'm not surprised if you don't. Risk calculation and ethereal things don't seem to go together very well." She'd found that out firsthand when she'd dated Beckett. He'd wanted to change so much about her, starting with the way she did business. She expected Graham to ease his hold like most guys did when they realized she wasn't the conventional thinker they were used to.

He tightened his grip, slow dancing to the new fast song the band was playing and said, "Enlighten me. Tell me what you see."

"Shades of blue and red mostly," she said.

"Not *gray*?" he asked with a smirk.

She shook her head. "Oh no, that's a low-energy, depressing color. No, cracker, you resonate inner peace, a quiet calmness and seriousness, and a strong sense of purpose."

He arched a brow, and she realized what he'd meant.

"Oh, you meant..." She laughed. "The primal urges you're trapping behind that cautious exterior? That's the *red* in you, not *gray*."

"Ah, that writer got it all wrong, I guess." His eyes went serious again and he said, "You can see all that from looking at me? Because I think you missed a few things."

He was clearly a thinker, no matter how much he claimed to thrive on danger. She was usually the opposite. Morgyn rarely took the time to think things through, but she found herself slowing down, wanting to figure him out.

"Like your connection to the earth?" she asked. "I get the feeling that you're not a guy who can be trapped in an office. I bet you have a passion for living life to the fullest and succeeding in everything you do, but cautiously. Like Zev alluded to, assessing risks before jumping in to adventures."

"Hm..." His gaze drifted around them for the first time since they'd met, and when his eyes found her again, they were even more intense. "If I'm mostly blue and red, what are you, sunshine?"

"You must already know, because of what you call me."

He cocked his head, and then a slow grin spread across his handsome face. "Yellow?"

"Yes, and I think we share that, actually. You have a touch of orange-yellow, which means you're creative and intelligent, but scientific and a bit of a perfectionist, while I'm more of a pale yellow. I'm an optimist, spiritually aware, and I'm definitely *not* a perfectionist. I usually act before I think, and I *love* exploring new ideas."

His gaze smoldered. "I do love *exploring*," he said in a low voice as his hands slid down her hips.

His hands were big and strong. Her mind traveled to his other *big* body part.

Oh boy.

Now her insides were humming.

She focused on the music, getting into the rhythm, the sound of the singer—who *wasn't* Sable. Had they been dancing long enough for the band to change? Had she been so lost in him she'd missed the break in the music?

They bumped and ground on their own tiny stage, surrounded by hundreds of people who were talking, dancing, laughing, and doing God only knew what else. Graham's eyes took on a seductive haze, and the sights and other sounds were drowned out by the electricity buzzing between them.

Your eyes have superpowers. Morgyn was sure of it because she had a hell of a time trying to look away from them. They were serious and sharp, everything she didn't consider herself to be. She was smart and she took her life seriously, but she didn't consider herself a serious or sharp *person*. She floated through her days taking everything in, seeing possibilities everywhere, and not stressing over the little things. Like the fact that she had to decide what to do about the rent increase on her shop and how she was going to manage it. But that was a worry for another day, not something to stress over when she was at her favorite festival, dancing with this handsome creature.

The longer she and Graham danced, the more intensely his rough hands moved over her skin and his eyes bored into her, bringing all sorts of naughty possibilities to mind. The kind of possibilities that Brindle and Sable would jump on, Grace would *secretly* take advantage of, and her most careful sisters, Pepper and Amber, would pretend didn't exist. The kind of sinful possibilities Morgyn wanted to explore but was a little afraid to, because doing so could lead to wanting more, and that never worked out well for her. But his tempting lips were *right there*. She wasn't laden with inhibitions, and she didn't have sexual hang-ups or a painful past to overcome, but this…Whatever this was—desire, lust, intrigue, something deeper—was *molecular*. It pulsed inside her, expanding and multiplying, filling her with a force she'd never imagined.

His eyes sought approval, and she arched into him. She *wanted* to kiss him, to give in to the pull inside her and experience all his pent-up passion firsthand. But she didn't need to feel the weight of desiring more and not having a chance at it. Maybe if he was a guy she wanted *only* to kiss, but she liked the man she was getting to know. He stirred emotions in her that made her want to slow down and think. She wanted to know more about him, and not to be remembered only as *that girl at the festival*. The festival noises came back into focus, clearing the lust from her brain enough for her to try to say what she was feeling, but all that came out was "Funnel cake."

Confusion riddled his brow, but his kissable lips tipped up again, giving her a peek at his sexy dimples, which felt like secrets even though everyone else could see them. "Funnel cake?"

"Uh-huh." She shoved her feet into her boots and jumped off the container.

He climbed down after her, mumbling, "Funnel cake…"

"Come on, cracker. I need it." She grabbed his arm as he

put the strap of his bag across his chest again and dragged him around tents and people, toward the funnel cake truck.

"Funnel cake? You actually eat that stuff?"

She looked at him like he'd lost his mind. "It's the food of festival goddesses everywhere."

"Festival goddesses? I guess I've got a lot to learn about festivals."

A guy stumbled out of a tent, nearly barreling into Morgyn. Graham tugged her against him, glowering at the guy. He settled his arm around her, keeping her close as they weaved through the crowds and got in line for funnel cake. He was looking at her with that curious expression again.

"What?" she asked. "Are you a nuts and twigs type of guy?"

"Aren't all guys? That's how God made us. Well, nuts and tree trunks..."

"Ha-ha." Great. Now she was thinking about *that* again. "You know what I mean. What's your go-to festival food?"

He waggled his brows.

"Seriously?" She pushed out from beneath his arm and said, "Are you one of those guys who comes to festivals just to hook up?"

He put that strong arm around her again and hauled her against him. "No, sunshine. I'm the kind of guy who'll take any reason to hang out with his family. I told you Zev travels a lot. He's leaving tonight for several weeks. He convinced me to come to the festival."

"You asked about the color gray, and I see a muddy or dirty gray in Zev, which doesn't mean what you think. It means he's blocking energies, overly guarded, despite his effervescent personality. That's why I think he's *foreplay*. It wouldn't matter which woman he was with; he's not open to that kind of long-term energy. I don't see that in you."

His face grew serious again. "I guess there is some truth to how you read people. He's had a tough time."

"What do you mean *tough*?"

"He carries guilt for something he shouldn't."

"Oh. I'm sorry. All that energy he throws out is probably to cover it up."

Graham nodded as the line inched forward. "So, intuitive one. Why are *you* here? Are festival goddesses like tour groupies?"

"Probably, but not me. I love festivals, but this is my favorite. It's been going on for like a hundred years. My grandparents met at this festival, and they were together from that day on."

"Really? That's great. Do they ever come anymore?"

"Unfortunately, we lost my grandma when I was little, but my grandfather brought us until he passed away when I was thirteen." She touched her necklace, thinking of her grandfather. "My parents brought us after that, until my oldest sister got her driver's license. She took us once and swore never again. I guess we drove her mad, because she was thrilled when Sable got her license. By then only me, Sable, Brindle—the sister who ditched me today—and Axsel went to the festival, because my other sisters decided they didn't need the craziness."

"I can't believe you have a family almost as big as mine. No wonder you're not afraid to talk smack with Zev."

"Comes with big-family territory."

They bought one funnel cake to share, and Graham handed the plate to Morgyn. "Can you hold this for a sec? I've got a tarp and a towel in my bag. We can sit and listen to the band while we eat."

"You carry a *tarp*?" She stifled a laugh as he spread it out.

"You must have been a Boy Scout."

"Eagle Scout," he said with a smirk as he spread the towel over the tarp.

"What else do you have in that bag?"

"Still begging for secrets?" he said with a cocky smile. "Come on, sunshine. Sit with me."

"I'll get your towel wet. Oh, that probably doesn't matter. I bet you have a portable, battery-powered clothes dryer in your bag, too."

He sat down and pulled her down beside him. "Smart-ass."

"Thanks. I try." She tugged off her boots and set them beside the tarp.

He glanced at her painted toenails—purple with little white daisies. "Did you do that?"

"Mm-hm." She wiggled her toes. "I hate plain toenails. They're like little wasted canvases."

"You're talented."

"Hardly, but they make me happy." She inhaled the sweet aroma of the funnel cake. "Mm. Look at it. Isn't it beautiful?"

He glanced at the twisted fried batter and powdered sugar piled high on their plate and arched a brow.

"Oh, come on, cracker. *Really?* A scrutinizing guy like you doesn't see the intricacies that make this beautiful?" She gazed down at the plate between them. "*Look* at it. Every funnel cake is unique, which I think is beautiful in and of itself. All those different twists and curls, powdered sugar landing wherever the air takes it? It's art on a plate. And it tastes delicious, which makes it even more special."

She lifted her gaze and found him watching her with an intense expression. "Sorry. I'm waxing poetic about fried dough. My family teases me because I see the world differently than most people. I can't help it. My grandfather was the same way. He worked on the railroad, and he was also crafty. He made beautiful pieces of furniture, art, and accessories out of other people's discarded items, which I know sounds like something a hobo might do, but he brought so much joy to people. He helped me appreciate every little thing."

Graham's eyes filled with a curious, deep longing. Without a word, he reached up and ran his fingers down her cheek, light as a feather. "You're something else, sunshine."

Despite the intimate touch, which made her insides turn to liquid, she thought he was teasing her. "I know you're going to say I'm *out there*, or *flighty*, or—"

"Spectacular," he said firmly, eyes serious again.

She swallowed hard.

"Your grandfather sounds like a special man. I'm sorry you lost him."

"Thank you," she said softly. "He was special."

He broke off a piece of the funnel cake and held it up to her lips, a small smile on his face. She opened her mouth, and he fed it to her. His eyes were riveted to her mouth as she ate, making her acutely aware of every move she made. When she licked the powder from her lips, he licked his lips as if he were tasting hers.

"Good?" he asked.

She answered with a nod, for fear of her voice failing her. She broke off another piece and held it up for him. He opened his mouth, then closed it around her fingertips. Her heart raced as she slipped her fingers from his lips and he kissed the tips of them.

"Even sweeter than I imagined." His eyes drilled into her as he broke off another piece and fed it to her. "What do you do for a living, Morgyn?"

How was she supposed to talk with him looking at her like he wanted to devour her?

"Um, I do a few things. I own a boutique called Life Reimagined, where I sell clothing, jewelry, accessories, and odds and ends that I make from gently used items."

He ate a piece of the funnel cake. A hint of his dimples appeared as he chewed. She figured out why those dimples affected her so deeply. He was seriously strong and sexy, which turned her on in a visceral, touch-me-please way, but those dimples were as adorable as a puppy, which made her want to cuddle up with him. The coalescing of the two was new and unfamiliar and had her completely swept up in him.

"Like your grandfather," he said, bringing her back to the moment.

She realized the music had stopped and the bands were changing again. "Yes, like him. I also make teas and herbal remedies."

"That's fascinating. I'd like to see your shop while I'm in town."

"You're not from around here? I just assumed…"

"I'm from a little town called Pleasant Hill in Maryland."

"Really? My friend Trixie goes there all the time to work with another ranch owner. Geez, small world." Trixie was Trace's sister. She and Trace helped run her family's ranch.

"It's about to get even smaller," he said with a surprised expression. "I assume you mean Trixie Jericho? How many Trixies can there be who travel between Maryland and Virginia? She works with my brother Nick, who owns the ranch."

"Six degrees of separation." She didn't know why that comforted her other than the fact that Trixie often talked about how great—*and ornery*—Nick was and how much she liked his family. Trixie liked ornery guys. Morgyn, on the other hand, had no interest in ornery, but she sure liked the man standing before her.

"Life Reimagined. I'll look it up."

"It's not big or fancy or anything."

"Fancy is worthless, unless your business is built on elegance or luxury, like a resort. Who's running it while you're here?"

"I closed it for the weekend. And don't think just because I work when I feel like it and I don't follow trends that I'm airheaded or *flighty*. I take my life seriously. If I'm anything, I'm *floaty*."

He smiled. "Floaty?"

"Yeah, you know, I sort of drift through this beautiful life, taking it all in and not stressing over little things. Or big things, really. I don't see a reason to get all wigged out because something isn't working right. It'll either get fixed or it won't."

He nodded, brows dipping like he was trying to make sense of that. "*Floaty*. I like that description. Did you make those boots? Is that why they were in your van?"

"Yes, and I know they're a little loud, but that makes them extra fun."

"They're different, but so are you. How do you decide what to make?"

"I don't know. Inspiration is funny. When it hits, I usually have no idea where it came from. I don't analyze *why* I do what I do, but I only create things that make me happy, and I love breathing new life into the old *and* the new. I see possibilities in everything from furniture and clothing to people and places, and I want to chase down those possibilities and bring things to life in a different way. Brighter, happier, more colorful. Nothing is exempt from my calling to change it up."

"How would you change *me* up?"

I'd like to strip you down, but… "From what I've seen, you don't need changing."

"Oh, come on," he said with a tease in his eyes. "No bedazzling my hat? Adding rhinestones to my boots?"

"Your lucky hat?" She gasped dramatically. "And risk being beheaded? I wouldn't think of it."

"Good point. The punishment would be quite severe. I wouldn't go as far as beheading, but a spanking might be in order."

He winked and the temperature rose by about a zillion degrees. Then he broke off another piece of funnel cake and held it up for her.

"I've never been *fed* before," she admitted.

"Sorry." He lowered his hand. "I got carried away."

"I like it. It's kind of romantic being here with you as the evening rolls in, while life goes on all around us." She realized what she'd said and quickly added, "Not that we're…that you're…like *that*."

SHE WAS CUTE when she backpedaled, but she'd have to be a robot not to feel the chemistry thrumming between them—and this passionate woman who followed her heart and walked in her grandfather's footsteps was no robot.

"Aren't we *exactly* like that?" he said, and then he fed her the funnel cake.

He could watch her eat all day long. Pleasure rose in her

eyes the way passion had inhabited them moments ago when she was describing her work. She held his gaze, darker passions pushing that innocent pleasure aside as she swallowed and her tongue slid seductively across her lips, leaving them glistening and painfully tempting. He leaned forward to wipe powdered sugar from the corner of her mouth, and her breathing shallowed and her eyes took on an even more *wanting* look. For the second time in the last few hours, he didn't think, didn't weigh the consequences, as he cupped her cheek and licked the powder from her lips. Her breathing hitched and her eyes closed as he lowered his mouth toward hers.

"Seduction by funnel cake. I should have thought of that."

Zev. Instead of enjoying the warm press of Morgyn's lips, an incredulous laugh fell from Graham's. Morgyn's eyes flew open, meeting the curious—and protective—eyes of Zev, Sable, and Axsel, whom Graham recognized from the bands.

Sable's jeans-clad hip jutted out. "Well, lookie what we have here." She folded her arms across her chest, amusement playing in her eyes. "Did our sweet little Morgyn pick up a man?"

The ends of Axsel's dark hair poked out from beneath a knit cap, which he wore in almost all the photos Graham had seen of the band. He had kind hazel eyes, and they were currently raking down the length of Graham's body as he said, "He's definitely *all man* from where I'm standing."

"Oh my gosh, you guys!" Morgyn pushed to her feet, and Graham rose beside her, stifling a chuckle. "Graham, this is my sister Sable and my brother, Axsel. You guys, this is Graham…um…?" She turned a curious look to him.

"*Braden,*" he said, and offered his hand to Sable. "Nice to meet you. I see you've already met my brother Zev."

Sable glanced at Zev, who winked. "Foreplay? Yeah, we

met."

"Jesus, you too?" Zev shook his head.

"Relax, dude," Axsel said as he shook Graham's hand. "Sable loves foreplay."

Zev draped an arm over Sable's shoulder with a hopeful look. She shrugged him off and said, "Not happening, hot stuff."

"You'll change your mind," Zev said. "Who's up for a drink and a little dancing before I take off?"

Graham glanced at Morgyn. "What do you say, sunshine?"

"She's coming." Sable narrowed her eyes and said, "And not the way you think."

Graham knew Sable was just being protective, but Morgyn looked annoyed, and she sure as hell didn't need to be treated like a kid. He put a hand on Morgyn's back and said, "Choice is yours, sunshine. You lead, I'll follow."

A look of sheer appreciation smiled back at him. "It's okay. We should go or her claws will come out."

"I prefer *talons*," Sable said with a heavy dose of snark.

Morgyn shot Sable a rebellious glare, then ripped off a hunk of funnel cake, put it in Graham's mouth, and immediately pressed her lips to his in a sugary, stake-her-independence kiss—and he fucking loved it.

She flashed a satisfied smile. "I want to stop by the bathroom and then get out of my wet clothes." Morgyn said it so innocently it came across wickedly hot, and by the look on Sable's face, Graham wasn't the only one who interpreted it that way. "We'll catch up with you guys…but where?"

"My trailer," Axsel said. "Come on, Zev. I'll introduce you to some of my groupies." He grabbed Sable by the arm and dragged her away.

"As long as they're not dudes," Zev said.

Axsel snort-laughed. "Nah. You're not man enough for that."

The first blush of the day stained Morgyn's cheeks as she put on her boots and Graham gathered his belongings. "Sorry. I mean, I'm not sorry about the kiss, but sometimes Sable grates on my last nerve."

"She's just a little overprotective of her younger sister. I get it. I have four older brothers and an older sister. They're all protective of me, and I'm just as protective of them. It's called family, and it's a good thing."

"Then I could do with a little *less* of a good thing."

He put his arm around her, keeping her close as they headed back toward the tents. "Well, I have no intention of giving you less of a good thing, so if that's what you're looking for, you've got the wrong guy. And that kiss, as sweet as it was, *wasn't* our first kiss. That was just you marking your territory."

"Oh yeah?" She bumped him with her hip. "Why is that?"

"Because you're still standing."

She looked up at him as they gave two dancing girls a wide berth and said, "So you think when you kiss me the first time, I'll sleep with you?"

"No, sunshine." He leaned down and whispered in her ear, "When I kiss you for the first time, you'll *wish* I'd sleep with you."

Chapter Three

EVEN AS THEY jumped over puddles, walked around groups of people, and slowed to greet a few cute pups, Morgyn's mind spun. *You'll wish I'd sleep with you. Did he really say that?* She stole a glance at Graham, and the coy look he gave her confirmed it.

Holy smokes.

Usually when guys said things like that, it was cheesy and laughable, but not coming from him. He made her blood simmer, and the quick kiss she'd stolen left her hungry for more, but why on earth did he make her *think* so much?

"Where are we headed, sunshine?"

She pointed up ahead, squinting in the dimming light. "It's right there, between the big blue tent and the pup tents."

"Something doesn't look right." He grabbed her hand, walking quicker and holding her tight, as if she might run away if he didn't.

Fat. Chance.

She wanted that first kiss.

And a whole lot more.

They rounded the pup tents and dodged a group of shirtless guys. Graham stopped cold in front of her makeshift tent. The broken pole she and Brindle had fixed with duct tape had bent, collapsing one side of the canopy. The ground beneath was soaked, along with the pretty peace flags and cloth stars she'd hung up.

"This is your tent?" Graham rubbed his jaw. "Sunshine, a tent typically has sides. It looks like someone broke your canopy." He set his bag on her beach chair.

"It's been broken for a long time." She stepped inside and waved at the pole. "The rain must have weakened the duct tape. But that's okay. I can fix it again," she said as she dug through her backpack.

"You can't sleep in this." He inspected the broken pole. "This isn't something you fix with duct tape. You need a new pole, and a real tent."

"Yeah, I know, but like I said, I didn't know it was going to rain. I can dry off the chair and sleep on that." She whipped her dress over her head.

Graham ran over, shielding her with his body. "Whoa, you can't—" His gaze slid down her body, lingering at her yellow flowered bikini top, his eyes darkening. "Holy hell, sunshine. You're fucking gorgeous." His entire body seemed to grow bigger and *harder* as he pressed closer, his head swinging from side to side with a warning look in his eyes.

"Far from it," she said, "but I'm glad you think so."

She knew her body wasn't anything special. She was tall and too thin in some places, too fluffy in others, while most of her sisters were blessed with curves in all the right places. But maybe she'd been wrong about her body for all this time, because there was no faking the appreciative, wolfish look in Graham's eyes as his arms circled her waist. His hot chest pressed against her flesh, and her dress dropped from her fingertips. Her nipples rose to achy, needy points as his hands moved slowly and greedily up her back, holding her tighter. His big hand pushed into her hair, staking claim like he owned her. And at that moment, he *did.* She could barely breathe with the feel of his hot, hard body against hers, his heartbeat thundering against her chest and his eyes boring into her, growing darker by the second. Her pulse quickened as his other hand slid lower, settling at the base of her spine, his fingertips brushing over her bikini bottom. His body heat seared into her as his whiskers brushed against her cheek, sending titillating sensations rippling through her, and he pressed a tender kiss beside her ear. Goose bumps raced up her spine, and she closed her eyes.

She held her breath, waiting for him to say something, *anything.* Her whole body prickled with anticipation. His breath warmed her skin, his body ignited the inferno that had been building all afternoon, and he began swaying to a sensual beat. His lips touched her cheek again and again, kissing his way toward her mouth. He didn't hurry, and each touch amped up her need until it thrummed inside her, pulsing and wanting. Then his lips brushed over hers so lightly she opened her eyes, nearly drowning in the desire looking back at her. He threaded his fingers into her hair, holding on tight as he tugged her head back, angling her mouth beneath his as those incredible lips descended upon hers in a possessive, needful kiss. She felt dizzy and light, and at the same time, she'd never felt more grounded in her life as they swayed and arched, deepening their kisses. Her hands ran over the muscular ridges of his back as his arousal ground into her belly. All she could think about was how badly she needed him. She groped at his shoulders, holding on tight as she pressed her entire body harder against him. Their tongues tangled as they devoured each other's mouths, and the world spun away. She wasn't even sure she was breathing anymore. She'd never—*ever*—gotten lost in a kiss. In a *man*. And that was exactly what was happening as they groped and ground, caressed and kissed. He cupped her ass, his thick fingers pressing and lifting as he bent his knees and aligned their bodies. His hard shaft created the most erotic friction against her center. She went up on her toes, trembling with desire as she pushed her hands beneath the waist of his jeans and grabbed his ass. It was firm and soft, cold and hot at once. He made a guttural sound that wound around them, binding them together in an intoxicating cloud of lust and greed. Her knees gave out, and he held her even tighter. Her emotions whirred, dark and wild, as he eased their kisses to shivery soft titillating teases. She pushed forward, needing more. Wanting *all* of him.

"Morgyn," he said in a gravelly voice that sounded as desperate as she felt.

Fire blazed in his eyes as he crushed his mouth to hers again, deeper and rougher than before. His hands moved hot and hungrily up her back, and then his palms pressed against the sides of her head as they both came away breathless.

"You need to sleep in my arms tonight, sunshine." He brushed the tip of his nose over hers and said, "You just rocked my world."

She couldn't think straight enough to respond. She might have whimpered, might have moaned, or maybe she just breathed at him. Whatever she did brought his smiling lips to hers again in a deliciously sweet kiss.

"I don't want to move from this spot," he said in a rushed whisper. "But I have a feeling if we don't get going, your sister is going to come after me with a shotgun."

"Okay." She had no idea how she'd managed to answer.

Her body was on fire.

He continued staring at her, smiling just for her. "I think you'd better get your hands out of my pants first."

She gasped and pulled her hands out, instantly missing the feel of him. She couldn't believe she'd even done that right there in the middle of the festival. She tried to take a step back, though it was the last thing she wanted to do, but he kept her close and said, "Tonight it's all yours."

What could she do but grin like a dizzying fool?

After her legs stopped wobbling, she found a clean dress and slipped it over her bathing suit, moving as if in a dream. Graham looked at her differently as she put clothes in one of her bags to bring with her to his...*tent*? Like he wanted to devour her, but there was something much deeper and more meaningful in his eyes, something she could feel as he touched his fingers to hers and kissed her shoulder.

"Ready, sunshine?" He slung the strap of his bag crosswise over his body, then reached for hers.

"I can carry it."

Those killer dimples appeared as he tugged her against him and kissed her slowly and tantalizingly perfectly.

"Didn't you ever have a guy carry your books in school?"

She shook her head. "Guys weren't interested in touching my *books*."

He made a growly noise in the back of his throat, as if he didn't like what she was implying, and then he said, "I want to touch your *books*." He kissed her again. "Your *bags*." His lips captured hers, longer this time. "And everything else you'll let me touch."

Hearing him say it brought the truth of where they were headed rushing at her. She wasn't a virgin and she certainly wasn't a prude, but what if she changed her mind? What if he did? *God, I hope he doesn't.*

He took a long look at her stuff. "You sure you want to leave all this here?" He touched one of the cloth stars. "This is really cute. Someone might walk off with it."

"You like those? Most of the guys I know think I'm really *out there* for putting up stuff like that."

"You're obviously hanging out with people who have bad taste. Why don't we take whatever you don't want stolen?"

She surveyed her belongings and said, "If someone needs my stuff more than I do, that's okay. They can have it."

He opened his mouth to say something, then closed it, looking over her things again. "You don't want the tie-dyed blanket or those funky pillows?"

She shrugged. "I can make more."

"You *made* them?" He took off his green bag and set it on a chair. Then he put the blanket in his bag. He unhooked the string of cloth stars and carefully put them in, too. He slung the bag across his chest again and grabbed the colorful throw pillows she'd brought to sleep with. "Okay, I think that about does it."

"They're not that special," she said as he draped an arm over her shoulder.

"Clearly your friends are wearing off on you. You made them, and in my book, that means they're special." As they walked across the muddy ground he said, "Mind if we stop by my truck so I can get out of these wet pants?"

She felt her eyes widen at the thought of him naked and tried to school her expression. "Um…no."

He laughed and dropped a kiss on the side of her head.

A few minutes later they arrived at Graham's campsite, or

rather, his cool old Land Rover, which he'd converted into a camper's dream. He'd built a bed that fit between the cushioned bench seats in the back and hidden compartments for storage. Shelves were built around the windows on one side, chock-full of books and other items, and a guitar was strapped to a contraption on the interior of the roof.

"You play guitar?" she asked.

"Mm-hm."

"That makes you a hundred times hotter. I hope you'll play for me later. I play, too." She touched the bed cushion, which looked like something she would make. Batik curtains covered the windows, and when he hung the stars she'd made from the end of the curtain rod, they looked like they belonged there. "This is all so amazing."

"It's got four inches of memory foam on a thin mattress. I made the bed cover from wall hangings I picked up in India when I climbed Mount Jopuno with my cousin Ty and our buddies."

"You made them? You? With your own two hands?"

"Yup." He held his hands up. "The only two I've got."

"I don't know what's more impressive, the fact that you made this cover and reconfigured your truck, or that you *mountain climb*. In India! I've never left the East Coast. Is that a big mountain? What's India like?"

"You're adorable," he said, pressing his lips to hers like he'd been doing it forever. "Mount Jopuno is in western Sikkim, which is in the Himalayas. It's just under six thousand meters, and the views are phenomenal. But getting there was just as magnificent. On the trek from Yuksom to Tshoka, we went through a forest of magnolia and rhododendron. That part of India is so serene, unlike anything I've ever seen, and I've seen a lot. Ty and I climb and cross-country ski together. I love hiking, biking, boating, just about anything that'll give me an adrenaline rush."

"Wow, cracker, you've got all sorts of cool stuff going on. I'm a little jealous. Is that why you're such a risk assessor? To make sure you don't die on one of your adventures?"

"Sort of. I followed in my father's footsteps and went to school for engineering, but that's more of a hobby for me now. I had dreams of working side by side with him, but I had a hard time staying put and realized I needed adventures in work *and* in life."

"Your zest for life! That's *exactly* what I see and feel coming off of you. So, you're a mountain-climbing, thrill-seeking, engineering hobbyist? That leaves a world of possibilities."

"Exactly. Luckily, I have a cousin who helped me find my way. When I was in college I was working on engineering plans for one of my cousin Pierce's properties. He owns real estate all over the world, and I apprenticed for him to get my feet wet. I told him my dilemma, that I loved analyzing and planning but felt too hemmed in. He suggested I try my hand in acquisitions. He taught me the ropes and I worked with him on a few business deals. I had a real knack for it, and more importantly, I loved doing it. But Pierce's investments are all over the map in terms of businesses, and I didn't want to bring more big businesses into the world that would ruin our ecological footprint. Gotta leave a green world behind for future generations, right?" He didn't wait for an answer. "My business partner, Knox Bentley, and I went to MIT together. He was born with a silver spoon in his mouth and did everything he could to separate himself from the pomp and circumstance that came along with that materialistic lifestyle. Together we formed

B&B Enterprises, our investment company."

"Investments?"

"Yes. We help companies get off the ground, buy and sell properties. Our specialty is eco-friendly businesses. You know the Eco-Sleep hotel chain? That's ours." He swatted her butt and said, "Now, enough about me. Step aside and let me grab dry clothes."

He climbed into the truck and came back out with clean clothes as he said, "Seems like you have more in common with this risk-assessing guy than you thought, huh?"

"Yes, I do." She looked up at the luggage rack on top of his truck and noticed a barrel strapped to it. "Why is there a barrel on your roo—" She turned around and lost her train of thought at the sight of Graham standing between the open doors of the truck, tugging off his wet jeans and underwear. He was blocked from the view of strangers, but she had a clear view of his thick thighs and perfect ass.

"It's a rain barrel." He glanced over his shoulder, catching her staring, and that slow grin slid across his face.

She whipped her head around, cursing herself for getting caught.

"Like what you see, sunshine?"

"God! I'm really not a Peeping Tom! I swear." She might not be, but she couldn't help peeking over her shoulder again—only to find him standing in clean, dry briefs with a big-ass cheesy grin on his face. He reached through the doors and hauled her against him, kissing her as they cracked up. "I like you, sunshine. I like you a whole hell of a lot."

"Because you think I'm a slutty festival girl, and I don't blame you for thinking that. I can't believe..."

"What? That you're attracted to a guy who straddles a very

fine line between risking my life on dangerous adventures and knowing I've taken every precaution to keep myself safe?"

"No! That I'm sneaking peeks at your nakedness and I have my stuff in your truck after knowing you for only several hours!"

"Really?" His brow wrinkled in confusion. "First of all, I don't pick up slutty girls, but *that's* what worries you? That's basal instinct, male-female attraction. That should be the least of your worries."

"The *least*? Then what should I worry about?"

He glanced over her shoulder and said, "The fact that your sister's staring us down and I'm in my skivvies."

MORGYN SCRAMBLED OUT of Graham's arms so fast Sable took a step back and said, "Don't hurry on my account. I was just making sure the hotshot hadn't absconded with you."

"He didn't." Morgyn crossed her arms, then uncrossed them, huffing anxiously. "We were…"

"I *know* what you were doing," Sable said as Graham pulled on his jeans and T-shirt. "You might want to do it *inside* the truck."

"Noted," Graham said as he put on socks and shoved his feet into his boots. He realized the sun was setting and wondered how the time had passed so quickly. "Sorry we took so long."

"God, Sable. Why are you creeping around like that?" Morgyn took a step forward, and Graham reached for her hand.

"Oh, you know," Sable said sarcastically, "because it's so

easy to creep when you're surrounded by *five hundred* people. I got worried, so shoot me."

"It's okay. How did you find us, anyway?" Morgyn asked.

Sable pointed to Zev, talking with a group of women by a tent across the field. "It's amazing what Zev will give up with a *maybe* instead of a *no*."

Sounds like Zev.

"Glad you're not lying in a ditch, sis. I'm out of time. I've got to get back up onstage soon. Axsel's hanging out with Beckett and JJ down by his trailer if you want to catch up with him." Sable nodded in Zev's direction; he was heading toward them now. "He's a great guy, and I swear there was a line of women trailing behind him like he was the pied piper."

"Yeah, he gets that a lot," Graham said. "I didn't mean to monopolize Morgyn's time."

"Yes you did," Sable said with a smile. "But that's okay. She's a good egg. Hurt her and I'll castrate you in your sleep."

"Sable!" Morgyn snapped. "Ignore her. She's got more testosterone than half the guys I know."

"Damn." He pulled Morgyn against him, her back to his chest, and said, "She can't hurt the goods if they're blocked."

Sable took off as Zev approached, giving Graham an approving grin. He gathered his things from the truck, slung his backpack over his shoulder, and said, "An Uber's picking me up at the gate to take me to the airport."

"We can take you," Morgyn offered.

"Nah. I like to go by myself. I kind of hate goodbyes. But I'll take a see-you-soon hug." He opened his arms and embraced her. "Be good to my brother, will ya?"

She looked sweetly at Graham and said, "He's pretty easy to be good to."

"You've got her fooled." Zev pulled Graham into a manly embrace and slapped him on the back, whispering, "Sable said your sunshine's never this free with herself. Take care of her, bro."

"Of course," Graham said, struck by his brother's sudden thoughtfulness. Zev was usually too caught up in his own life to slow down and worry about others. Graham had always chalked that up to Zev's need to remain detached from almost everyone. "Be careful out there, and if you don't return my texts I'll hunt you down." He should be used to Zev taking off with almost no worldly possessions and his refusal to say a real goodbye. Graham always worried about him, but knowing Morgyn had sensed the weight of his brother's troubles and seen through his effervescent smoke screen made him wonder if Zev's taking off and trying to outrun his pain was only making things worse.

"Let me know what you decide about that deal overseas," Zev said.

Graham and his business partner were considering investing in building homes for the residents of a small village in Belize. It would mean staying overseas for eight to ten weeks. It was a sweet deal. They had a couple of weeks before they had to make a decision, which had seemed like plenty of time...until he'd met Morgyn.

"Will do," Graham said.

"Ready? Might as well bring your girl in." Zev put an arm around her and dug out his phone. "Smile pretty, sunshine."

"What are we doing?" she asked as Graham put his arm around her.

"It's what we call a last-time-we picture," Graham explained. "Zev takes them each time he leaves."

"What a great idea!" She put her arms around both of them

and Zev took the picture. "Take another!"

She gave them bunny ears, and Graham tickled her in retaliation. She huddled against Zev, pleading, "Save me!" but Zev was busy taking selfies of the three of them. He jumped on Graham's back, loaded up with his bags and all. Morgyn grabbed his phone and took pictures as they tumbled to the ground in a laughing heap and wrestled. Graham rolled off him, and they both lay with their arms outstretched on the wet grass, smiling.

Morgyn reached down to help Graham up, and he pulled her down on top of him and kissed her. "Welcome to my life, sunshine."

Zev pushed to his feet. He helped Morgyn up, and then he pulled Graham up and tugged him into another embrace.

"See you later, asshole." Zev walked backward away from them.

"Till then, dickwad."

Morgyn waved and hollered, "See ya, foreplay!"

It was an awesome send-off, and seeing that playful, roll-with-the-punches side of Morgyn, along with her sensual side, attracted him to her even more. He wrapped her in his arms and said, "What now, sunshine? Want to catch up with your brother and friends?"

She shook her head. "I want to sit on top of your truck and listen to you play the guitar, but you probably need to go through a mess of mathematical calculations first to see if it's worth the risk."

He poked her ribs, making her squeal. "You're worth the risk, sunshine. No mathematical equations necessary. In fact, with you around, all the blood from my head rushes south. I probably can't do math right now anyway."

She giggled. "I might use that to my advantage, but that barrel worries me. With my luck it'll spill all over us."

"Do you think I'd put something on my roof so shabbily that it could be knocked over? I'm an engineer, remember? I know how to do a few things." He pressed his lips to hers and then said, "You'll be glad I have that. You can take a shower without waiting two hours in the shower lines."

"Oh my gosh. I didn't think it was possible, but you just surpassed risk-taking-guitar-playing hotness and got me hot and bothered with your *preparedness.* Is that a word? Preparedness?"

"I'm not sure," he said as he brushed his lips over hers. "I'm still stuck on *hot and bothered.*"

Chapter Four

GRAHAM COULDN'T REMEMBER the last time he'd spent almost an entire day with a woman, much less a day when he'd had this much fun. Morgyn was so impressed with his portable heater and the drying line he rigged between the doors of the truck to dry his clothes and her blanket and pillows that they packed up her campsite and hung her clothes out to dry, too. He was glad it was her suggestion, because he'd wanted to suggest it earlier but had worried it might scare her off. He'd never been a guy who moved too fast, but with Morgyn he wanted to plow ahead. For the first time in his life, it took restraint to slow down and remember to think, to be smart, not foolish. She was too special to risk scaring off.

They toweled off the roof and sat on blankets beneath the starless night sky, taking turns playing the guitar, making up songs, and getting to know each other better. The bands didn't play during quiet hours, from ten at night until eight in the morning. They had about ten minutes before the guitar had to be put away.

"What are your three most favorite things?" Morgyn asked as she strummed the guitar.

"That's a hard one."

"Okay, and the next two?" She bumped him with her shoulder, looking as sweet as she did sexy wearing one of his flannel shirts over her dress.

He loved her quirky sense of humor.

"Shouldn't that be one of *your* favorite things?" he teased.

She shifted her gaze up toward the sky and strummed a faster tune, singing, "It's *your* turn, not mine."

"I've got a lot of favorite things." He ran his fingers along her leg. "Your sexy legs."

Her eyes darkened, and she played a little slower.

"And the way flecks of darker blue glitter in your eyes when you get turned on."

"Cracker," she said just above a whisper.

"I can't help it that you're beautiful."

"Stop. You're embarrassing me. Tell me something real."

"That was real, and number three would be your free spirit."

"Says Mr. Prepared, who brought a pop-up shower stall, a battery-operated heater, and a Coleman stove like my grandfather used. I'm willing to bet there's a kitchen sink around here somewhere."

"No sink, but I can rig one up if you need it." He leaned in for a kiss, lingering because her kisses were unlike any others. She kissed with the same energy she seemed to do everything else, giving herself over to it completely, savoring every second.

Her eyes remained closed for a few heated seconds after their lips parted. When she opened them, a sated smile appeared like a gift. He wondered if she kissed other guys like that, or if she felt the same unfamiliar, unstoppable connection he did.

"I like kissing you, sunshine." He brushed her hair behind her ear and kissed her again, slower and sweeter than the last. "I'm adding that to my list. I think I need more than three things."

"Okay, ten, but only if six of them don't include me."

He'd gone out with a lot of women in his life, but he'd guess that most would have wanted to claim all ten items, if they'd ever had the notion to ask. Which they hadn't. Because they weren't inquisitive and deeply emotional like—although she tried to hide it—*Morgyn.*

"Ten. *Go*, cracker. It's still your turn."

"Easy. Family is right at the top of those six things, along with any extreme sports event that I'm a part of. It doesn't matter what it is—biking, rafting, skydiving, climbing."

"You have to tell me why," she said.

"They all take focus, determination, strength, and competitiveness. Knowing it's me against the elements makes me push myself harder than I think I can. It's a better feeling than almost anything I've ever known."

"I think I know that feeling, but not from sports." She looked out over the tents and set the guitar beside her. She touched her necklace and said, "I get that feeling when I hear a train. It brings back memories of my grandfather, and for the briefest of moments, even after all these years, I get a rush of excitement, like I might see him again. Then I remember he's gone. But in those first few seconds, I can feel his energy and it seems impossible that he's no longer here. That's how I know that when people leave this earth, they don't fail to exist. Their energy lives on."

She looked at him, and her expression was so peaceful, he wanted to learn from it. To borrow it. To experience whatever she was experiencing.

She sighed and said, "There I go showing my weirdness again." With a quick shrug she added, "I get a rush from other things, too. Like when I saw your smile? Oh my gosh, Graham…"

He couldn't suppress his smile.

"That's it, right there," she said. "I see guys smiling all the time, but my stomach never gets swarms of butterflies from it. And then there's mint chocolate chip ice cream, and puppies, and creating a new outfit out of something old. They're all rush worthy. Oh, and hikes at daybreak, when the world is barely awake and the dew is still glistening on the grass. And the first blooms in my garden, that's definitely on my list. The sight of a deer grazing on the side of the road. Gosh, I love that. They feel very elusive to me. Like you're being given a gift from this amazing creature. It bums me that they're so frightened of us, so I built a deer garden in my yard. Now I get to see them a lot more often."

He had no idea how she went from one topic to the next so quickly, but her outlook was fascinating. "A *deer* garden?"

"Mm-hm. I have an area by the woods where I let the shrubs and grass grow wild so they have cover, and I put in a pond so they have water. I also have corn feeders and salt licks out so they want to stick around." She pulled her knees up to her chest and wrapped her arms around them. "I'm rambling, sorry."

"Don't be. I love hearing about your life." *And seeing your eyes light up when you talk about it.* She was more of a preparer than she thought, at least when it came to the deer, and he'd imagine it didn't stop there.

"I like my life, but it's not very exciting, at least not the way yours is. You said you have a big family and you put them at the top of your list. Are you as close to them all as you are to Zev?"

"You're from a big family, so you know how it goes. We're

all close in different ways. Nick and I get shit done. We're both headstrong, so we can butt heads, but for the most part we get along fine. The adrenaline junkie side of me is closest to Zev, because he runs on the stuff. And the meticulous, overthinker in me, which doesn't seem to exist much when you're around, is closest to my oldest brother, Beau, and probably to Jax, too. Jax and my sister, Jillian—*Jilly*—are twins. Jax is totally chill all the time. Nothing rattles him, but Jilly's like you, a bundle of energy and game for anything."

"I can't believe you have twin siblings. Sable is Pepper's twin, and they are completely opposites in almost every way. Pepper is a scientist with no musical inclination. She prefers research to just about anything else."

"Isn't it weird how that happens? But life would be boring if everyone were alike."

"Yes, it would. Do you travel a lot for work?"

"Mm-hm. For work and pleasure. I take it you don't, since you've never left the East Coast?"

"I'm a road-trip girl. I'm always going somewhere, to festivals, craft shows, that kind of thing. Just day trips, usually. Sometimes with friends or my sisters, but mostly alone. I love finding treasures to use in my shop and seeing other people and how they live. But I've never even flown, and it kind of freaks me out. That's probably okay, though, because no one's ever said, 'Hey, let's go to Maui.'"

"Hey, let's go to Bali," he said, and he was surprised to realize he wasn't kidding. His mind leapt ahead, envisioning them going on adventures together. How strange was it to have that reaction to a woman he'd only just met?

Her eyes narrowed and she said, "Too much risk in Maui?"

"No. You're too interesting a person to take someplace so

typical." He laced their fingers together and lay back, bringing her down beside him. Then he went up on one elbow so he could see her face. "I have a confession."

"If you tell me you're married, I'm calling Sable."

"I'm not married, sunshine. I've never even been in love."

"Me either," she said softly.

"That's hard to believe. You seem like you *feel* so much. I really like you, sunshine."

"Is that your confession? Because I have to admit, I like it."

He ran his fingers through her hair, and then he kissed her softly. "No. I want you to know that I'm not one of those guys who hooks up with women everywhere I go. And I don't take it lightly. If you don't want to do anything more than kiss tonight, that's okay, and if you do, you should know I've never had a disease, or any of that. I'm clean and careful."

"Thank you," she said softly. "I haven't either, and don't worry, I'd tell you if I changed my mind. And, cracker? I haven't changed my mind."

Thank God, because he'd never wanted a woman like this before. "Good. There's just one more thing. As much as I want to sit here and get to know everything there is to know about you, if I don't kiss you like I did this afternoon *very soon*, I think I'm going to lose my mind. But I've been sweaty and dirty all day, and to do the things I want to do with you, I really need to rinse off."

She laughed. "I was thinking the same thing. Not about you. About *me*. I got hot and sticky putting all my stuff away. Can we shower?"

"We can do anything you want."

He kissed her deeply, and then she sighed dreamily and said, "Is it hard to set up?"

"Hearing the word *hard* come out of your sexy mouth…*Mm.* If you only knew what you were doing to me."

A mischievous glimmer rose in her eyes. "I'm having a *hard* time processing that information."

She rose, rubbing her body against his, and he pressed his lips to hers. She went down on her back as he took the kiss deeper. His body sank into hers, and she arched beneath him, making sweet, sexy sounds as he moved over her, aligning their bodies even though they were fully dressed. Her innate sensuality was like a drug, luring him in. He had to feel her, explore, *taste…shower.*

Fuck.

He tore his mouth away, leaving them both breathless.

"Shower," they said in unison.

He helped her down from the truck, stealing several more kisses as they tossed the blankets into the truck and put away the guitar. He connected the shower faucet inside the pop-up stall and hung two towels on the rope inside it. Then he gathered Morgyn in his arms and said, "The water takes a minute to heat up. I'll rinse off quickly; then it should be warm enough for you to get in."

"I have a confession, too." She wound her arms around his neck. "When we went to use the bathrooms after carrying my stuff over, I washed up and took off my bikini. I'm completely naked under this dress."

He pushed a hand under the hem of her dress and *holy hell,* her bare ass had been right beside him all evening.

"Christ, sunshine. Now I *need* that cold shower."

MORGYN KNEW SHE should probably be nervous about hooking up with Graham, especially since she wasn't the kind of girl who normally jumped right into bed with guys. But she wasn't, and she also wasn't worried about what he thought of her, because he'd already made that clear. It was a hazy, moonlit night, and the neighboring campers were either inside their tents or too busy to pay attention to Graham stripping off his jeans and shirt. He stood before her in those dark briefs she hadn't stopped thinking about since she first saw him in them hours earlier. His formidable erection strained behind the cotton, filling her with white-hot desire. He leaned in, kissing her so tenderly, she got all melty inside. Being with Graham felt good and right, and there was no way she was going to miss out on him.

He pulled off his hat and tossed it into the truck, revealing short, thick brown hair, making him impossibly hotter. "I'll be quick."

He stepped into the pop-up shower, and a second later he peered out of the flap and tossed his balled-up briefs into the open back of the truck. Morgyn's heart rate spiked. He winked and disappeared behind the vinyl.

What am I doing?

He was naked behind that thin sheet of vinyl, taking a cold shower so she didn't have to. She inhaled a deep breath and before she could chicken out, she stepped into the shower. Graham stood beneath the cold spray, goose bumps riddling his skin. She removed her dress, shivering from the cool shower spray. His eyes flamed as they trailed down her body. Thank goodness she'd remembered to wax. She reached through the flap and threw her dress toward the truck. Graham's arms circled her from behind. His chest pressed against her back, and his warm lips touched her shoulder.

"Hello, sunshine."

His voice was like liquid heat, warming her to her core. She turned as he gathered her closer, gazing down with pleasure and appreciation. His body was slick, sudsy, and hard—growing harder by the second. He smelled fresh and manly and looked at her like she was truly the only woman he desired. She no longer needed courage. She was positive that she was exactly where she was supposed to be.

"I thought it was silly for you to take a cold shower just so I could be warm." Eager to explore, her hands wandered down his arms and over his sudsy chest. She extended her index finger and wrote *C+S* in the suds on his abs.

He glanced down and smiled. "You are full of surprises. It's good we're not at a tattoo parlor. The way I feel right this second, I just might let them put that in ink."

Now she *was* a little nervous, because their connection was so magnetic, she wanted to put more stock in his words than she probably should. She knew he'd said it in the heat of the moment, but still, it felt more real than that.

She'd never showered with a man before, and there wasn't a lot of room in there for what she'd like to do. She tried to work it out in her head. She didn't have to think for very long because he moved her under the water and took her in a scorching-hot kiss that rocketed through her. *God*, kissing him was the best of everything all wrapped up in one man's deliciousness. Their bodies slithered against each other, arms and legs pressing and sliding, spreading suds from his body to hers. His erection ground temptingly hard and insistent against her lower belly. His hands slid up and down her body in a mesmerizing rhythm, dropping a little lower with each downward path. Water sprayed between them, washing away the suds and slithering between their joined lips as they kissed like they never wanted to stop. And she didn't.

She ran her hands down his back and clutched his ass, eliciting another of those sexy noises that made her insides clench in anticipation. He bit her lower lip, tugging it gently with a hungry look in his eyes, and *oh*, what that did to her! She thought about all the places she wanted his mouth and the places she wanted to put *hers*.

"I'm going to enjoy every second of us, sweet sunshine," he said greedily.

The way he said *us* gave her that bigger-than-life feeling again, and Lord help her, she clung to it. Because that's what you did when you saw the brass ring—and she didn't just see it. She felt it through and through.

He poured body wash into his hands and then kissed her ravenously as he bathed her shoulders, arms, and breasts. His rough hands played expertly over her nipples, caressing and tweaking, pulling sinful sounds from her lungs. His thick legs pressed against her, powerfully rooting him to the ground as his hands slid down her hips and he put space between them, allowing the water to wash the suds away. Rivers of water cascaded down his muscular chest and ripped abs, to his thick cock. She'd never seen so much power, so much *man*. She wanted to touch him, but it took all her focus to hold on to his arms as he followed the shower spray with his mouth, kissing and nipping at her neck. Every touch of his lips and graze of his teeth sent spikes of lust shooting through her. He dipped lower, fondling her breast and licking over and around her nipple until it burned with need. She went up on her toes, but he continued his relentless pursuit of driving her to the brink of madness.

She grabbed his head with both hands. "*Cracker—*"

He sucked the achy, taut peak into his mouth, sliding one hand down her belly and between her legs. His thick fingers teased over her wetness as his thumb found her most sensitive nerves and began moving in mind-numbing circles. She closed her eyes, and her head fell back as desire mounted inside her. Her senses were overloaded. She clung to his shoulders, trying to focus on the overwhelming pleasure coursing through her, but just when she caught the feel of his tongue, he applied more pressure with his thumb, sending her senses reeling. She whimpered and moaned as pressure built inside her, pulsing and throbbing, filling up all of her empty spaces. She leaned back—and kept falling backward—forgetting they were in a vinyl encasing. Graham's arm swept around her waist, bringing her upright again. He captured her mouth at the same moment he thrust his fingers inside her, stroking over the spot most men had no idea how to find. And there in the pop-up shower, with water raining down on them and Graham pleasuring every part of her, an electric shock scorched through her, and she shattered into a million magical stars.

As Graham's handsome face came back into focus he said, "We'd better get out of here before we collapse the shower."

He turned off the water and then wrapped a towel around her back and used it to pull her against him again. He slanted his mouth over hers, kissing her as they stumbled to the truck. It wasn't until he was closing the doors buck naked that she realized his ass hadn't been covered by the towel. But as he pulled the curtains closed and came down over her, she knew that had been the last thing on his mind. His hips nestled between her thighs, his thick cock perched at her entrance. He touched his lips to hers in a single, soft kiss.

"Hey, sunshine," he said softly, gazing down at her with as much tenderness as passion. "Still as into us as I am?"

Her heart swelled at his thoughtfulness. "More than before."

A hint of dimples appeared, but it was the emotions swimming in his eyes that had her reaching up and pulling his mouth toward hers. "I'm on the pill, but do you have protection? It could get messy."

"I do, and just so you know, I'm used to camping and always keep gallons of water in the storage beneath that bench." He winced and said, "Not for sex. *Man*, that sounded bad, didn't it? I meant for washing up, brushing my teeth…"

She loved that he cared enough to explain. He brushed his nose over hers as he had earlier, and the intimate touch felt incredibly meaningful.

"I'd never do this if you weren't properly taken care of before, during, or after," he said with a serious expression. He reached into a backpack behind the driver's seat and withdrew an unopened box of condoms. He tore it open and tossed a few packets beside the pillows. "Zev gave me his stash. I came prepared for a lot of circumstances but not for this."

The confirmation of what he'd said earlier about not taking sex lightly did undefinable things to her emotions.

Her heart fluttered erratically as he cradled her in his strong arms, taking her in a series of deep, intoxicating kisses, clearly in no rush to get to the next step. And she was glad, because in the space of an instant, everything had changed. A tangible bond had formed between them, and she felt it everywhere. His hands skimmed her hip as he rolled them onto their sides, their legs tangling. He lifted her leg at the knee and rested it on his thigh, bringing his thick shaft against her. The hair on his legs tickled. His hands moved over every inch of her, into her hair, between her legs, along her ribs, like he wanted to memorize *all* of her. She was right there with him, running her hands all over his body. Kissing his chest, his nipples, stroking his shaft, riding his thigh until it was slick with her arousal. She was dizzily happy, unable to hold on to a single thought past how good it felt to want someone that badly and be desired just as strongly. Everything felt so right. His strong arms felt like they were meant to hold her, and his mouth—his glorious, talented mouth—brought her to unfamiliar heights. When he rose up on his knees to sheathe himself, she reached up to help him, and together they protected themselves.

Neither one looked away as they aligned their bodies. A hot ache grew inside Morgyn as the broad head of his shaft pressed against her entrance. This wasn't just sex, or maybe it was, but it wasn't like any sex she'd ever had. She felt his energy melding with hers, their hearts beating in time, as he laced their hands together and kissed the edges of her mouth. Could he feel it, too? Could he sense the coming together of more than just their bodies?

"Why do I feel like this is going to change me?" he nearly growled.

Ohgodohgodohgod. She told herself to keep silent, because her thoughts were so often too outside the norm for others to accept. But his eyes bored into the far reaches of her mind, into her heart, and the truth came tumbling out. "Because synergy is the deepest desire of the human soul, and I think we might have found it."

"I have a feeling no matter how much I tried, I could never be fully prepared for you, sunshine."

He lowered his mouth to hers, kissing her passionately as he pulsed his hips, entering her slowly and carefully. She felt her body stretching to accommodate his girth as he pushed in one inch at a time, retreating and entering again, until he was buried deep inside her. She felt full and complete in a way she never had. Not just from the way their bodies seemed to be made for each other, but because of the way he held her and kissed her, making her feel special without ever saying a word. When they began moving and found their rhythm, every thrust sent shivers of pleasure rippling through her. Heat raced through her veins and prickled beneath her skin. He kissed her deeper, rougher, turning all of her nerves into live wires. He quickened his pace, and her insides swelled, reaching for the pinnacle of their passion. He took her right up to the edge, but she wanted to come *with* him, to feel him lose control *for* her. She dug her nails into his back, and a rumbling sound crawled up his throat, pulling her closer to the cliff. His corded muscles told her he was still holding back.

She wrapped her legs around him, craving his raw, unbridled passion, and tore her mouth away long enough to say, "Let me feel *all* of you."

"I don't want to hurt you."

"It would hurt more knowing you could have given me all of yourself and held back than it will to feel all of your energy poured into us."

His eyes flamed with a savage inner fire. He crushed his mouth to hers, holding and loving her with the power and magnificence of a hurricane, claiming *all* of her as they spiraled into oblivion together, groping and panting, crying out with pleasure.

Afterward, as they lay with their foreheads touching, legs intertwined, and his arm protectively around her middle, he said, "Where have you been all my life?"

She knew she'd never forget that moment, any of the things he'd said, or the look in his eyes—the one she was trying hard not to make too much of.

But it was too late. She had already woven the specialness of them into a treasured memory.

Chapter Five

GRAHAM AWOKE WITH his right arm numb, something silky smooth beneath his left hand, and a warm weight on his chest. He opened his eyes and found Morgyn fast asleep, straddling his shoulder. Her torso was curled around his head, his favorite MIT shirt bunched above her belly. Her panty-clad hip rested by his chin. One thigh lay across his chest, her toes tucked precariously close to his junk. Her other leg stretched along the right side of his body. Two more firsts—a woman sleeping in his truck, sprawled all over him. He pressed a kiss to her belly, inhaling the fresh scent of body wash. They'd made love like rabbits, and afterward they'd washed up and lain with the truck doors open, listening to the murmurs and sounds of other festivalgoers. Morgyn had called their quiet time of togetherness *just being*. It was amazing how little thinking was involved with simply being together and how good it felt.

He kissed her belly again, and she made a sleepy noise, curling tighter around his head. Her toes dug in just above his balls. Instinct brought his knees together as he guided her leg over his hip, kissing her again. She startled and shot up to her knees, hit her head on the roof, and fell on top of him with a loud "*Oomph.*"

"Ow," she said in a craggy voice.

"Aw, sunshine." He kissed her head as he gathered her close with one arm—because the other was asleep—and rolled them onto their sides. Her hair was a tangled blond mess, her brow wrinkled, and her expression was happy and pained at once. He held her tighter. "I'm sorry. I didn't mean to startle you. Are you okay?"

She buried her face in his neck and made a grunting, moaning sound, like a pouty child, tweaking more unfamiliar emotions. He felt her head for a bump, of which there was none, thank goodness.

"Was I lying across your whole body?" she asked softly.

"Yeah. I think you were a cat in your previous life."

She laughed and drew back with a smile. "I'm not used to sleeping with anyone. I have a body pillow I usually curl around."

"I like being your body pillow." He ran his hand up her thigh. "Your toes are deadly, though. For a minute I thought you were Sable in disguise, trying to castrate me."

She wrinkled her nose. "I'm sorry."

He kissed that adorable nose, and she snuggled closer. "If you don't have plans for the day and wouldn't mind leaving the festival for a while, I thought maybe we could take a hike, see what good old Romance, Virginia, has to offer."

"Really?" She leaned back, excitement dancing in her beautiful eyes. "I had this dream about us. Well..." She lowered her voice. "I had a *lot* of dreams about us, most of them dirty, but in one dream we were holding hands and walking through the woods. Sunlight streaked through the trees as pretty as a picture. You took both of my hands in yours, and then you kissed me. One simple kiss on the lips, but it was like a movie." She spread her fingers, making an arcing motion between them, and sighed. "Perfect."

He touched his lips to hers and said, "You're perfect."

She covered her mouth, speaking from behind her hand. "Perfectly stinky with morning breath." She wiggled away and said, "Let's go!" She reached over the front seat and grabbed her patchwork backpack. "I need to brush my teeth, but we can grab something to eat in town." She dug around in her bag.

He hauled her beside him, and she laughed, grinning up at him as he gave her a big, hard kiss. "I take it you're not a coffee drinker?"

She wrinkled her nose again.

"No breakfast before our hike?"

She shook her head. "But I'm sure you have a list of things to do, right? I just got excited to explore with you. It's okay. You can get your coffee, do your risk assessments of ticks, sunburn, and poison ivy—"

"I'll give you *sunburn.*" He tickled her ribs, and she curled into a ball, laughing as she pleaded, "*Stop, stop, stop!*"

He kissed her hip, then nipped at it, earning a sultry moan. "Stop? That's not what you said last night." He ran his hand along her leg and lifted her—*his*—shirt, kissing the dip at her waist.

"The tickling needed to stop." She ran her fingers through his hair and said, "*This* needs to continue."

He kissed her belly, and she said, "Mm-hm. You still have water to wash up, right?"

"Mm-hm," he said as he dragged her panties down—and *off.* He kissed her inner thigh, then gave it a long, slow lick.

She tugged her shirt off, eyeing his briefs. "*Someone* has too many clothes on."

He nearly growled, quickly shedding those pesky briefs. As he did, she changed positions, sitting beside him, her legs tucked beneath her. She leaned forward and began kissing his chest.

"Ah, sunshine. That's *nice.*"

He lay back as her fingers played over his pecs and her sweet, hot mouth teased his nipples. Her hair brushed over his chest and abs as she licked and kissed a path directly to his cock. He pushed his hand into her hair, brushing it away from her face and watching as she kissed the tip, then ran her tongue along the length of his throbbing shaft. He gritted his teeth as she did it again, driving him out of his mind. She kissed around the base, down his thighs, then up again, circling where he wanted her most. Her eyes flicked up to his, and the wonder in them sent warm gusts of emotions whipping through him. He didn't understand the power behind them, but he wanted to explore those emotions as badly as he wanted her to take a grand expedition over his entire body.

He reached for her, but she shook her head and whispered, "Not yet."

Fuuuck.

She wrapped her hand around his shaft and slicked her tongue over the tip. His hips bucked, and she smiled, licking the length of him again and earning another torturous rock of his hips. She was going to tease him until he came; he just knew it. She licked slowly, kissed longingly, like she was savoring every touch. Lust coiled deep and hot inside him. He was blessed with a thick cock and had been told enough times it was too uncomfortable for oral sex to know better than to expect it. No matter how desperately he wanted Morgyn's mouth on him, to claim her from the inside out, he'd never ask that of her. Her gorgeous eyes caught his again, and he saw a mix of anticipation and hesitation. As he opened his mouth to tell her she didn't even need to try, she lowered hers, taking him all the way to the back of her throat and drawing a long, low groan from his lungs. She gave him a hard suck, sending heat through his veins. He ground his back teeth to keep from losing it.

"Christ, sunshine…"

She must have liked that reaction, because she did it repeatedly, until he was shaking with restraint. Just when he thought he was going to lose it, she released him, and the air rushed from his lungs. She reached for a condom, and he took it from her, tearing it open as fast as he could. When he went to roll it on, she did it for him, and then she straddled him, slowly lowering herself down. Her tightness wrapped around him and the emotions brimming in her eyes sent his world careening away. When he was buried to the hilt, she leaned forward, her hands on his shoulders, and her hair tumbled around their faces.

"Confession time," she whispered. "I don't want to move. I just want to feel you inside me, knowing I just had you in my mouth."

"Sunshine, if you talk like that, whether you move or not, I'm going to come. Which means I have to move, because I'm not coming until you've had enough orgasms to never forget how this feels."

He pulled her into a passionate kiss and made good on that promise.

NEARLY TWO HOURS later Graham and Morgyn hiked

through the woods toward town. They'd been blessed with a breezy, sunny, perfect morning. Although Graham would have thought it was perfect whether it rained, snowed, or blazed as long as Morgyn was by his side. She was a funny woman. While he had coffee and eggs for breakfast, she drank ice water with lemon and scarfed a cookie from a vendor. She had sweet-talked her way into borrowing another one of Graham's favorite shirts, this one from the Hilltop Vineyards, the winery his mother's family owned. He'd had the soft gray shirt forever. The logo had faded so much it was nearly invisible. The shirt was so big on Morgyn, she'd tied it in a knot at her waist and paired it with sexy cutoffs that had colorful patches on the butt. She hadn't brought sneakers or hiking boots, but Graham was quickly learning that Morgyn was quite resourceful. While he'd dressed, she'd traded the embellished rain boots she'd worn the day before for a pair of black Converse high-tops from a woman at a neighboring tent. Not exactly proper hiking footwear, but she seemed happy and her feet were protected from the sticks and leaves they were traipsing over.

"Do you have goals?" Morgyn ducked beneath a branch, her eyes trained on the chain of wildflowers she was making.

"Doesn't everyone?"

She used her fingernail to make a slit on a stem. "Probably, but everyone's are different. What are yours?"

"That's a pretty open-ended question. Professionally or personally?"

She shrugged and threaded a stem through the slit and then made another slit.

"Well, today my goal is to enjoy this time with you."

She bumped him with her hip. "Big picture?"

"Let's see. Work-wise, I'd like to be even more hands-on

with my investments and do more than simply invest money. I want to make a bigger difference, although I haven't completely mapped out how yet. On a personal level, I hope to continue enjoying what I'm doing and to enter *and win* more sports competitions, do some rafting with my cousins, spend time with you…"

Her gaze flicked up, and she stopped walking. "You're not looking to make a billion dollars or prove that you're better than every other engineer slash real estate investor in the world?"

"I make a lot of money. Not billions, but I don't have to worry about my future, if that's what you're getting at."

She shook her head and they began walking again. "I don't care about money. I'm trying to figure out more about the man you are. What drives you, if not money?"

"Life. I want to experience as much of it as I can. Most of the competitions I take part in are for charity, and that drives me to work harder in my professional life so I can afford to give more time to the events. And yeah, money drives me to some extent. Of course I want to be great at what I do, but not at the expense of living a fulfilling life. And eventually, I'd like to get married and have a family, but not necessarily settle down."

"What does that mean?"

He leaned closer and said, "It means I don't want to have a house and a white picket fence where everything is always the same. I'd like to love and be loved and to be able to travel with my family. Homeschool the kids, whatever it takes. What about you? Do you have goals?"

"Yes, but I could *never* homeschool children. Math is my enemy. My kid would be in sorry shape if they had to rely on my knowledge to learn more than the basics. But I could teach them all about art and botany."

He chuckled. "You realize they make online tutorials for kids, and you'd probably have a husband in there somewhere, right? He could help out?"

"It's not necessary to be married to have children," she said matter-of-factly. "I've never been one of those girls who dreams of her wedding day. I don't believe real connections, the type that last forever, need a piece of paper to keep them together or honest. I don't want to be waiting at home for a cheating husband. I want to be my significant other's best friend, someone he can't wait to come home to, even if I'm knee deep in daisy chains or dancing in the rain because it feels good."

He lifted her chin, taking in the honesty and hope in her eyes, and kissed her smiling lips. "I can't imagine anyone not wanting to come home to you. And I've definitely never met a woman who wasn't looking for a ring on her finger."

"Well, now you have," she said sassily.

"So I have. You know my goals. What are *yours*, mysterious Morgyn?"

"I'm hardly mysterious, but my goals change from time to time. Like you, I want to enjoy what I do, but not so I can afford to do other things. I want to enjoy it because I want to enjoy my life. If I don't love what I do"—she shrugged—"why do it?" She fiddled with her flower chain and then put it around her neck. "What do you think?"

"I think it's almost as gorgeous as you are." As he pulled her in to a kiss, he spotted poison ivy by her leg and swept her against him, away from the plant. "Careful where you're walking. That's poison ivy."

She glanced at the plant and said, "Thanks. But if I got poison ivy I could just pick that jewelweed, cut open the stem, and rub the inside on it. It's an instant remedy for soothing and healing skin. I've used it for cuts and burns, insect bites, all sorts of things."

"I forgot you were an herbalist, and full of surprises."

She went up on her toes, flashing a cheesy smile, and kissed him. "Want to race to town?"

"I thought you didn't like sports."

She rolled her eyes and said, "I have never gone mountain climbing or run in a race, but that doesn't mean I *can't.* Ready? No risk or *any* kind of calculations, cracker. We're a team. We're racing against time." She climbed on his back and said, "Piggyback race. Go!"

MORGYN WAS LEARNING a lot about Graham, like the fact that those thick legs of his could run wicked fast, even when burdened with her weight on his back and her kisses on his neck. And that sometimes he studied her as though he was trying to work the pieces of a Morgyn puzzle into some semblance of normalcy he could understand. *Good luck with that.*

When they reached Main Street, they walked hand in hand. Romance, Virginia, was a quaint small town, much like Oak Falls. Pretty flowering dogwood trees lined the sidewalks. Large picture windows graced the front of old-fashioned shops with faded awnings and cheery welcome signs. Colorful flowers spilled out of large planters by shop entrances and trailed over the edges of window boxes. There were flyers for the festival posted on shop windows and a big banner across the main road announcing the festival. They lingered in a bookstore and learned they both enjoyed reading crime novels. Graham seemed surprised about that. Almost as surprised as Morgyn was when he bought Zev a postcard from the gift shop, wrote *Thanks for the donation. Xox, Cracker + Sunshine*, and mailed it to a post office in the town where Zev was headed. As they walked by the antique shop, a big gold cat lying in the window lifted its head, giving them a cursory glance, then hunkered down again and closed its eyes.

It was wonderful spending time with Graham, sometimes talking and sometimes just walking in comfortable silence. He didn't rush her through shops or seem annoyed when she spotted a thrift shop and hurried toward it. A bright green sign read FUNKY JUNK. VINTAGE. UPCYCLED. LOCALLY MADE.

"This store is a must!" she said as they entered.

Bells above the door chimed, and they were greeted by the scent of fresh linens. Brick walls held metal racks loaded with clothing, old pictures, and funky mirrors. A velvet sofa, eclectic end tables, and a number of gorgeous, distressed dressers created an aisle through the center of the store.

"Howdy, y'all!" a petite brunette called out as she hurried up the center aisle with her arms full of clothes. She wore bright red leather shorts, cowgirl boots, and a black mesh shirt with a yellow tank top underneath—an outfit Morgyn would kill for. "I'm Magnolia Love," she said with a bright smile. "Jewelry, household items, toys, and footwear are in the back. We have a make-your-own section with everything from frames to key chains on the counter in the right rear of the store. And don't worry, handsome, we have plenty of tools and guy stuff, too. A whole roomful right through that curtain." She pointed to a batik curtain hanging to their right. "If you need anything, just holler *Mags* and I'll come running." She headed to the opposite side of the store to hang the clothes.

"What a great name," Morgyn said as Graham reached for her hand.

"Not as great as *Morgyn.* Where do you want to start?"

"Right here," she said. "We'll work our way back."

They walked through the store admiring everything Magnolia had to offer.

"Does this remind you of your store?" Graham asked.

"Sort of, because of the variety she sells. Thrift shops are precursors to my shop. I find a lot of the things I sell in my shop in places like this, and then I put my own twist on them."

"So you don't sell anything that you haven't embellished?"

"I don't just embellish. I tear apart clothing and make it into something completely new. A dress might become a top, or I might turn a scarf into a skirt. I also make jewelry from scratch using different parts." She spotted toy trains and gasped, heading for them. "Like these!"

"That one's cracked." He looked at the others and said, "That one's missing a wheel. Are they all broken?"

As he surveyed the trains she chose two of them. "I'll buy these two and use the parts for jewelry or on clothing or bags. I *scavenge,*" she whispered. "I want to look through the clothing."

"Here, give me the trains," he said, taking them from her. "I'll check out the *guy stuff.*"

She watched him disappear behind the curtain, feeling like they'd been shopping together for years. She found him sometime later at the register with Magnolia. He was admiring a brass piece of equipment with a wide, dark base, upon which was a flat semicircular brass piece with decorative swirls and an inlaid compass. A flat brass bar was secured at the center and divided the semicircle. Standing upright from each end of the semicircle and each end of the brass bar were vertical pieces of metal with two slots in them.

"What is that?" she asked. "It's so elegant."

"It's a 1750s graphometer, a surveying instrument used to measure angles. My father collects them. This one's in perfect shape. I think he would love it." He pointed to the upright pieces of brass attached to the semicircle. "These are the sights. They're fixed at either end, and a pivot carries the sighting rule across the divided semicircle. See?" He moved the sighting rule.

"It's a great piece," Magnolia said. "I didn't know what it was when the woman who owned it brought it in, but I knew it was special. It's amazing what you can learn online. Now I'm practically an expert in all types of graphometers. Not that I'll ever find another beauty like this one."

"It's gorgeous. Can you ship it for me?" Graham asked.

"I can wrap it, ship it, embellish it, whatever you'd like." Magnolia grabbed a piece of paper and said, "Just write down the address."

He wrote down his father's address and asked for a piece of paper and proceeded to write a note to his father. "I bought your trains, too."

"You did?" Morgyn was surprised, and touched. "Thank you. I would have bought them."

Graham blew her a kiss.

"Your man is pretty sweet," Magnolia said with a smile.

Morgyn's pulse quickened at *your man*. She wasn't sure if it was okay to claim him like that, so she waited a few seconds before answering to see if he cleared things up. But his heated glance was all the confirmation she needed. "He sure is."

"He said you were at the festival," Magnolia said. "Isn't it great? I went for a while yesterday. It's such a fun event."

"I try to go every year, but I've never taken the time to check out the town. Your shop is great. I run a similar business in Oak Falls called Life Reimagined."

"Really? You should join our cross-country Junk in the Trunk event." She handed Morgyn a flyer and said, "It's an annual road-trip event. Last year we had fifty-seven shops take part, and we saw more than five hundred customers the first day. Buyers drive from one shop to the next, and at each location they get something for free, like a flag, a key chain, a button…But most of the customers come with trailers or trucks, expecting to buy things. It's a great event."

Graham smiled at Morgyn and said, "That sounds like an event you and I could have a blast following."

Morgyn thought her heart might leap out of her chest at the suggestion. "I would *love* to do that."

She and Magnolia exchanged contact information, and Magnolia told them how to sign up online for the event. Morgyn tried not to put too much stock in Graham actually meaning that he might like to do the event with her, but it was hard not to fantasize about it.

When they left the store, Graham reached into the bag and said, "I made you something." He withdrew an ultrathin turquoise, gold, and white braided bracelet with three tiny silver charms.

"You made this?"

"Remember the do-it-yourself area she had at the counter? While you were busy shopping, I put it together." He showed her each charm. "A compass, so you never lose your way. A heart, because we're in Romance, Virginia, and a sun, because it's you, sunshine."

Other than her father and her grandfather, no man had ever

made her anything. Her throat clogged with emotions, and she threw her arms around his neck. "I love it so much. Thank you."

As he put it on her wrist, looking at her like she made him the happiest man in the world, she struggled to keep her emotions in check.

"I hope you never forget today. I know I won't." He pressed his lips to hers and said, "Come on, beautiful. You might be able to live on air, but I need sustenance."

They bought sandwiches from a cute café called Birdie's and ate them as they walked around the town square. The square was picture perfect with brick pavers surrounding an enormous fountain. In the center of the fountain was a statue of a man and a woman dancing. The woman was sculpted midtwirl, her dress lifting at the hem, and the man was gazing happily into her eyes. Morgyn glanced down at the special bracelet on her wrist, feeling like today was something out of a dream. She watched Graham, gathering the trash from their lunch. He smiled, looking rugged and tender at once.

If today was a dream, she never wanted to wake up.

After they ate, they walked around the square, which was surrounded by interesting old brick and stone buildings with decorative elements carved into the stone. Across the street was a beautiful park with a gazebo, wooden benches, and colorful gardens along walking paths. Graham's gaze lingered on one of the old buildings, and she wondered if that was his engineering side taking over, assessing and meticulously figuring things out, or if, like her, he was just soaking in the beauty of the town.

She wrapped her arms around his waist and said, "I'm not the kind of person who holds a guy like this or takes off from a festival where my siblings are playing. So why does it feel so right to be here, holding you and wishing it was snowing so I could experience the hope of the holidays with you in this pretty little town?" The words poured out, and she was unable to stop them. "How can that be when we've only just met?"

"I was wondering that, too, but for the first time in my life, I don't want to overthink. I just want to go with it and see where it leads. You must be wearing off on me." He pressed his lips to hers in a sweet kiss. "What do you think, sunshine?" he asked as they walked toward the fountain. "Are you up for a wish?" He pulled a handful of change from his pocket.

"Do you really need to ask?" Morgyn snagged a penny. "Are you going to make one?"

"Yes, but I'm using a quarter so it has a higher chance of coming true."

She looked over the remaining change in his hand and then scooped it all into her palm. "Okay, now I'm ready."

He laughed. "Nothing like increasing your odds. You go first."

Ever since she was a little girl, she'd wished for things for others on her birthdays because she worried that too much wishing for herself would be greedy and nothing would ever come true. They were little-girl wishes for Amber to be cured of epilepsy and for Pepper to win the science fair. As she matured, her wishes were practical, though still for the benefit of others, like that Axsel would be safe traveling all over the world with his band and that Grace would find her way back home. So far those wishes had come true. Axsel was safe, and Grace had recently moved back home. But today she wanted to be selfish. Maybe all those years of wishing for others would pay off.

She closed her eyes tight and held her breath as she made her wish. *I wish this day would last forever.* When she opened her eyes, she found Graham watching her intently with a knowing smile on his lips, as if he'd somehow heard her wish.

"Make your wish and we'll throw our coins in together," she said.

"I already wished while you were making yours." He took her hand and said, "Let's do it together and make it count. One—"

"Two," they said in unison. "Three!" They threw their change into the air, and Graham swept her into his arms and kissed her deeply, serenaded by several tiny splashes.

The rest of the afternoon passed in a whirlwind of stolen kisses, fun conversations, and interesting little shops. When the sun began its slow descent from the clear blue sky, a cold knot began forming in Morgyn's stomach. She knew they had to go back to the festival and then she had to leave. Grace's rehearsal dinner was tonight, and tomorrow was the wedding. Sable and Axsel had planned to leave early today, and they'd texted her to make sure she was safe and would make it home in time for dinner. They'd be gone by the time she and Graham got back to the festival. She didn't want her day with Graham to end because despite wishes and heat-of-the moment words, she knew the likelihood was that this was all they'd ever have, and the last thing she needed was to pine for a man whose life was so far away from hers.

As they headed back the way they'd come, she felt his energy change, too. Without a word about the heaviness bearing down on them, they bought a sundae from Scoops and sat in the gazebo in the park while they shared it.

Graham kept her close, his eyes reflecting the same sadness she felt as they reluctantly gave in to the ending of their blissful, romantic afternoon and began their hike back to the festival.

They didn't talk much on the way, but they didn't have to. The way he held on to her, the kisses he gave her, and the way he slowed every so often just to touch her face or gaze into her eyes spoke louder than words ever could.

By the time they reached the festival, the sea of tents had become an expanse of crushed grass and mud, as many festivalgoers were already gone, and the rest were leaving in droves. The place was emptying out, and as they headed to Graham's truck to gather her things, that's how Morgyn felt—like she was about to be empty, too.

After getting her belongings together, Graham helped her take down her canopy and pack her van. With every glance, touch, and kiss, she tried to silence the voice in her head that wanted to ask all the unanswered questions—*Can we stay in touch? Will I ever see you again? How can our time be over?*

"I'm buying you a proper tent," he said as he set the broken poles in her van and closed the doors.

"I don't want a proper tent." She draped her arms around his neck and rested her face on his chest. *I want you.*

He kissed her forehead, holding her so tight she knew he was struggling, too. He pressed his hands to her cheeks, tilting her face up to his, and the knot in her stomach invaded her chest, making it hard to breathe. His dimples appeared, but the anguish in his eyes overshadowed them.

He touched his forehead to hers and said, "How did you change my world in a little more than twenty-four hours?"

Tears welled in her eyes. Unable to speak, she fought to keep her tears from falling. He thought *she'd* changed *his* world, but she knew they'd changed each other's. She filled with a sense of despair that once she left the festival grounds, her world would never feel as full, as bright, or as happy again.

He took off his hat and put it on her head. "I have plans I can't break tomorrow, but I'll find you Monday."

Happiness bubbled up inside her. "You're staying in town?"

"I am now. How can I leave us behind?"

"I'll give you my number—"

"No. My girl believes in ethereal things. How many boutiques could there be called Life Reimagined? I'll find you. I have to. You've got my lucky hat."

There was no stopping her happy tears from falling as he sealed his promise with several greedy kisses, and his words—*my girl*—and his promise—*I'll find you*—burrowed into her heart.

She slipped her flower chain over his head, and as she drove away, watching him disappear in the rearview mirror, she still felt Graham's strong arms around her, his heart beating against her own, and the hope of something more.

Chapter Six

AFTER SPENDING SUNDAY morning and most of the afternoon with her five sisters and Sophie Roberts-Bad, Grace's best friend and matron of honor, Morgyn had already had enough *wedding* to last her a lifetime—and they hadn't even gotten to the actual wedding yet. The wedding was being held in the field behind the Majestic Theater, where Grace and her fiancé, Reed Cross, claimed their love story began back in high school. Morgyn didn't want to know those dirty details. Reed had recently purchased the magnificent old theater. Although he planned to begin major renovations after they returned from their honeymoon, Reed had renovated the dressing room just for Grace to use before the wedding.

Sophie's sister, Lindsay Roberts, the wedding planner and photographer, was taking pictures as Grace wore a path in the floor in the dressing room. They had invited practically the entire town of Oak Falls and Meadowside, which made sense, since the night Reed proposed practically the whole town had been present. But it wouldn't matter how many people showed up. There was only one person Morgyn really wanted to see, and she had no hopes of seeing him until sometime tomorrow when he *found* her.

"Morg, I think you'd better look at this." Brindle fidgeted with the neckline of their sister Amber's dress.

Morgyn had made the short, champagne-colored bridesmaids dresses from gowns she'd purchased off Craigslist. The original dresses had been hideous, with hoop skirts and frilly necklines and sleeves, but the color and fabric were gorgeous. She had made each dress unique, to match her sisters' personalities.

"Stop messing with it," Morgyn said too impatiently as she went to them.

Brindle held her hands up and backed away, looking stunning in her sleeveless dress, with her long blond hair cascading over her shoulders. "*Sorry.* What's got your panties in a bunch?"

"Just tired," Morgyn said as she fixed Amber's neckline.

"Is it too low cut?" Amber reached nervously down to pet her service dog, Reno, a golden retriever. Amber was epileptic, and she wore a seizure-alert necklace their sister Pepper had developed when she was in graduate school. The device was now sold all over the country. It featured a button that Reno could push with his nose if Amber had a seizure, and it included an internal GPS system to alert family members and emergency services to Amber's location. Morgyn had painted the device the same champagne color as their dresses.

"No, and you look gorgeous," Morgyn reassured her most reserved sister.

Amber's dark hair was swept over one shoulder, secured with a ribbon. A few pretty tendrils framed her face. It was the perfect hairstyle for the draped neckline.

Morgyn pointed to Sable's plunging neckline on her spaghetti-strap dress and said, "Her neckline is too low, but you know Sable."

Amber lowered her voice to just above a whisper and said, "She said there won't be enough water to douse the flames when Chet Hudson sees her."

Chet was a firefighter from Meadowside, the next town over. He assessed risks the same way Graham did, and he was probably a smart man to keep his distance from Sable. Guys who went out with Sable always wanted more—more of a relationship, more hot dates, more of *anything* she'd give them, because Sable was *that* intriguing—but while Sable had a voracious appetite for men, like Brindle, it would take an act of God to get her to settle down.

"I swear, Gracie," Sable said from across the room, "if you don't stop pacing I'll tie you to a chair."

"Now, that would be a picture worth having," Lindsay teased.

"I'm allowed to be nervous. It's *my* wedding." Grace pushed her long dark hair over her shoulder and continued pacing, looking gorgeous in the simple and elegant halter-style wedding gown with a lace bodice and a slit up the right side of the skirt that went above her knee. "I know I'm going to trip down the aisle, or rip my dress, or throw up on Reed when I try to say my vows."

"Aw, Gracie," they said in unison.

"You're not going to do any such thing," Sophie said as she took Grace's hand and guided her to the couch. "But just in case, how about if you sit down until your mom comes to get us? Think about your honeymoon, Gracie. Ten days in Cornwall. You've always wanted to see the Minack Theatre, and now you get to see it with *Reed.* What could be more exciting than that?"

Pepper sat beside Grace and crossed her legs. More interested in research and technology than men who couldn't hold an intelligent conversation, Pepper had insisted on showing *no* cleavage. Her dress had a high lace neckline and capped sleeves, which fit her slender body perfectly. What Pepper didn't realize was that it didn't matter if she showed cleavage or wore a parka; she was beautiful, and her intelligence made her even more so. The truth was, Morgyn had always been a little jealous of her.

"You won't trip, Grace," Pepper said. "The minute you step onto the lawn, you're going to see Reed standing at the end of the aisle and all those butterflies will disappear. It's a known fact that you can't think of more than one thing at a time, and you'll be thinking of getting to him. Afterward, you probably won't even remember the walk down the aisle."

Grace sighed. "That's a relief, but how can I distract myself from it all right this second?"

"Morgyn can tell you all about Foreplay's brother!" Sable grabbed Morgyn's arm and dragged her toward Grace.

"Me? How about you tell her about Foreplay?" Morgyn suggested. She didn't want to talk about Graham, because she felt too much for him. And even if he was coming to see her tomorrow, what would happen after that? She'd been trying not to think about that particular question since she'd left him yesterday, an impossible feat.

Brindle pushed between Sable and Morgyn and said, "Hold up! Is *Foreplay* a *guy*?"

"Yes," Morgyn and Sable said in unison.

"He's Mr. All Nighter's brother," Sable said.

Although she was amused by her sister's name for Graham, she hoped to steer the conversation away from him and said, "He had the hots for Sable."

Sable rolled her eyes. "He had the *hots* for sex, and you

know I won't sleep with a guy who's prettier than I am."

"Whoa! Prettier than you? I would have liked to see him. What else did I miss at the festival?" Brindle turned wide smoky eyes on Morgyn. "*Who* is Mr. All Nighter?"

"The guy with the legs," Morgyn confessed. "And you saw Foreplay. He was the guy with the long hair."

"The gay guys? You slept with a gay guy?" Brindle asked.

"Must have been bi if he slept with Morg," Pepper pointed out.

Amber rushed over. "Morgyn, you had a one-night stand? I thought you weren't into that."

"Oh my God, you guys!" Morgyn began pacing. "He's not gay, and he's not bi, and it wasn't a one-night stand. I'm seeing him tomorrow."

Brindle squealed and hugged her. "I want all the details. He was wicked hot. Is his joy stick as thick as his legs? You guys should have seen his ass. Talk about *nice*."

"Brindle!" Morgyn glared at her.

"What? It was nice and—" She made squeezing motions with her hands. "Where did you do it? I know you didn't do it in your tent. You'd be too worried about people seeing you."

"I'm *not* having this conversation." Morgyn's heart was racing. The last thing she needed was for Brindle to make her incredible time with Graham into a dirty tryst. "And stop thinking about his ass."

"Someone's jealous," Sable said.

Morgyn turned a hot glare on Sable.

"Is he from around here?" Amber asked.

"No, and I have no idea how long he's going to be here, but I really like him and it's not what you guys are making it out to be."

Sable arched a brow. "So it *wasn't* hot sex with Mr. All Nighter? Then why bother seeing him again?"

"God, you're impossible." Morgyn turned to leave just as their mother appeared in the doorway.

"Hey, sugar. What's wrong?" Her mother reached for Morgyn's hand, forcing her to stop.

I want to strangle my sisters, turn the clock back to yesterday, and stay there forever. Knowing that would only incite more annoying comments, she said, "Nothing."

"Bull hockey." Her mother eyed Sable, who was smirking. "Fess up, Sabe. What did you do?"

Sable crossed her arms, looking put out. "Why do you think it's me? Look at this motley crew of gossipers."

"I don't gossip," Grace said.

"I have a new baby. I have no time to gossip," Sophie said.

"She thinks it's you because it's either you or Brindle," Pepper said. "And Brindle would have admitted it by now."

"That's true," Brindle said.

"It's nothing, Mom," Morgyn said. The minute her mother heard about her spending the night with Graham there would be even more questions. "We're all just antsy to get started."

Her mother brushed Morgyn's hair away from her face the way she'd been doing since Morgyn was little and said, "Are you sure, honey?"

No. She was pretty sure it wasn't even her sisters' taunts that had her so upset. She'd been an emotional wreck since she and Graham said goodbye.

"*Honey?*" her mother urged.

I have all these feelings whirling around inside me and I have no clue what to do with them. She could tell her mother that and trust it to stay between them, but there were too many eyes on her to fess up about something so real and confusing.

"Yes," she lied. "I'm sure. Are they ready to start?"

"They are. It's time, Gracie." Their mother held a hand out toward Grace. "And I think your future husband is even more nervous than you are. The Jericho boys have been trying to distract him, but you know Reed. There's only one thing on his mind—marrying the woman he's loved since he was a googly-eyed teenager."

A flurry of commotion ensued as they checked Grace's dress one last time, grabbed their orchid bouquets, and then headed down the hall. Sable and Brindle flanked Morgyn.

"Don't," Morgyn warned. "Can I just get through today without any more crap about his body parts?"

Sable's expression turned serious. "You really like this guy."

"Gee, you think?" she said sarcastically. "I'm a wreck, and all your jokes just make it worse."

"You could hook up with another guy at the wedding to get your mind off him," Brindle suggested.

Morgyn rolled her eyes. "I don't want to hook up with anyone else. I just want today to pass so tomorrow can arrive and I can see him again."

"MY GRANDDAUGHTER LINDSAY would be perfect for you," Nina—*call me Nana*—said for the third time in the last twenty minutes. She looked like Helen Mirren and acted like the mother in *Meet the Fockers*. She pointed to a pretty blonde taking pictures of a fair-haired man and said, "Look at her over there. She's a little sexpot, isn't she? She owns a wedding planning and photography business. She's a *catch*."

Nana and her silver-haired friend, Hellie, had been talking Graham's ear off since he sat down—like dirty-grandma matchmakers.

"Don't forget Haylie Hudson." Hellie leaned closer to Graham and said, "She's got the cutest little boy, Scotty. Do you like children? You look like a man who likes kids."

"Of course he likes children," Nana said. "You can tell when a man dislikes children. You can smell them coming a mile away." She elbowed Graham and giggled as she said, "No pun intended."

"I like children," he said, "but I'm really not looking for a date."

Hellie waved her hand dismissively, flashing several colorful rings. "That's *okay*, honey. We get your drift. We know a few good men we can introduce you to."

He choked out a cough. "I'm not gay. I'm just biding my time until tomorrow, when I can see my girl again."

"Oh, you don't have to cover it up," Nana said. "We're a very open community."

Nana had seemed so innocent when he'd sat down beside her, but then Hellie had taken the chair on his other side and everything had changed. He wondered if the two women waited for unsuspecting men to home in on like hawks stalking prey. "I'm not—"

Music sounded, and Nana and Hellie both said, "Shh!"

Glad for the interruption, Graham swept his gaze over rows of white chairs to the floral arch at the end of the center aisle, where his friend Reed stood beside his uncle Roy, who had raised him, looking nervous and happy in a dark suit. He knew Reed's father, who was suffering from a terminal illness and from whom Reed had been estranged since he was a baby, was there somewhere. Graham was glad Reed had been able to find closure in that part of his life.

Nana nudged his shoulder. "All the girls who are going to walk down the aisle are single except my granddaughter, Sophie, the matron of honor, and, of course, Gracie. So keep your eyes peeled. You just pick one out and we'll introduce you."

Graham followed her gaze toward the women coming through the back door of the theater. He thought he saw Sable walking with a petite blonde, both wearing short dresses and cowgirl boots. "Is that…?"

"Those are two of Grace's sisters. Sable's the brunette, and Brindle's the blonde."

"Brindle," he repeated, piecing together more of Morgyn's family.

"You'd better buckle up for a wild ride with that gal," Hellie said with a shake of her head.

Graham watched as the bride and two slim brunettes filed out the door.

"That's my Sophie, on Grace's right," Nana said. "And those two pretty gals are also Grace's sisters. Pepper has the lace collar. She's a big-time scientist, and Amber, the one with her hair pulled to one side, standing beside the dog, owns a bookstore. They're more *pretty fillies* than *wild rides* like Sable. But to each their own…"

Her voice turned to white noise as Morgyn came into view and Graham's heart rate skyrocketed. He squinted, trying to get a better look. Her hair was tied back, a few wispy bangs framing her face. She wore a short dress with a single ruffled strap over one shoulder. The dress accentuated her curves and showed off her long legs. Legs he could still feel wrapped around him. All the other girls wore brown cowgirl boots, but Morgyn's were brown and turquoise, with glimmering silver and gold embellishments. His fingers itched with the need to hold her. She was carrying a bouquet. While the other girls were smiling and huddled together, Morgyn stood a few paces away with a sad look in her eyes. How come no one was tending to her? Couldn't they tell her smile was forced? Couldn't they sense it the way he could?

"Sunshine," he said absently. It took all of his control not to go to her and fix whatever was wrong.

"It is a beautiful day," Hellie said. "And look at Morgyn. That girl's got more style in her pinkie than half the county put together."

"Mm-hm," Nana agreed. "Morgyn's a feisty one, and she's sweeter than cherry pie. She's got a wanderer's soul, though. It'll take a special guy to keep up with her."

"Yes, it will," he said as the wedding began. *A wanderer's soul.* He wondered about how far she'd wander. Soon there was no room for thought. There was only beautiful Morgyn and the distance stretching between them as the ceremony took place. Morgyn stood off to the side with her sisters, the half-hearted smile on her face tugging at Graham's heartstrings.

Was she thinking of him, the way he'd been thinking of her since yesterday?

Morgyn's gaze swept over the crowd, and he sat up a little straighter, hoping she'd see him, but her eyes moved past, and his heart sank. As he tried to rein in his disappointment, her gaze zipped back to him, connecting with the heat of a laser. He couldn't suppress his smile as her eyes widened with delight, and her radiant smile followed. She went up on her toes, like she wanted to get a better look, and he couldn't help rising up as well. He lifted his chin and blew her a kiss. Even from that distance, he could feel her energy lighten. Brindle leaned closer and said something to her, but Morgyn never took her eyes off him. She said something, and then Brindle was going up on her toes, searching for him, he assumed. On Morgyn's other side, Sable looked at the two women, then searched the crowd.

He tried to stop a chuckle, and a tortured sound escaped before he could stop it. Nana put her hand on his and whispered, "It's very emotional, isn't it? Weddings get me every time."

"Gets me every time," he said, looking at Morgyn.

The ceremony went on for what felt like forever, but in reality it was probably little more than half an hour. When Reed finally kissed Grace, everyone clapped and cheered, rising from their seats. Graham eyed the distance between him and Morgyn, wondering if it would be in bad taste to race down the aisle and sweep her off her feet.

The wedding party followed Grace and Reed up the aisle. Morgyn was walking with a tall, dark-haired man, but she only had eyes for Graham. His heart thundered harder with her every step. Her eyes were glistening, and her smile was so big it had to hurt. His legs moved forward without thought.

"Excuse me," he said to Hellie. She said something about waiting another minute, but he couldn't wait another second. "I'm sorry," he said as he pushed past her.

Morgyn ran up the aisle, pushing past her sisters, and leapt into his arms. Their mouths came together like an unstoppable force. Smiling into their kisses, he twirled her around, unable to believe she was right there in his arms.

"Sunshine," he said, and then there were no words, only his lips pressed to hers, her fingers in his hair, and his heart beating a mile a minute.

"It's *Legs*!" Brindle said from behind them as hoots and hollers rang out from the crowd.

"Cracker!" Morgyn kissed his lips, his cheeks, his chin. "How did you find me?"

"Mr. All Nighter must have a GPS tracker in his—" Sable said.

"Sable!" Grace glared at Sable as she and Reed hurried back down the aisle. Reed arched a brow as his new bride flashed an approving gaze and said, "I think we need to rename you Mr. Wedding Crasher. Thanks for waiting for us to finish our kiss before you took yours."

Graham realized they were blocking the aisle and everyone was watching them. He lowered Morgyn's feet to the ground. Several of the groomsmen were openly assessing him with serious expressions. *Go ahead, assess all you want.* He squared his shoulders and said, "I'm sorry for interrupting the wedding." He reached for Morgyn's hand and noticed she still had on the bracelet he'd given her. He filled with happiness. "I'm Graham Braden, a friend of Reed's."

"And of mine," Morgyn added with a beaming smile.

"Guess that answers the gay question," Nana said from behind him, causing everyone to laugh.

Graham scoffed and shook his head. "Why does everyone think I'm gay?"

"Because you're too pretty, man." Reed pulled him into an embrace. "It's good to see you."

"You too. Congratulations." He looked at Grace and said, "I really am sorry for interrupting, but your sister..." He gazed at Morgyn, pulling her against his side as he said, "There's no excuse. I honestly couldn't wait a second longer."

There was a collective "Aw."

"Reed has told me a lot about you," Graham said. "Big-time play producer turned community theater enthusiast. Sounds like you'll do great things for Oak Falls."

"I don't know about great things, but we just put on our first play and—"

"It was amazing!" Morgyn said. "Grace is the best producer, and she's teaching classes on screenplay writing and working with local companies to fund future events. I'm in awe of her."

Grace's eyes teared up and she hugged Morgyn.

"Grace is already making a world of difference," Reed said proudly. "And once the theater is open, she'll make an even bigger impact." He looked between Graham and Morgyn and said, "I had no idea you two knew each other. Morgyn, Graham is the investor I told you about, the one I wanted to evaluate your business."

"Evaluate her business?" Graham asked. "I thought I was here to check out your theater."

"You are," Reed said. "Tomorrow morning at eight. Grace and I leave for our honeymoon at noon. Morgyn's on the cusp of some changes with her business. I thought you might be able to check it out while you're here, go over her books, offer some suggestions…"

Graham tried never to mixed business and pleasure. Sure, he helped a few friends but not friends he was sleeping with. "I don't think it's a good idea, since we've got a personal relationship."

"Oh, come on, cracker. It's a *very* good idea." Morgyn went up on her toes and whispered, "You might have to inspect my goods."

He cleared his throat to stifle a hungrier noise.

"Morgyn's gonna get lucky," Brindle said in a singsong voice.

Morgyn smiled up at him and said, "I already have."

"As if we had any doubt?" Grace said under her breath.

Morgyn gasped. "No! I meant because he's *here*. I didn't know he was going to be at the wedding."

"Who is this handsome devil kissing my little girl?" A dark-haired woman pushed through the crowd, eyeing Graham and Morgyn with the same spark of life in her eyes that Morgyn possessed.

"Mr. All Night—"

Amber elbowed Sable and said, "His name is *Graham*, Mom. They met at the festival."

"Hi, *Mom*." He extended his hand. "Graham Braden, professional wedding procession crasher. It's nice to meet you."

"Aren't you just the cutest thing. Look at those dimples. No wonder Morgyn's all pink cheeked." She embraced him and said, "I'm Marilynn Montgomery, the mother of all these noisy girls. I'm so pleased to meet you." She pointed to a fair-haired man with sharp blue eyes standing beside Axsel and watching every move Graham made. "And that handsome man over there is their father, Cade, standing with their brother, Axsel. They will probably have a few questions for you, so I suggest you go get yourselves a drink before the inquisition starts."

As they made their way out of the aisle, Morgyn leaned against his side like she couldn't stand to have any space between them. And he loved it.

"How did you and Reed meet?" Morgyn asked.

"He renovated a project I funded in Michigan, and we hit it off. We've been friends ever since."

Reed and Grace got swept up in the crowd, and Morgyn's

parents stopped to greet the other guests. Morgyn and her sisters guided him off to the side. Trixie Jericho, who Graham knew through his brother Nick, stood with four guys a few feet away. The men stood shoulder to shoulder, arms crossed, sizing up Graham. Two wore cowboy hats, reminding him of his brother Nick. One was dressed sharper than the others and looked like he was chewing on nails, and the fourth wore a serious expression, like Graham's oldest brother, Beau, used to before he'd fallen in love with his fiancée, Charlotte Sterling.

"This is Pepper," Morgyn said, motioning to her tall, slim sister. "She and Sable are twins. Pepper's a research and development scientist in Charlottesville."

While Morgyn and Brindle were fair like their father and her other siblings were darker, like their mother, Pepper had shades of brown and blond in her hair. She had a serious air about her and warm, intelligent eyes.

"What type of things do you develop?" he asked.

"Neurological devices mostly," Pepper said, "but I'm researching a few other areas."

"That's fascinating. I'd love to hear how you got into that field."

"She's amazing," Morgyn said. "She made Amber's seizure-alarm necklace."

Amber lifted a necklace from her chest with a shy smile. "*Epilepsy*, in case you're wondering." She reached down and petted the golden retriever standing beside her. "This is Reno, my service dog. Our mother trains service dogs and teaches them all to use the device."

"It's nice to meet you both," Graham said, mentally noting information about each of her family members. He wanted to know everything about Morgyn's family and the parents who had raised such an amazing daughter.

"Amber owns the best bookstore in Meadowside," Morgyn explained. Her adoration for her siblings was apparent despite her claiming to have wanted a little less love from them at the festival.

"Ahem," Brindle interrupted with a wiggle of her shoulders. "And your *hottest* sister…?"

"He already met Grace," Morgyn teased. "This is Brindle. She teaches at the high school, runs the drama club for the elementary school, and has issues with modesty."

Graham laughed. *Drama.* That made sense. While Pepper and Amber both seemed fairly demure and Morgyn and Sable were outgoing, Brindle gave off an overly dramatic, flirtatious vibe.

"Ah, yes," Graham said. "The one who left you high and dry at the festival—"

Brindle rolled her eyes. "Oh, *please.* Morgyn might have been high on life, but she ended up with you. There's no way she was *dry.*"

"Brindle!" Morgyn turned away, but not before Graham noticed her blushing.

Graham pulled her closer. "Your family is great," he said for her ears only.

"Nice save, Mustang," one of the cowboys who was sizing up Graham said as he walked over and draped an arm possessively over Brindle's shoulder. The other three guys and Trixie followed him over.

"You must be Brindle's boyfriend?" Graham asked. "Bet I can get a few tips from you on how to romance a Montgomery girl."

Brindle and the guy both laughed.

"No," the guy said. "We're not…"

"Do *not* take relationship advice from *this* one," Amber said. "From either him or Brindle, actually."

"Again with this?" Cowboy shook his head.

"I give good relationship advice," Brindle said. "Don't commit and no one can get hurt. There. *Done.*"

"Hey, Montgomerys!" Nana's granddaughter, Lindsay, shouted as she approached. She carried a camera and looked like she was on a mission. "Family photos before drinks. We can't have any stains on those pretty dresses. Let's go." She glanced at Graham and said, "I'm Lindsay Roberts, photographer extraordinaire and the master planner of this great event. Don't worry. I got a great shot of your impromptu make-out session. I'll blow it up to poster size for you, but first I need to steal your girl."

Brindle grabbed Morgyn's and Amber's arms and said, "Come on, Pep!" as she dragged them all away.

"I'll be fast!" Morgyn hollered over her shoulder. "Go have a drink!"

Graham watched Morgyn race away.

"Get used to it," the guy who *wasn't* Brindle's boyfriend said as the other three guys and Trixie, the woman who worked with Nick, converged on Graham. "I think it's time we get to know each other. I'm Trace Jericho and this is my brother Justus; you can call him JJ."

JJ tipped his cowboy hat.

"I hear you know my sister, Trixie," Trace said.

Trixie waved. "Small world."

"Nice to see you again," Graham said. He was used to seeing Trixie working with the horses, wearing jeans, boots, and a flannel shirt tied at her waist. She looked like a completely different person in a dress. Nick would probably lose his mind seeing the hourglass-shaped brunette in a short dress.

"And these are my buddies." Trace motioned to the other guys—the sharp dresser and the serious-eyed dude. "Beckett Wheeler and Chet Hudson."

"How's it going?" Chet said.

Beckett's jaw clenched and Trixie elbowed him. He grunted out a "Hey."

"Nice to meet you," Graham said as they headed toward the open bar. "I take it you're the welcoming committee?"

"Something like that," Beckett ground out.

They ordered drinks and Graham prepared for the inquisition, doing his own sizing up. Trace, JJ, and Chet had the type of brawn that came from hard physical labor, while Beckett was fit, but not bulky. Graham guessed he had an office job. The way Trixie was keeping an eye on the guys, he had a feeling she was there to keep the peace.

"Think of us as Morgyn's big brothers," Trace said. Then he took a sip of his beer.

"Okay, that's just gross," Trixie said. "You're sleeping with Brindle, and now it sounds incestuous."

"She's right, dude," JJ said with a chuckle.

Graham took a drink, his eyes shifting to Morgyn and her family taking pictures by the trees. She was all smiles, and he liked to think that was because they were together, but it could be because she and her sisters were goofing off while Lindsay tried to wrangle them into a pose.

"Did I hear you're an investor?" Beckett asked, eyes narrowed and trained on Graham in what he probably thought gave him an edge.

Graham wasn't impressed. This was a wedding, not a

throwdown. "That's right. Real estate, capital investments, that sort of thing. What is it that you do?"

"Uh-oh," Chet said. "Investor versus investor."

This could get interesting.

Graham wondered if the chip on Beckett's shoulder was because they shared a field. "You're an investor? What's your market?"

Beckett took another drink, biding his time responding, an old negotiation tool used to gain the upper hand. It had no effect on Graham.

"Started out in banking," Beckett finally said. "Now I do mostly personal investing, company startups…"

"He invests his time in giving Morgyn's boyfriends grief," Trixie teased.

"And why is that?" Graham asked, holding Beckett's stare.

"Because she dumped him a few years ago, and he doesn't think anyone else is good enough for her," Trixie explained.

Beckett sneered. "She didn't dump me. It was the other way around."

"Does it matter?" Chet said. "Christ, Beck, give the guy a break. That ended years ago, and nobody wants to hear about it. Listen, Graham, we don't know you, but we know and care about Morgyn. You waltz into town and sweep her off her feet…" He shrugged. "We just want to make sure she's with a good guy."

"He knows *Reed*," Trixie pointed out. "Do you really think Reed would invite a jerk to the wedding? He's Nick's *brother*. You guys know Nick, and I've met Graham a dozen times over the last few years at Nick's ranch, so back off already."

"Listen, I'm sure there are people who think I'm a jerk," Graham said. "And there are people who would kiss my feet.

The fact is, I'm just a normal guy. I make a good living, travel a lot, put my family first, and feel lucky to have connected with someone as amazing as Morgyn." He looked at Beckett and said, "I'd say I'm sorry it didn't work out for you two, but that'd make me a liar, because she wouldn't have been single when I met her. So let's just get past the bullshit, assume we're both good guys, and move on."

"Here, here." Trixie lifted her glass.

Trace elbowed Beckett, and Beckett reluctantly lifted his glass as Morgyn and her sisters approached.

"I hope you guys aren't swinging dicks," Brindle called out, "because from what Morgyn says, Graham will put all of y'all to shame!"

"I did not!" Morgyn insisted as she came to Graham's side. "But he *definitely* would."

Graham put his arm around her, pride filling his chest as he kissed her. "Thanks, sunshine."

"Well, that's more information than I needed to hear. Catch y'all later." Beckett turned and stalked away.

"Be warned," Trixie said to Morgyn. "Beckett has a bug up his butt."

Morgyn turned worried eyes to Graham. "I hope he wasn't a jerk. We went out for a little while."

"He wasn't, and it wouldn't have mattered if he was. If I'd lost you I'd probably have a bug up my ass, too."

Chapter Seven

THE RECEPTION FLEW by, or maybe *floated by* was a better description, because Morgyn was definitely on cloud nine. Dinner was delicious and the conversations were hilarious, as her siblings and their friends had ribbed her and Graham relentlessly. One of Morgyn's pet peeves with the guys she'd gone out with was their inability to just be themselves, to live without pretense and roll with the punches without getting competitive. She'd known from the festival that Graham wasn't like that, but being at the wedding, surrounded by so many people who were eager to see what he was made of, really put him to the test. Graham took it all in stride, blessing them with his dimples throughout the evening and kissing her without any hesitation. It was obvious that he was used to big families and the commotion that often came with them.

Now, as Sable's band got ready to play another set, Morgyn watched Graham and her father cross the field toward the table carrying fresh drinks. Graham looked devilishly handsome in a white dress shirt, sleeves rolled up to just below his elbows, and a pair of dark slacks. Without his baseball cap he looked more serious, making it easier to picture him in a boardroom negotiating business deals. She might never understand the business world the way others did, but she respected it and was glad that so far he seemed to respect her world, too.

"What do you think Daddy's saying?" she asked her mother.

"Let's see. An engineering professor and an engineer slash investor? My bet is that they're figuring out a better way to build the sound stage for Sable's band." Her mother patted her hand and said, "Either that, or he's telling Graham about the time you and Brindle took off your clothes and did a rain dance at the Strawberry Festival."

Morgyn covered her face. "Oh God. I hope not."

"It's better than him telling the story about the two of you sneaking out to go to that creek party when you were teenagers. If he tells that story, he'll probably follow it up with a threat or two."

"He would not." She laughed, remembering how angry Brindle had been when their father had shown up. She glanced at Brindle and Trace on the dance floor. They were so right together, but they both fought it so hard. "Do you think Brin and Trace will ever become a *real* couple?"

"Honey, every time I think I have one of my daughters figured out, they surprise me. I don't even try to figure you guys out anymore. But that doesn't mean I don't worry. She leaves for Paris Friday, and she's going to be so far away, all alone..." She patted Morgyn's hand and said, "But like you, Brindle has always done things her own way. I have faith she'll figure things out in a way that's right for *her*. And I have a feeling you might be figuring something out, too. I've never seen you this smitten with a man before. By the way, you're welcome to bring Graham to Brindle's going-away dinner Tuesday night."

"I don't know if he'll still be in town, but thank you." How long *was* he staying? Her stomach dipped at the thought of him leaving. "Mom, how did you know that Dad was *the one*?"

"Oh, sweetheart, there were too many signs to ignore. Some so big they felt like billboards and some so small I was sure I dreamed them up," her mother said. "But I think the biggest thing was that before your father and I met, I was sort of like you, drifting happily through life. Then he showed up, and suddenly he was front and center in every thought I had about my future. We were inescapable."

"Inescapable," she said softly.

Graham and her father had stopped a few feet from the table, their foreheads nearly touching like they were sharing secrets. Her father put a hand on Graham's shoulder, both of them looking serious. Then her father said something and Graham cocked his head, and his gaze slid to Morgyn. Electricity arced between them. She drank in his broad chest and muscular forearms as his thick legs ate up the distance between them. She could still feel his body bearing down on her, his hips moving in slow, powerful thrusts, his tantalizing mouth sending her higher as he—

"I'd say that right there is a *very* good sign, sweet pea."

Oh shit. Morgyn swallowed hard, feeling her cheeks burn. "You can *see* it?"

"I think everyone here can see that he passed your father's test, don't you?"

Relief rushed from her lungs as the men arrived and Graham stopped beside her chair.

He reached for her hand, bringing her up beside him. "Ready to light up the dance floor, sunshine? It's calling our name."

"Oh my, you are a sweet one, aren't you?" her mother said.

Her father pulled her mother up to her feet and said, "Hey,

Mare. That guy's got nothing on me, except about twenty years." Her father winked and said, "Let's show these kids how it's done."

Morgyn loved seeing her parents dance almost as much as she enjoyed being in Graham's arms again. They danced for a long while. As the sun went down, the lights that were strung across the field and the balloon lanterns hanging from the trees lit up, giving the night an even more magical feel.

"I still can't believe you're here," she said as they swayed to the music. "What are your plans? How long are you staying?"

"My original plan was to assess the theater with Reed, then head across the country to visit relatives on my way to meet my business partner in Washington. We're thinking of buying a property just outside of Seattle. Then I'm heading to New York to discuss another investment. We've also got another international deal in the wings, but..."

"Wow, you travel a *lot.*" Drive across the country? Then to Seattle and New York? An international deal? She had a feeling that no matter how great this was between them, it was probably temporary.

"I do, and those were my *original* plans. But then I met a sexy woman at a festival, and now I'm in no rush to leave." His eyes darkened and he said, "I booked a room at the Meadowside B and B until Friday, when I have to leave for the West Coast. I figured we'd see how things went."

"Five days," she said, feeling lucky and knowing that would never be enough.

"It's a start..." He held her a little tighter as they danced.

Her heart raced with the thought of seeing even more of him. "I was thinking you might want to stay with me, but if you've already paid—"

"Do you think I give a damn about a few bucks? There's no place I'd rather be than with you. When I saw you come out of the theater with your sisters, I thought I conjured your image from thinking about you so much."

He pressed his lips to hers, showing her just *how much* he'd rather be with her. His kisses sizzled through her, stealing her ability to think, and she melted against him. His lips were warm and sweet as he eased his efforts to a series of feathery, tantalizing grazes of his lips against hers.

They danced to several songs, kissing and holding each other. Morgyn loved Grace, and she wanted to support her, but the longer she danced with Graham, the deeper she longed to be alone with him, to feel their bodies melding together as they disappeared into each other.

Suddenly there was a commotion, tearing her from her fantasy.

Grace ran up to the stage and tapped the mic. "Who's ready to catch the bouquet?"

A bunch of girls rushed toward the stage.

"Oh, no." Morgyn tried to back away, but the crowd pushed forward. She was trapped.

"Aren't you going to try to catch it?" Graham asked.

"No. If you catch the bouquet, everyone starts betting on wedding dates and babies. I don't want that pressure."

He looked amused *and* confused. "You're really afraid of commitment, aren't you? I don't get it. Your parents seem happily married."

"I'm not afraid of commitment. I'm good at committing. I just don't need"—she waved her hand at the crowd—"all this to prove it's real."

"Ready?" Grace's voice boomed over the speaker. She

turned around and said, "One!"

Brindle ran over and said, "Let's go, Morg. Come on, *legs*. We gotta get out of here."

"Two! Three!" Grace threw the bouquet, and Morgyn and Brindle screamed and ducked.

The bouquet landed right in Graham's arms. There was a collective gasp, followed by an uproar of laughter and congratulations.

Graham uttered, "Oh shit."

"No. No, no, no." Morgyn shook her head, waving her hands. "Drop it! Quick, just let it fall to the ground."

"You're screwed, Morg," Brindle said.

Graham chuckled and held the flowers out toward Morgyn. "For you, sunshine."

"Excuse me!" Nana pushed through the crowd and planted her hands on her hips. "I'm not sure what it means when a man catches the bouquet, but I'll gladly give these to Lindsay!"

"You sure, Morgyn?" Graham arched a brow.

"Yes!" Morgyn took the flowers from him and handed them to Nana.

Nana's arm shot up into the air, and she traipsed victoriously toward the stage, saying, "Lindsay! We've got the bouquet!"

The crowd cheered and followed Nana, giving Morgyn room to breathe.

"She takes her granddaughter's love life very seriously," she said lightly, but the concern in Graham's eyes made her heart hurt.

"Uh-oh. Looks like Morg's got some explaining to do." Brindle leaned closer to Graham and said, "Rule number one. Never push a Montgomery into a corner. We'll always come out fighting."

Graham pulled Morgyn into his arms. "Never underestimate a Braden." A coy smile appeared on his lips. "I just scratched Ask Morgyn to Marry Me off my bucket list."

She went up on her toes and kissed him. "Cracker, you just got a thousand times hotter."

"At least I'm heading in the right direction. The guitar only made me a *hundred* times hotter."

"You should see what getting her an extra piece of wedding cake will get you," Brindle suggested.

Graham took Morgyn's hand and dragged her off the dance floor.

Hurrying to keep up she said, "Where are we going?"

"Dessert table, and if it's empty, we're hitting the bakery I saw on the way in."

TWO HOURS LATER, after they shared sugary kisses and danced until the band stopped playing, the wedding came to an end. Grace and Reed drove away in Reed's truck with JUST MARRIED painted on the tailgate and noisy cans tied to the bumper. After saying goodbye to everyone under the stars and giving Pepper and Axsel extra hugs because they were both leaving town early the next morning, Morgyn and Graham made their way to his truck.

"Hey, Braden!"

They turned at the sound of Trace's voice and found him with his arm around Brindle, heading for his truck.

"We're all heading over to JJ's Pub," Trace hollered. "You and Morgyn want to come?"

Morgyn was elated that over the course of the evening her friends and family had gotten to know Graham. Trixie mentioned that Beckett had given him a hard time when they'd first met, but even Beckett was coming around.

She turned to Graham, and the hungry look in his eyes told her the answer before she asked. Just in case she wasn't reading him right, she said, "Do you want to go?"

"Don't take this wrong. I like your family and friends, but they don't hold a candle to you, sunshine, and right now all I want is to finally kiss you like I've been dying to do all day."

Morgyn waved without turning around and hollered, "We're good. It's been a long day."

Sable brushed past them carrying her guitar and said, "Guess it's going to be an even longer night." She turned, walking backward as she added, "Nice to see you again. Hope you stick around for a while and live up to your new nick-name."

Graham turned a curious gaze to Morgyn.

"Don't ask me. I have no idea what she's talking about." She looked at Sable and said, "What new nickname?"

Sable unlocked the door to her truck and said, "Next in Line. Nice job catching the bouquet." She laughed and climbed into her truck.

"Your sister is awesome. She's not afraid of anything, is she?" Graham asked as they came to his Land Rover.

"Yes," she said as he opened the door. "She and Brindle are both afraid of commitment."

"What is with you Montgomery girls?"

"It's not all of us. I don't think Amber and Pepper have issues with commitment or marriage, and obviously Grace doesn't." Morgyn climbed into the truck, noticing the flower necklace she'd made hanging from his rearview mirror. Happiness wound through her as he settled into the driver's seat.

She touched the necklace and said, "You kept it."

"Yeah, I'm sentimental like that." He leaned across the seat and drew her into a long, slow kiss. "At least when it comes to you."

He started the truck and she said, "To get to my house, you take a left out of the parking lot and then go through town. When you see the Marriott, turn left." She knew he deserved an answer about why she wasn't sold on marriage, so as he drove out of the parking lot she said, "Do you want to know why I don't want to get married?"

"I am curious."

"You brought up my parents' marriage, and there's no doubt that we have great role models. Around here, for whatever reason, couples seem to stay together. But I went to college at UVA in Charlottesville, and most of my friends had divorced parents. It kind of freaked me out. It made me wonder if I lived in this little bubble where everything is so focused on family, it helps keep couples together."

His brows knitted. "You don't trust that whoever you fall in love with won't love you outside of Oak Falls?"

"Not exactly. I don't know what it is, but I know that I want a love that will last no matter where we are. Our community focuses so much on family that even the idea of divorce is shocking. But in college, when I talked about Friday-night family jam sessions, when everyone goes to the Jericho barn to play music, or going to a pot-luck dinner hosted by Nana and her friends, people my age couldn't relate. They couldn't imagine wanting to hang out with their parents that much. And

I get that, you know? My friends and I have our own parties and get-togethers without parents, but there's something wonderful about those family events. Everyone's so busy all the time, and none of us live at home anymore. It's a time for us all to reconnect, and I know my parents reconnect with each other as much as they do with us, because during those events, they're even closer than they normally are. I guess it made me wonder if those events, and being in a community where long marriages are the norm, help keep couples together."

She pointed up ahead and said, "Turn there, right before the Marriott. And then take the second right."

"I think I need to take you traveling with me, sunshine, so you can see the world from another perspective. Trouble isn't caused by the effects of a bigger community on a marriage. Life is full of choices, from how you'll bedazzle your boots to who you'll let kiss you." He followed her directions and turned down the road leading to her house. "If someone is going to fall out of love, it's going to happen no matter where they live. For a lot of people it's easier to move on than it is to work through a rough patch." Graham glanced over with a serious expression. "You might not have more family events here than other places. Where I live we have parades and all sorts of family events, and I'm sure they're offered in bigger cities, too. Your community is so small, it might only seem like you have the majority of residents attending. If you looked at statistics, you might find that the number of attendees in larger cities doesn't differ much from your own, but because the size of the city is larger, it would seem like fewer people attended. But I bet if your parents lived in Washington, DC, Chicago, Illinois, or anywhere else, they'd seek out family-related events because it's what they enjoy *together*. I don't think it's the location that changes love.

It's the people making the choices."

She thought about that as they drove down the long narrow road toward her house. "When you pass the mimosa tree, you'll see a colorful mailbox. That's my driveway."

"You live way out here alone?"

"Mm-hm. My grandfather inherited the property from his father. He called it their hunting property, although they never hunted. That's what his father had called it, because the two of them used to scour the land for interesting sights and treasures, so the name stuck. After the railroad stopped running, which was around when my grandfather retired, we would come out here and walk along the tracks. We found all sorts of cool stuff, and then we'd make things out of them in his barn. When he passed away he left the property to me and my siblings. Nobody wanted it but me. Grace moved to New York for college right after high school and didn't come back until a few months ago. Sable lives above her auto shop. She's a mechanic, by the way. Music is just a side gig for her. Pepper moved out to Charlottesville, and Amber is afraid to live this far away from everyone in case she has trouble. Medically, I mean," she said as he turned onto her dark tree-lined driveway. "And Axsel travels all the time. But I couldn't wait to live here. I built my house over summer break during my sophomore year of college."

"You *built* a house when you were in college?" he asked incredulously.

"Mm-hm."

"How did you afford it?"

"Bartering, of course," she said as the woods fell away and her gorgeous property came into view. Seven lush acres of woods, grass, flowering trees, and a beautiful little creek. Wild roses and other flowers sprouted up throughout the property. A mulched footpath led from the driveway to her 238-square-foot tiny house and to the greenhouse near her vegetable gardens and the barn.

He parked at the end of the driveway and said, "Holy shit, sunshine. This is gorgeous. Your barn is adorable. It looks like a tiny house."

"That *is* my house. The barn is way back on the property and four times the size of my house."

"You live in a tiny house?" He leaned across the console and pulled her into a toe-curling kiss. And then he brushed his lips over hers and said, "Sunshine," with so much emotion, it sent a rush of adrenaline through her. "I didn't think it was possible, but you just got a hundred times hotter."

She laughed at his throwing her own words back at her. "Only a hundred?"

"You haven't invited me inside yet."

"Mr. Braden," she said seductively, "would you like to come inside my tiny house?"

"Inside the house, in the yard, and anywhere else the feeling hits us."

He reclaimed her lips, devouring her so intensely, she tried to climb over the console to get to him.

"Forget a hundred times hotter," he said in a husky voice. "You just broke a million."

THEY STUMBLED INTO her adorably rustic tiny house in a tangle of gropes and hungry kisses. They toed off their shoes and stripped off their clothes as they ascended the narrow staircase that led to a loft above the kitchen, ducking at the top of the stairs to keep from hitting their heads on the angled ceiling. Morgyn wrapped her arms around his neck, and he lowered them both to the mattress, which was on the floor. Just like his.

"God, sunshine," he said between hungry kisses. "How can I possibly miss you this much?" He rained kisses down her neck. "I feel like we've been apart for years, and we've known each other only a few days."

"Spiritually, we've known each other much longer," she panted out as he kissed his way south. "Our paths—"

She gasped as he took her breast in his mouth, and arched beneath him, moaning as he teased the taut peak, then sucked it into his mouth. His hands moved eagerly over her body, loving her softness against his hard frame. He lavished her other breast with the same attention, and then he took his time memorizing every dip and swell as he tasted and nipped his way down her body, learning every luscious spot that earned a sinful noise or a gasp of pleasure. He splayed his hands over her thighs, trailing kisses over her inner thighs. Her fingers curled into the covers as he lowered his mouth between her legs, taking his first taste of her.

"*Oh... Graham*," she said breathlessly.

He lifted his gaze, drinking in the pleasure on her face as he loved her. Every slick of his tongue brought another sweet sound, a bite of her lower lip or a rock of her hips. Reading her like a map, he loved her harder when she moaned or grabbed his hands, her nails cutting into his flesh. When she pleaded, "There, there, there," he eased his efforts, drawing out her pleasure. The way she writhed and mewled, angled and guided amped up his arousal. He ached to be inside her, to become as close as they had been at the festival. He dipped his fingers into her slick heat, earning a long, surrendering moan, and he used his mouth to send her over the edge. A string of erotic sounds rang out from her lungs as her inner muscles pulsed and her body quivered. She was so beautiful, he could barely control himself. When she sank back to the mattress, he moved up and over her, taking her in a rough and wild kiss as he clutched her ass, his cock perched at her entrance.

"You're protected?" He needed to make sure he hadn't dreamed that when they were at the festival.

"Yes."

She rocked up at the same moment he thrust forward, burying himself to the root. They both groaned, clinging to each other. He touched his forehead to hers, eyes closed, and whispered, "My God, sunshine…" There were no words for the immensity of his emotions.

"I know," she said. "I feel it, too."

They moved slowly at first, savoring every second of their coupling. Their bodies were in perfect sync, and their kisses quickly turned fierce, more possessive. She wrapped her legs around his waist, and just when he was sure he'd lose his mind, she tore her mouth away and her eyes slammed shut. His name flew from her lips like a plea—"Graham!" He slowed his pace again, keeping her at the peak even as she begged for more, clutching at his arms, his shoulders, anywhere she could find purchase. Every graze of her nails and every thrust into her tight heat sent a bolt of lightning down his spine. He was stuck between heaven and hell in the most blissful torture of all, staving off his own release to enjoy hers. Lust coiled tight and hot inside him like a viper ready to strike, until he was shaking with restraint. Unable to resist for a second longer, he drove into her harder, kissed her rougher, and followed her over the edge. His world spun, careening on its axis as pure, explosive pleasure tore through him. They clung to each other through the very last quake of their releases, gasping and panting as they collapsed to the mattress.

He buried his face in her neck, kissing her warm flesh and wondering how in the hell his life would ever feel complete without her by his side.

Chapter Eight

BRINDLE SWORE THAT if Morgyn ever had a man spend the night in her tiny house, she'd wish she had more space. But Morgyn and Graham had woken with the sun, their bodies still intertwined, and it was the most glorious feeling Morgyn had ever experienced. When they were together, everything felt *right*. Waking up in Graham's arms, his breath warming her skin and his body cocooning hers, was as wonderful as their lovemaking. Co-showering had been a little tight, but that had made it even more enjoyable, and there was no risk of knocking over tiled walls like there was in the flimsy shower at the festival. A shudder of heat tiptoed down her spine with the memory of his slick body against hers. Now music streamed from Graham's phone as he cooked breakfast and she sketched at the bar. He stood tall and relaxed in cargo shorts and a T-shirt stretched over his broad back and narrow waist, bopping his head to the beat, his hair still damp from their shower. Her rust-colored kitchen might have been small, but it was efficient, with an under-the-counter refrigerator, shelves instead of cabinets along the back wall, and hanging hooks for pots against the wall that adjoined the bathroom. The window above the sink let in plenty of natural light, and the bar offered ample counter space.

The apartment-sized stove was perfect for how little she cooked. Brindle was wrong, she decided. Her tiny home was *perfect* for the two of them.

"Sure you don't want eggs, sunshine?" He glanced over his shoulder, gracing her with the dimples that made her melt.

She shook her head. "Unless *eggs* is code for *a kiss*."

He sauntered over, leaned across the bar, and kissed her. His lips were soft and warm. He touched her wrists as he rubbed his nose along hers. The intimate move felt familiar and special.

"What are you drawing?"

"A necklace I'm thinking about making using pieces of the toy trains we bought in Romance." She turned the notebook toward him and showed him how she'd connect the three wheels in a triangular pattern and set a jewel in the center. "I have some tracks in my workshop, and I'm thinking about threading the chain through them, one on either side midway up the necklace so it's a little more substantial."

"It's amazing how you can see a toy train and come up with a necklace."

"It's amazing to me how people can't."

"That's what makes you so special."

As he ate breakfast, Morgyn let her mind play with the idea of a future with Graham. Could they always be this happy? She knew she was getting way ahead of herself, but why shouldn't she? The universe had brought them together. It would be a cruel joke to give her such immense joy only to break her heart.

He washed the dishes and said, "I have to meet Reed at eight, but I'd love to see your workshop and your deer garden."

"You remembered." She slipped off the stool in her summer dress and he pulled her into his arms.

"How could I forget? Your eyes lit up when you told me

about it."

Well, that filled her with all kinds of goodness. And the kiss that followed felt even better.

She grabbed her cowgirl boots from beside the front door and sat on the futon to put them on, watching Graham check out the funky blanket hanging over the back, and her colorful throw pillows. He crouched beside the coffee table, which she'd made out of a shutter using the iron base from an old end table.

"Did you make this?" he asked.

"Yes." She popped up to her feet and said, "The shutter is from a house that burned down. The family had to rebuild, so I snagged it." She tapped her toe on the wide-planked hardwood. "The floors are teak. One of my father's friends owns a construction company. They were replacing the floors at a monstrous house in Meadowside because these were scuffed and worn. I traded for babysitting their granddaughter. My father and I sanded and laid the floors. We used something we got at the flooring company in town to fill in the deepest grooves. I think they came out pretty good."

"They're better than pretty good. They look great." He glanced at the stairs and the loft railing. "Repurposed barn-wood?"

"Yup. Our friends renovated their barn and built an apartment upstairs. They were happy to give it to me." She waved at the walls and said, "I worked over Christmas break to pay for the lumber for framing. I bought the siding and shingles on Craigslist. And you probably noticed that the windows and door are odd sizes. They were custom orders a family purchased for their pool house, and then they changed their minds. I made their daughter's class costumes for a play in exchange for them. I bought all of the appliances secondhand. And the guys you met last night? Trace, JJ, Beckett, Chet, and the others? They all pitched in to help me build the house. But I helped every step of the way, from digging footings to hammering nails. It cost me about twenty-two thousand to build, and that's already paid off."

"Like a car payment," he said. "You're brilliant."

She rolled her eyes. "That's Pepper. I'm just *crafty*."

He wrapped his arms around her again and said, "You can call it whatever you'd like, but the truth of the matter is that you saw something you wanted and you found a way to make it happen that didn't break the bank. You created your life in a way that most people only talk about or dream of. That, my sweet sunshine, is *brilliance*."

"Oh, cracker, you see me in a way no one else does. I was never a great student, except in art class and in the holistic herbalism program I took to get certified. I excelled in those courses. One day you'll wake up and see the errors of your ways, but until then I'm going to enjoy each and every misguided compliment you give me."

"And I'll convince you how on target I am about each and every one."

"Maybe you can just build me up at dinner with my family tomorrow night. My parents are having a goodbye dinner for Brindle. She's leaving for Paris Friday morning for the rest of the summer. I'd love it if you'd come with me."

"*Coming* with you happens to be my favorite thing. I'd love to." He gave her another steamy kiss, and then he smacked her ass and said, "Now, show me this deer garden before I carry you upstairs and see how creative you can get in *that* room."

"Like that's a threat? You're crazy." She laughed, grabbed his MIT baseball cap from where she'd hung it by the front door, and put it on as she stepped outside. "Did you forget you lent me this?"

"Of course not. You look cute in my hat. I figured I'd let you wear it while I'm here. But if you get it dirty I might have to punish you."

"I'm seeing dirt in my future," she said sassily, earning another ass smack.

They followed the towpath, which was lined by verdant billowing plants and vibrant wildflowers. The sun warmed Morgyn's shoulders as she gave Graham a tour of her massive herb and vegetable gardens and the small greenhouse where she grew herbs over the winter.

"How did you get into herbs?" he asked as they headed for the barn.

"My aunt Roxie makes all sorts of homemade soaps, shampoos, lotions, tinctures, and *love potions.* She lives in Upstate New York in a small town like ours called Sweetwater. I've always been enamored by the things she makes. You'd love her. She's got tons of energy, and she's like my mom, warm and friendly."

"We might have to take a trip out there sometime," he said as the barn and the deer garden came into view.

"Oh my gosh, I would *love* that! We could water ski and hang out with my cousins, who are a trip. You'd get along so well with them." As she said it, she realized she was jumping way ahead of herself again and that he'd probably said it off-the-cuff. He was leaving in a few days, not making long-term relationship plans. She tucked away that disappointment, refusing to, as her mother always said, *borrow trouble.* He was there for five days, and he'd called it a *start.* That said something, and she knew in her heart that what they had *was* special.

"I'm sure I will," he said casually.

I will. Maybe she wasn't getting so far ahead of herself after all. She held on to that nugget of hope as he shaded his eyes, looking across the yard.

"Damn, sunshine. That barn's at least three times the size of your house."

"I know. It's been here forever, but it's perfect for my workshop."

"And that must be the deer garden? It's exactly how you described. If I were a buck, I'd hang out there."

"If you were a buck, I'd put out more than salt licks."

He laughed and helped her slide open the barn doors. As always happened, her spirits soared as the timeless scents of wood and earth intertwined with happy memories.

"Welcome to my world," she said.

His truck was so organized, she imagined the plethora of long wooden worktables littered with items in various stages of creation looked to him like the room had thrown up on itself. She hoped the chaos of her life wouldn't scare him away. Stacked milk crates lined half of the right wall, each one filled with fabrics and sewing paraphernalia. Various metal objects—old fireplace tools, planters, bases from tables—lay on the floor in what probably looked haphazard but was organized by types of metal, possible purposes, and stages of development. Shoes, boots, sandals, and various other items sat on tiered shelves in the far back corner, and along the back wall, long metal shelves held a plethora of birdhouses, kitchen crocks, vases, jewelry, and outerwear. Along the left wall were tall dressers with labeled drawers for embellishments she'd picked up over the years. Metal clothing rods hung from chains draped over exposed beams in the ceiling, displaying gowns and dresses.

"I know it looks like a badly organized thrift shop," she said. "My sisters tease me about my hoarder ways. But this is how I work best, with it all at my fingertips. I collect things and then use them when inspiration hits, which is sometimes years later."

"This is just what I thought your workshop would look like, except it's much larger."

She followed him inside. "And you're not running for the hills?"

"My brother Jax designs wedding gowns, and Jilly makes all sorts of dresses. The only difference between your workspace and Jilly's is the structure in which it resides. She has two work areas—one at home and one above her shop. Jax's workspace is just as busy, but he makes such high-end stuff. I'm afraid to touch anything for fear of a bridezilla coming after me."

She laughed. "I think I'd like your siblings."

He kissed her and said, "Another trip to plan."

"You'd better stop saying things like that. You make me think five days could lead to more."

"You're doubting it?" he asked casually.

"Well, not doubting, but…"

He picked up a tennis shoe on which she'd painted a beach scene and had added fringe around the edge and said, "The girl who creates one-of-a-kind beauties like this and believes in universal connections *doubts* our spiritual bond?"

Oh my. He was even *hotter* when he was making a point about their relationship. She couldn't suppress her smile as he narrowed his eyes and set the shoe on the table. He stalked toward her, bringing a heat wave so strong she was surprised her hair didn't blow back from her face.

"You're wearing my lucky hat, sunshine. That means a whole hell of a lot more than how long we've been seeing each other. *Know it. Trust it. Accept it.* And don't get any crazy ideas about marriage, either. Marriage is not on the table." A tease shone in his eyes. He pressed his lips to hers and then said, "Come on, girlie. Let's get this show on the road so I can meet with Reed and get back to you."

He grabbed her hand and headed out of the barn, acting as natural as could be—as if he weren't leaving a trail of happiness and hope in his wake.

GRAHAM WAS STILL smiling an hour later, as Reed showed him around the Majestic Theater, which was built near the railroad tracks and marked the line between Meadowside and Oak Falls. The name fit the old stone theater well, with two grand entrances, one curved, one straight, and stone pillars with Ionic capitals on either side of the large arched doorway. The horizontal portion above the columns had alternating patterns usually found in Greek architecture. Although it was in disrepair, he had seen worse, and Reed was a leading historical restoration expert. Graham knew the regal theater would be gorgeous when it was done.

"You've got months of work ahead of you. Even with a cursory glance you can see there's evidence of deterioration around the foundation. My bet is that once you dig into it, you're going to find more," Graham said as they walked inside.

The lobby had as much character as the exterior, with inlaid marble floors and intricate woodwork around the counters. As they strolled through to the auditorium, Reed said, "Did I tell you my uncle proposed to Ella right here in the lobby?"

"No way."

Reed nodded. "Yeah. Small world, huh?"

"Is that why you had the wedding here?" His buddy looked happier than he'd ever seen him. Reed was a formidable guy, with brown hair and a heart of gold. Months before moving back to Meadowside, he'd practically been engaged to a woman whom everyone except Reed had known was a stopgap for his one true love. *Grace.* His fiancée had saved him a lifetime of unhappiness by cheating with his business partner. Although it was a devastating blow, in the end it had been the best thing that could have happened to him.

"Married life agrees with you," he said. "And Grace seems great."

"My first and only love." Warmth washed over Reed's face. "We got married here because when we were in high school we *christened* our relationship in the field out back." His eyes narrowed and he said, "That's for your ears only. Got it?"

"Hell, yes, I've got it." Man, he wished he had that kind of history with Morgyn. Damn, she'd been adorable this morning in his hat, getting all doe-eyed when he'd said they had a future together. "Can you imagine if Sable heard that about you? She'd start calling you *field fucker* or some other cockamamie name."

"She's got balls, that one. She's a good person, though. She would protect her siblings with everything she has."

"Yeah, I got that impression. I still can't believe Morgyn was at your wedding. What are the chances?" Graham surveyed the domed ceiling, elaborate chandeliers, and multi-level balconies in the auditorium. "You know I can't possibly complete an assessment on this building before you leave town at noon. You mentioned you're keeping the rigging for hanging show elements?"

"That's right. Replacing whatever's necessary."

"Why didn't you ask me to come out a few weeks earlier? Or after you get back? I've got to inspect the supporting structures, the grid-iron and fly systems, and the rest of this place from roof to basement. I had no idea you were leaving town right away. You know what goes into an inspection. Not that I mind sticking around. I mean...*Morgyn*...but, dude, what were you thinking?"

Reed rubbed the back of his neck, cleared his throat, and a sly smile appeared on his face. "I had no idea that you and Morgyn would meet at the festival. I thought you'd meet at the wedding, and..."

It took a moment for Graham to put the missing pieces together. "Holy shit, man. You were *setting me up*? With Morgyn?" He laughed. "Seriously?"

Reed shrugged, grinning like a fool. "Do you blame me? She's totally your type. She's earthy, creative, smart, beautiful, and a doer, like you."

Graham paced, trying to wrap his head around what he was hearing. "How could you know? She has all those qualities, but, man...You know me. I am *never* unprepared. I'm not sure Morgyn prepares for anything."

"I know."

"If I'm the eye of the storm, she's a hurricane."

Reed laughed.

"Seriously. She didn't even check the weather before going on an overnight camping trip at the festival." He laughed, remembering the state of her tent and belongings.

"I don't know about all that. I just know that when I talk to Morgyn, I get the same feeling as when I talk to you. She's got this energy that radiates off her and breathes life into everything around her. She's a whirlwind, always taking off for a day trip, staying out until all hours with her friends, listening to music. I doubt most guys could keep up with her. But she reminds me of you."

"That's some crazy shit, because from the moment I saw her dancing in the rain, I've thought of nothing else. I've never connected with a woman like I have with Morgyn, and yeah, she's out there. But for some damn reason I totally dig that—and everything else—about her. She's got no hang-ups, no desire to follow the pack. She's exciting and spur-of-the-moment, and beneath it all, she's careful even though she doesn't think she is. Did you know she *bartered* her way into that house?"

"I've heard the stories."

"I've never met anyone like her."

"I can see that. Dude, you're glowing," Reed teased. "You're rambling and you never ramble. You're like I was when I first saw Grace again. I would have followed her anywhere."

"That's the other thing. I've known her three days, and I cannot imagine leaving town Friday without her. I just can't even picture it, and I don't want to. That's fucked up for a guy like me who has never needed anyone by my side."

"No, man, that's *love*."

Graham scoffed. *Love?* "That's not even a word that was on my radar before..." *Before you said it?* No. Before this *morning*. *Holy fuck.* The realization momentarily struck him mute.

"It sneaks up on you and stings you in the ass like one of those green flies at the beach," Reed said.

"This is all too much to grasp. I haven't even had a chance to process the overwhelming emotions that have consumed me since we met. How about we focus on business."

"You can run, but you can't hide," Reed said with a laugh.

"Dude, I don't want to hide. I just want to wrap my head around what it all means. And what's up with wanting me to evaluate her business? You know I don't do business with women I sleep with. Why would you think that would be okay if your goal was to set us up?"

"Because I trust you, and Morgyn's family now."

Of course. That made perfect sense.

"The building where she rents space was sold recently, and the new owners are raising the rent by something like thirty percent next month. Apparently the previous owners were charging below fair market value."

Graham wondered how she could be in such a good mood and so carefree for the last few days with *that* weighing on her mind.

"I don't know anything about her finances," Reed said, "but Grace asked if I knew anyone who could help her figure her business out. There's Beckett, but they have history."

"So I've heard." He wasn't about to ask Reed for details, but he was curious about what had happened between Morgyn and Beckett. He also wondered how she was making ends meet in such a small town. How many boots and unique types of furniture and jewelry could a community that small need on a daily basis?

He'd never let Morgyn flounder, and hell if he'd let Beckett try to help her. "I'm heading over to her shop when I'm done here. I'll check it out." He looked around the theater, and an incredulous laugh slipped out. "So this was all a setup? You don't want me to inspect this place? What the hell, man?"

Reed shrugged. "Your old man came out a few weeks ago to check it out."

"My *father*? Did he know about your matchmaking scheme?"

"Well." Reed pushed a hand through his hair, guilt rising in his eyes. "Hey, you can't be pissed because I want you to be happy, can you?"

"Not pissed, no. *Floored. Shocked.* I'm not sure if I should beat the hell out of you for making a fool of me or bow at your feet for your matchmaking superpowers."

"I didn't make a fool out of you. If anything, you two made fools out of us. Who did we think we were, setting you guys up? According to Grace, Morgyn's the *fate* fairy. She goes through life relying on the universe to guide her."

Morgyn's voice sailed through his mind. *I take my life seriously. If I'm anything, I'm floaty. I sort of drift through this beautiful life, taking it all in and not stressing over little things. Or big things, really. I don't see a reason to get all wigged out because something isn't working right. It'll either get fixed or it won't.*

Graham pulled his vibrating phone from his pocket as his sister's name flashed across the screen. He opened and read her text. *So?! How was the wedding? Meet anyone special?*

"Morgyn?" Reed asked.

"No. It's Jilly." He loved his pushy, nosy sister and he knew she'd love Morgyn, but he didn't want to spend his time texting when he was with Reed. "Obviously my father has a big mouth. She's fishing for details."

His phone vibrated with another text from Jillian. *Come on! Dad told me you were being set up, and Zev told me you hooked up with someone at the festival. We've got a bet going. BIG stakes! I want to win, so give me a clue! Pleeeeaassseee!*

"This ought to be fun." Graham turned the phone toward Reed for him to see.

"Just give her Morgyn's number. They'll get along great."

"I can't. I don't have her phone number. When we left the festival we didn't exchange information. Hell, I didn't even know she lived here. We were supposed to meet up today at her shop, but then the wedding—*aka setup central*—happened."

Reed laughed. "You let her leave without getting her number?"

"I knew I'd find her. Or die trying."

"Oh yeah, buddy. You're *perfect* for each other."

Chapter Nine

AFTER CATCHING UP with Reed, Graham climbed into his truck and typed a response to Jillian. A reminder to get his oil changed popped up on the screen. He remembered seeing an auto shop in town and decided to call Jillian on the way to getting the oil changed before heading over to Morgyn's shop.

Jillian answered on the first ring. "Finally. I texted you *hours* ago."

"You have the patience of a flea. How about, hey, Graham, how are you? How was the wedding?"

She groaned, and he imagined her rolling her eyes. "Hi, Graham. How are you? How was the wedding? Now give me the good stuff. Dad said Reed was setting you up."

"I think I'll keep the details of the *good stuff* to myself, but yes, I was supposed to be set up."

"So you didn't get set up?" All the gusto drained from her voice. "Bummer. I figured you didn't answer my texts because you were too caught up in the girl Dad told me about. She sounded amazing. Wait! What about the girl Zev met?"

"They're one and the same—Reed wanted to set me up with her, but we'd already met. Her name is Morgyn Montgomery, and she's..." He tried to think of the best way to describe her.

Great felt insignificant, *special* wasn't significant enough, and *amazing* could be used to describe anything. *Mine.* That one was perfect, but that would leave him wide-open to too many of Jillian's incessant questions, so he settled on, "*Everything.*"

"Everything? Like, everything you've ever wanted or everything I'd expect in a woman you're with—interesting, funny, smart, outdoorsy, *ballsy*..."

"I love that you know me so well," he said as he drove past the Oak Falls library. It had wide stone steps. Three little girls and a woman sat on a blanket out front leafing through books. Graham pictured Morgyn's big family doing something like that when they were younger—but he imagined Morgyn twirling and picking flowers in the field behind them.

"Well, she has to be ballsy to keep up with the crazy shit you and Ty do, and she has to be smart, because you know, you're *you*. So...how much *everything* is she?"

"I don't know, Jilly. We just met," he said, even though he felt like he'd known Morgyn forever. "I thought I'd use this morning to try to separate the hot and hectic lust fogging my brain from the deeper emotions stacking up inside me, but they're too tangled up to separate."

"Wow," she said, bringing his head back to their phone call.

Fuck. He hadn't meant to say that aloud. He ground out a curse and tried to change the subject. "Anyway, you spoke to Zev?"

"Oh no, you're not changing the subject on me. Tangled-up lust and something deeper is significant. Even I know that."

"Jilly," he warned, not wanting to be analyzed. He heard the pecking of fingers on a keyboard and assumed she was at work.

"Don't *Jilly* me. My most careful brother has been thrown off-kilter. Let me enjoy Mr. Perfectly Organized and Always

Prepared being knocked off his pedestal."

"Christ, Jilly. I'm not perfect, and I don't claim to be."

"Well, you never screw up."

"You're nuts. I screw up a lot. Just ask Mom and Dad. I'm sure they can give you a litany of examples. Now can we move on?"

"Not yet. I'm looking at her Facebook page. Her status says she's feeling very *pink* today. Okay, not sure what that's about, but she's super cute and I *love* her style. She's always smiling. Where does she get her boots? They're fantastic."

He pulled into the auto shop parking lot wondering what feeling *pink* meant. "She probably made those boots, or rather embellished them. She's really creative. She makes clothes and jewelry and—"

"I know! I'm on her Life Reimagined page now. I need to take a trip to Oak Falls. Her stuff is awesome. I can't believe you won't be here for my show." Jillian was introducing a new clothing line, Multifarious, in her annual fashion show next week. She'd rented out an old warehouse, and Graham had worked with her to create floor plans and lighting schematics.

"I'm sorry, Jilly. Do you want me to cancel my meetings in New York?"

"No, of course not. Besides, I spoke to Riley, who's in Colorado with the baby. She said Josh is looking forward to having dinner with you."

Their cousin Josh and his wife, Riley, split their time between Colorado and New York. Graham was looking forward to seeing Josh, too.

"But since you'll miss it," Jillian said, "maybe you can make it up to me by doing me a favor. About that bet..."

"I'm not lying for you to win the bet."

"Oh, come on! I'd do it for you," she pleaded.

"No way. I've got to go. It was good talking to you."

"Are you meeting Morgyn?" she asked with a conspiratorial tone to her voice.

"I'm getting my oil changed; then I'll see her."

Jilly squealed, and he pulled his phone away from his ear.

"I'm going now," he said loudly. "Love you." He ended the call, pulled up Google, and typed *what does a pink mood mean* in the search bar. The page filled with information on mood rings and the psychology behind the color pink. He typed *what does a pink aura mean*, hit the search button, and read the first result.

> *Pink aura people are natural healers, highly sensitive to the needs of others, and have strong psychic abilities. They are very romantic and once they have found their soul mate will stay faithful, loving, and loyal for life. They hate injustice, poverty, and conflicts and strive to make the world a better place, often making personal sacrifices in the pursuit of this ideal.*

That sounded just like Morgyn, but at the festival she'd said she had a yellow aura—*an optimist, spiritually aware, and I'm definitely not a perfectionist. I usually act before I think, and I love exploring new ideas.* He searched the meaning of a yellow aura and found that people with yellow auras create a sensation of brightness and warmth and attract those looking for joy and light. *Sunshine.*

He took out a pad and pen from his glove box and scribbled down the main points of each aura, so he could try to figure out how they worked together. He started at a knock on the truck window and was surprised to see Sable, wearing an Oak Falls

Automotive shirt. He remembered Morgyn mentioning that Sable owned an auto shop.

As he stepped from the truck Sable said, "Nice wheels, All Nighter. You lost?"

"No. I need an oil change." He glanced at the two-story building, from which country music was blaring. The first story was covered in metal automotive signs touting Goodyear, Firestone, Pennzoil, and about a dozen other automotive businesses.

"Shouldn't you have done that *before* you drove here from Maryland?" She stepped back as he closed the door.

"I have an app on my phone that's synced to my odometer. It reminds me to change the oil every three thousand miles."

"Quite geeky of you," she said as she walked around his truck. "Better than you having Tinder or some other shit on your phone."

Tinder? That was laughable. If she only knew him. The risks associated with online hookups were off-the-charts. "No Tinder, but uh, I get your drift. Think you can fit me in sometime before Friday?"

"How about now? I'm working on a bitch of an engine repair and could use a break." She waved to a truck with its hood up in the garage. "Pull into the third bay."

"Great, thanks." He drove the truck into the bay. "This is going to sound weird," he said as he climbed out, "but can you give me Morgyn's cell number?"

Sable looked confused. "Didn't you stay with her last night?"

"Yes, but we didn't exchange numbers and I want to let her know I'm running late."

"You act like she has a schedule." She pulled out her phone

and said, "What's your number? I'll text it to you."

He gave her his number, and she sent the text.

"Thanks," he said. "And thanks for fitting me in. I'll just..." He motioned toward the field beside the shop.

"Go say sappy things to Morgyn. She loves that shit." Sable chuckled as he walked away.

He saved Morgyn's and Sable's numbers, and then he called his girl. It went to voicemail. "Hey, sunshine. I'm over at your sister's shop getting an oil change. I'll see you soon." He ended the call, fighting the urge to say more. What else, he wasn't sure, but *see you soon* seemed far more appropriate than pouring his heart out over voicemail.

He saw a patch of wildflowers and walked into the field to pick some for her. His phone rang a minute later, and Morgyn's name flashed on the screen. "Hey, beautiful."

"Hi. Sorry. I don't answer calls from unfamiliar numbers."

"Ah, my girl is a risk assessor after all," he teased, hoping she'd like the flowers he'd picked.

"I'm a time saver," she said sassily. "You're at Sable's? Do you know how to get here? If you go to the end of her street, then take a right on Main and a left on Arbutus, you'll see my shop on the left."

"Want me to walk over? Pick up my truck later?" he asked as he noticed a few shingles missing from the roof of Sable's garage.

"No. It's okay. I need to walk down to the bank, but I'll be back by the time you get here. Then you can help me figure out what to do with my business."

He still wasn't keen on the idea of mixing business and pleasure, but a thirty percent rent hike could throw a small business into a downward spiral, and he wanted Morgyn to succeed. "Sure, sunshine. Whatever you'd like."

"Well, what I'd *like* we can't do in my shop," she said seductively.

Oh man. He had visions of sweeping her merchandise off a display table and making love to her. Heat coursed through his body, and he tried to push away those dirty thoughts, but then she said, "But you *do* have curtains in your truck..."

A groan escaped, and Morgyn giggled.

"I love knowing I can get to you over the phone."

"Babe, you get to me in person, on the phone, and I have a feeling if you wrote a fucking letter telling me what you'd like to do, I'd get hard reading it. So let's keep it to a minimum while I'm at your sister's shop."

"Okay, gotta go," she said too fast.

"Customer?"

"No. I have to find some paper and a pen!" She blew a kiss into the phone and ended the call.

"Damn, sunshine," he said to himself. "Just the idea of you scripting your fantasies has got me hot and bothered."

To distract himself from thoughts of Morgyn's fantasies, he focused on the garage.

By the time Sable was done with the oil change, he'd created a list of items that needed attention.

"Just a heads-up," he said as he paid. "I sent you a text with a list of things on the exterior of your building that should be checked out. Nothing major. A few missing shingles, flashing issues, loose siding. And there's a crack in the foundation that should get repaired before winter."

"And you're delivering that message with *flowers*?" She smirked, eyeing the wildflowers he'd picked. "If I wanted a man to tell me what to do, I'd be married. Sheesh, Braden. You're so gaga over my sister it's coming out your ears."

There was no use denying it. "Tell me something I don't know."

Her eyes turned serious. "She *deserves* someone to be gaga over her. She's a diamond in a town of pebbles."

"I said something I *don't* know," he said snarkily.

Sable pointed a wrench at him and said, "She's got a heart of gold. Break it, and I'll break that pretty face of yours."

He laughed. "Again, that's not new information." He looked over her shoulder at a water stain on the wall and said, "You should probably get that stain checked out, too."

Sable looked behind her. "Damn it. I just had some renovation work done upstairs. Maybe that happened when they worked in the bathroom."

"Usually they turn the water off for that. That's an old stain, so maybe they fixed whatever caused it. But that's the type of thing you should get checked out, just to be sure you don't run into bigger issues down the line. I'd be happy to take a look if you'd like."

"Thanks, but I'll get the guys who did the work back out here. They cost a bloody fortune."

"If you change your mind, let me know. And thanks again." He turned to leave and then he said, "You should have Morgyn barter for you next time. I hear she's awesome at it."

Sable snort-laughed as he walked out the door.

MORGYN'S SHOP WAS nestled between a florist and a diner. Bright yellow awnings shaded big picture windows. LIFE

REIMAGINED was painted in bold blue script on one window with sixties-era flowers and hearts painted around the words. LOVINGLY ENHANCED TREASURES was painted beneath in smaller white print.

Lovingly enhanced. That fit what she did perfectly.

On the sidewalk outside the door, several dresses hung from an iron coatrack. A red upholstered chair with brightly colored sunbursts and stars embroidered all over it had a pretty fringed scarf draped over one arm. A few women's handbags that had been painted and embellished with pretty charms lay on the cushion. Upbeat music drifted out the open front door. He peered inside, catching sight of Morgyn swaying to the beat as she draped several necklaces around the neck of a tie-dyed-bikini-clad mannequin. Morgyn was still wearing his baseball cap—backward—and looked cute as hell. Her short red sundress drifted around her thighs, and she wore a pair of strappy leather sandals that wrapped all the way up her calves.

As he stepped inside he took in bright yellow and pale blue walls and a ceiling fan with patchwork material adhered to the panels, the center painted bright red. He glanced at the price tag hanging down. $78. His girl was smart not to undersell her wares. To his right, tires hung from ropes with wooden shelves secured inside them, displaying lamps, shoes, vases, and other items—each embellished by Morgyn's talented hands. One wall featured the front end of four bicycles, each with a brightly colored metal basket attached. The tires were cut in half and secured flush against the wall. The handlebars were painted vivid colors. One basket held billiard balls. The others contained plants, socks, and spools of yarn. They were so unique, he thought about buying one for his mother. There were displays of clothes, shoes, furniture, wreaths, knitted animals—

each and every item was unique. The shop was filled with textures and colors and interesting merchandise unlike any he'd ever seen. She offered antiques, but they'd all been enhanced with items not normally found on old things, making them appear chic and new. He could see them in shops in New York City. Morgyn had put her creative touch on everything, and he wanted to take his time exploring all of it. No wonder she needed all that workspace in the barn. Her type of originality should not be limited in any way—including to this space or this small town.

Morgyn hadn't noticed him yet. She was singing "Praying" by Kesha. Jillian loved that song, and she sang it with the same vehemence and vigor as Morgyn. Morgyn held her hands up, fingers splayed, making a pushing motion as she sang about hoping someone was praying. Her hand covered her chest as she sang about being proud of who she was—and then she belted out the next few lines, hands fisted, raising them to the ceiling, her hair whipping from side to side. Suddenly she spun around, eyes clenched shut as she sang about hoping someone finds peace and how she prays for them sometimes. She was so passionate about everything she did, he was utterly and completely mesmerized.

When the song came to an end, she exhaled loudly, her shoulders slumping. She opened her eyes, laughing before she even noticed Graham, as if she had completely entertained herself. He felt like he'd been given a sneak peek at a secret part of her. He closed the distance between them, falling even harder for her.

The song "Just the Way You Are" by Bruno Mars came on as she lifted her gaze.

"Cracker," she said with an embarrassed gasp. Her gaze

dropped to the flowers, and that embarrassment turned to appreciation. "You brought me flowers…?"

Without a word, he took her in his arms and began dancing, singing the lyrics and knowing they were written just for her. She fell into step without hesitation, smiling up at him. After the song ended, he gazed into her eyes and said, "You make my head spin, sunshine."

"You make *lots* of my parts behave in ways they're not used to. You know that song that Kenny Chesney sings about setting the world on fire? That's us, without the hotel, and obviously we're not wherever they were." She took his hand and walked through the store. "Let's put these gorgeous flowers in water and I'll show you around so you can *evaluate* my business." She looked at him seductively and said, "I'm really looking forward to hearing your suggestions."

He hauled her into his arms again, earning a giggle. "You keep doing that and I'll drag your pretty ass behind that rack over there and *suggest* you do all sorts of dirty things."

"I bet you say that to all the girls whose businesses you evaluate." She slipped out of his arms and took his hand, but he twirled her into them again, bringing their bodies flush from chest to thighs.

"I don't normally mix business with pleasure," he said as seriously as he could with her rubbing against him. "You're my exception, and I'm not very comfortable with it. Business can get sticky."

"I can feel how *uncomfortable* you are," she said with feigned wide-eyed innocence. "What *should* we do about that? And just for the record, I happen to be a fan of *sticky*."

"Christ, sunshine," he ground out as he lowered his lips to hers.

"Morgyn!" A little boy darted toward them with Chet chuckling behind him.

"Hold that thought," Morgyn whispered. Then her brow wrinkled and she said, "For about an hour. Sorry!" She scooped the little boy into her arms and twirled him around. "Hey, Mr. Big Guy."

Graham pulled his T-shirt down to cover his arousal. Seeing Morgyn cuddle the sandy-haired little boy who was rattling on about fixing his mother's favorite beach bag warmed him in a different way. She looked natural with him in her arms, but then again, he had yet to see Morgyn looking less than natural in anything she did. The little boy's big blue eyes widened as she told him what she had planned for it, which had something to do with beads.

"Good to see you again, man," Chet said, shaking Graham's hand.

"You too."

"Scotty," Morgyn said as she lowered the little boy's feet to the ground, "this is my friend Graham, but you can call him *cracker* if you want."

Scotty giggled. "Dat's a funny name."

"He's a funny guy," Morgyn whispered.

Chet gave Graham an I've-got-your-back look, which surprised *and* pleased him.

"We can reschedule if you two are busy," Chet offered.

"Don't be silly," Morgyn said. "I'd never let Scotty down. Did you bring my fireman calendar?" She looked at Graham and said, "Chet's a firefighter. Meadowside and Oak Falls firefighters do a big calendar shoot every year for charity, and we always watch. This year they convinced Axsel to be in it as Mr. December. Chet and all the firemen wore only their turnout pants and boots, and poor Axsel sat in the middle with his guitar trying not to drool."

"The calendars won't be ready for a while," Chet said with a laugh. "And Axsel wasn't the only one drooling. I seem to remember the Montgomery sisters making all sorts of comments about our *hoses*—"

"Uncle Chet has a big hose!" Scotty said so loudly Graham had to laugh. "When I grow up I'm gonna have a big hose, too! Right, Uncle Chet?"

Chet tousled Scotty's hair and said, "I sure hope so, buddy."

"Okay, no more *hose* talk," Morgyn said. "Chet, we just need a few minutes. Graham's going to help me figure out a couple things. I have bunches of ideas, and I put some fun embellishments on the round table over there." She pointed across the room. "Why don't you check them out while I get Graham whatever he needs to get started."

"Come on, Uncle Chet." Scotty ran through the store, and Chet followed him.

"So, drooling over firemen, huh?" Graham teased.

"Oh, come on. Not *really* drooling, but they were hot. I mean, they're friends, so it's not like I wanted to jump their bones or anything. But I think Axsel would have liked to." She smiled and said, "Sorry about having to do this with Scotty. He's Chet's sister Haylie's little boy. She's a single mom, and Scotty's fixing her favorite bag for her birthday."

"No worries, beautiful."

"Thanks. What do you need to get started on checking things out?"

"I usually start with the books to get a handle on finances. What do you use for bookkeeping? Quicken?"

"Quicken?" She wrinkled her nose. "I hate computer programs. They take too long to learn."

He followed her to a dresser in the back of the store. She took off the long necklace she wore around her neck and opened the locket charm, revealing an old-fashioned key.

"This is the key to the top drawer. My books are in there." She pointed to a desk near the table where Scotty and Chet were checking out their supplies and said, "You can work over there. Is that okay?"

"Yes. Perfect. I'll grab my laptop from the car and get started, but first…" He took her hand and pulled her closer, lowering his voice. "Sunshine, the reason I don't mix business and pleasure is that it can get weird when people talk about money. I want to help you figure things out, but I don't want this, or anything, to come between us."

"You really *are* an overthinker. The good thing is I'm not. Well, not usually. I mean, you have made me think about things a lot more than usual. But whatever is destined to work *will*, and things that aren't meant to be *won't*. If we don't stay together, it won't be this business that tears us apart." She patted her hand over his heart and said, "Have faith in something bigger than your brains. You'll see."

"But—"

She put her finger over his lips and said, "'Know it. Trust it. *Accept it*,'" and walked away with a bounce in her step.

After retrieving his laptop, Graham unlocked the dresser drawer and peered inside.

A shoe box.

Why doesn't that surprise me?

He carried the box to the desk and lifted the lid. On top of a few spiral-bound notebooks was an envelope with *Cracker, read this first* written in pink ink. Her handwriting was loopy and big with tiny suns dotting the *i*'s. He glanced at Morgyn across the room, sitting with Scotty and Chet. She and Scotty were placing colorful embellishments on the bag. Had she scripted her fantasies after all? He opened and read the letter.

> *Dear Dimples (did that make you smile? I hope so, because I love your dimples).*

He felt himself smiling and lifted his gaze to Morgyn again, catching her watching him. He blew her a kiss and she pretended to catch it.

Chet glanced at the two of them, smirked, and then went back to texting.

Graham returned his attention to the note.

> *Roses are red, violets are blue, I can't wait to show you all the dirty things I want to do to you. Xox, Sunshine.*
>
> *PS: Have I told you I kind of suck at dirty talk? Maybe we should practice. A LOT.*
>
> *PPS: Thank you for helping me today. This business is my baby. Please be gentle with her.*
>
> *PPPS: (Picture me fanning myself from the hot sun, standing by the deer garden wearing nothing but my bikini.) Whew, I sure could use a few licks of your big Creamsicle right about now. I wonder how many licks it would take to get to the creamy center. (See? Told you I need practice.)*

He chuckled. *That's a Tootsie Pop, babe.* Christ, she was adorable.

MORGYN STOOD ON the sidewalk in front of the shop later that afternoon talking with Brindle on the phone. "Maybe this was a mistake. Graham's been looking over my books and poking around on his laptop for hours. He keeps rubbing his temples, and his face looks pinched, like it's a painful process."

"Worried he'll figure out you're not a millionaire? Because from what I read about him online, the guy makes more money than God himself."

"I don't care how much he makes or if he sees how much I make. But you know Beckett suggested I close my store and get a real job. I'm not doing that. What if he suggests the same thing?"

"He's not Beckett," Brindle reminded her. "And so what if he does say that? You don't have to do what anyone else says, Morg. I never do."

Morgyn sighed. "I know. Hey, I found that dress you wanted for Paris. The black one with the silver thread. Do you want to swing by, or should I bring it to Mom's tomorrow night?"

"Bring it tomorrow. I'm out at the falls and I think I'm going to be busy tonight."

"With Trace?" Morgyn asked.

"No. He pissed me off. The jerk told me all these horror stories about single women going missing when they travel overseas. And then he proceeded to tell me about goddamn Suzie Surrats. Remember her from that ski trip he went on last winter? That skanky ho who kept texting him?"

"Doesn't she live in Pennsylvania or Ohio or someplace out that way?"

"Yes, but he said she's traveling through Virginia on her way to Florida."

"And…?"

"I don't know! I think he tells me this shit just to piss me off."

Morgyn rolled her eyes. "He's doing it to get you jealous. Why can't you two just admit you want to be exclusive with each other?"

"Jesus, you too? You don't want to get married. Why push me in that direction?"

"I never said *get married.* There's a difference between wanting a commitment and wanting to get married. What are you so afraid of?"

"Hold on. I have another call."

Morgyn wandered back inside as Graham closed his laptop. "Done?" she asked, worried about the serious look in his eyes. He nodded and she said, "I'll be right off."

She waited another minute, and when Brindle still didn't come back on the line, she ended the call and texted her. *Had to run. See you at Mom's tomorrow. I'll bring the dress. In the meantime pray Graham doesn't end things with me because of my lack of accounting skills. And go tell Trace how you feel about him. Don't lose him to Skanky Suzie!*

With her heart in her throat, Morgyn said, "Is it that bad?"

Graham reached for her. "No, sunshine. Although I admit it took me a while to piece together and understand your accounting practices."

"I didn't know I had accounting *practices.*"

"Well, you do. Your check register is great for tracking major expenditures, but what about the things you pay cash for? Like when you buy boots or clothes to fix up and sell, and the embellishments and other stuff you stockpile in your barn? Did you keep your receipts for them? Did you write them off over the years?"

"No, but whatever I spend I earn back when I sell them."

"Maybe so, but how do you know if you don't track it? Those are expenses against your income. You might be paying too much in taxes. That's something we'll want to get our arms around at some point. We'll set up an easy way for you to track the true cost of goods sold, meaning the sales price less the original purchase price, and the cost to fix them up. But we can deal with all of that later. The more pressing issue is your rent hike."

"That's the *whole* issue. If it weren't for that we wouldn't be having this conversation. My lease renews next month, and I need to decide before then."

"Right, well, I did have a few questions before I make any recommendations. I didn't see any income between the middle of November and the end of January last year."

"I closed for the holidays. Friends and family were in and out of town and there was a lot going on."

He rubbed the back of his neck, his brows slanting with concern. "And there were a few weeks in the spring…?"

"Oh, right. I almost forgot. I took off to go to a garden show, and I met some girls who were traveling together. They invited me to camp with them and to go tubing with some other friends of theirs. It was really fun. We hope to do it again next year."

"You do realize that with a retail business, time off comes at a cost?"

"Of course it does. But I'm not going to spend my life trapped in this space. I want to see and experience life, not just dream about it."

"I really like that about you, Morgyn, and I'd never suggest changing it, but with your rent increase, something's got to give. Have you run the numbers to see if it's worth hiring someone to work when you're not around?"

"No. I don't love the idea of having someone I'm responsible for paying. That's a lot of pressure. Besides, people around here are used to my hours. They know there are times when I'm closed. They just come back when I'm open. And please don't suggest that I take out a loan to keep my shop open, because I hate owing money."

"I would never suggest that."

She breathed a little easier. "You wouldn't?"

"No. I love everything about you, sunshine, but you're not exactly what I'd call a *reliable investment*." A playful smile tugged at his lips. "You need a sugar daddy, not a loan."

She swatted his arm, laughing. "I do not!"

"I wasn't suggesting you find one." He pulled her in for a kiss. "You could never be tied down to someone in that way. I can see that even after only a few days together."

"That's because you see *me*, cracker. The real me, and you understand who I am. Even when guys understand me, they usually don't accept the way I live my life. Beckett said I should close my shop and get a real job."

Graham's jaw clenched. "It doesn't sound like he knows you very well."

"He's known me forever."

"What happened between the two of you?"

"On the surface we should have clicked, but the fundamentals of who we are were too different. He's a great guy, and everyone loves him. *I* love him—as a friend—but we clashed about everything. I was always running late, or making last-minute plans, and that drove him crazy. I think fancy cars and big houses are a waste of resources, while he loves creature comforts. We never spent any time at my house because it was too confining for him, and he was always trying to fix me, to teach me about business and life and the *right* way to do things. It's not his fault, really. That's who he is, and his right way of doing things isn't mine. We're just too different."

Concern washed over Graham's face, and her stomach sank.

"Oh no," she said softly. "You're risk calculating, aren't you?"

"No," he said with a smile. "I'm just wondering how anyone could know you for any length of time and not adore those things about you. Morgyn, there are ways to make this work without giving up your business. You're incredibly talented. You have the potential to earn well beyond what you're earning now."

She could count on two hands the number of people in her life who believed she could ever be something more than she was—and her family and her grandfather took up nine of the ten people. Graham was number ten. "Thank you for saying that."

"Don't thank me for telling you the truth. I admit, I wasn't sure how you were making ends meet selling boots and repurposed items. But I understand it now. You're selling unique merchandise that no one else can offer. Have you thought about not letting your business go, but letting your space go and selling out of your barn or on consignment? Consignment would allow you to actually expand your marketplace. Or sharing space with someone else to cut down on overhead?"

She shook her head. "No to the barn. I don't want people traipsing all over my property. That's my quiet place. And I can't imagine giving up this space, either. It will feel like I'm going backward. I started my business on a hope and a prayer. Growing up as one of six siblings, we didn't often have money for new things. We were always going to thrift shops, and from the time I was old enough to work with a needle and thread, I made my stuff special. It wasn't long before my friends started asking me to make things for them. I didn't finish college, and I know that's not something to be proud of, but I am. I sell my herbal remedies and teas and some of this stuff online. I admit I'm not great at getting the word out about my site, but *I* created all of this." She waved her hands. "This is where my vision came to life. What will I have to show for my hard work if I close the doors?"

Graham took her hand in his and said, "If you sell on consignment, you're not closing your doors. You're opening many more of them. I think you're dreaming too small, sunshine. What you've accomplished is incredible, but this space is limiting and far too costly for the lifestyle you lead."

"But—"

"Wait. Just hear me out. If you were selling coffee or ice cream, that would be easy. Every small town needs a coffee shop or an ice cream parlor, right? You'd likely have a constant stream of customers. But right now you are primarily limited to selling these incredible things you're creating to the residents and visitors of this town. Oak Falls is cute, but it's not a resort town where you have hordes of tourists coming through. Imagine collecting items from all over the world, gaining inspiration from other cultures and places. There's no limit to what you can create, and if you're selling on consignment, your customer base can expand. With the right marketing touting your products as one of a kind, you can increase the purchase price to include whatever percentage you'll have to offer the companies who are selling them. It's something to think about if you want a traveling lifestyle while maintaining your business."

"That sounds *wonderful. Beyond* wonderful. Almost *impossible.* Wouldn't I spend everything I earn on travel, or marketing, or have to work twice as hard to keep up inventory in several stores?"

"Morgyn, look around you. You have a huge space filled with inventory. You could spread this out to a dozen stores across the country. You'd have to come up with a plan, work the numbers, talk to other shop owners. But think about that shop in Romance as an example. I bet Magnolia would happily sell your products. It's something new to offer her customers, plus she gets a piece of the pie. And you can travel frugally if you're careful about when and where you go. But that's just one option off the top of my head. I'm sure I'll come up with more."

It was such an exciting idea, she could barely process it. And the thought of working through it with Graham made it even more appealing. But she knew her downfalls, and they couldn't be ignored. "Cracker, I love that idea, but you know I'm not a planner or an organizer. I could screw it up just by being me."

"Lucky for you, you have a boyfriend who can help you with planning, organizing, and strategizing."

Her heart soared at *boyfriend.* He made it sound possible, like their staying together was a given. Everything was happening so fast, which was okay in her personal life, but she didn't want to make a mistake with her business. "I appreciate your help, but I think I need to be able to understand and handle whatever I do on my own."

"Of course. I can teach you how to figure out expenditures and put together a program for you to pop in numbers and see if it works for your bottom line."

"Just *pop* in numbers?" she said with a smile. "You make it sound so easy."

He pulled her onto his lap and pressed a kiss to her shoulder. Then he trailed kisses up her neck. "Business is never easy, but it doesn't have to be hard."

"Cracker…" She moved her hair over her shoulder, giving him room to explore, which he did with more tantalizing kisses. "I like your ideas. But what if I can't figure this out? To you it's popping in numbers, but what if I blow it? What if I forget to pop them in?"

He drew back with a perplexed expression. "There's nothing you *can't* do, sunshine. Look at all that you have accomplished. The key is, what do you *want* to do? Where do you want to be in a few years, traveling and still making your creations, or maybe selling from a smaller store here in the area?"

"I don't know. I don't usually think ahead like that. But with you I want to, and I know that's a little crazy since we've only just met…"

"You make me want to be crazy, sunshine. I say we go for it."

His mouth came coaxingly down over hers, sweeping her into a world of hope and desire. She deepened the kiss and he groaned, going hard beneath her. She drew back, both of them breathless, and said, "Cracker, you make me *feel* so much. You make me *think*."

He chuckled. "And you make me feel so much thinking is

almost impossible." He kissed her tenderly and then said, "Nothing has to be decided today. I'm just tossing out ideas for you to mull over."

"I'm not sure about giving up my shop," she said honestly. "Even though your idea sounds fantastic, it's scary. What if I fail?"

"Is my girl risk assessing?"

"Oh my gosh. I *am*. But seriously, if I took that chance and it didn't work I'd have to start all over."

He wrapped his arms around her and said, "That's why you take the time to do research and a complete risk assessment before making any decisions. I worked through some projections. You make a good income, but once your rent is increased, you'll need to tighten your belt. That's why you should research and prepare, decide on a strategy that works for you. And if you decide to travel, then how far you want to go, what countries or cities you want to see. You'd never walk a tightrope without a net, right?"

"I'd never walk a tightrope, *period*. I've never even been on a plane or traveled very far. What if I don't like traveling, or if I miss my family or my home too much?"

"Then you travel only to the places you love. But...what if you love it? What if you find inspiration in the forests of the Amazon or on the sandy shores of Bali? What if you get inspired by Georgia peaches or New England lobsters?"

"Now who sounds floaty?" she teased. "You're supposed to be the grounded one."

He pushed his hands up her thighs and held on tight. "I am grounded, but you have big beautiful wings that should never be clipped. If what you want is to live your life on a whim, experiencing all of what life has to offer while maintaining your business, then I think we should find a way to make that happen. Or you'll always wonder *what if…*"

"We…?" She wound her arms around his neck and said, "Every time you find out more about me, I expect you to run the other way, but you don't."

"I'd have to be crazy to run away from you. You're everything I never knew I wanted."

"Impulsive and floaty?"

"I need floaty in my life, and I think maybe you need this overthinker in yours."

She soaked in the emotions in his voice. He was the yin to her yang, the cushion to her fall, the only person who made her want to think beyond tomorrow. But she couldn't help teasing him. "Even though I'm not a good investment?"

He brushed his lips over hers and said, "You might not be a solid business investment, but, sunshine, you're the only woman I'd invest my heart in."

Chapter Ten

MORGYN AWOKE TUESDAY morning draped over Graham's big body, wondering when she'd become such a bed hog. She was lying sideways across the bed, her torso spread over his stomach, one arm stretched across him, her other hand splayed over his *package*. She stifled a giggle, in no hurry to move. She closed her eyes and thought about last night. They'd gone over Graham's projections and talked all afternoon about the idea of selling her products in other people's shops. He was so smart about business and finances. He'd projected best- and worst-case scenarios and said if she was interested they'd work together on getting their arms around the other expenses she hadn't noted. He wanted to completely understand all aspects of her business, and although that wasn't her thing, through Graham's eyes, she was beginning to see the value in keeping better records. She'd spent most of the evening combing through the Internet looking at different types of businesses where she could sell her merchandise. Graham had suggested thinking *outside the box*, not just looking at thrift and consignment shops, but specialty stores that sold high-end, one-of-a-kind products. The longer she'd looked, the more excited she'd become. But was her stuff good enough? Would anyone else *want* to sell her merchandise?

He shifted beneath her, running his rough hand along her back. "Why's my girl wide-awake at the crack of dawn?"

"I can't stop thinking about your suggestion."

"Which suggestion might that be? The one where you agree to let me show you the world?"

Her pulse skyrocketed as he swept her beneath him. He grinned wolfishly, his panty-melting dimples in full force. She had no doubt they'd work *if* she had panties on.

"What? When did you suggest that?"

"Just now." He kissed her softly. "What do you say, sunshine?" His chest hair tickled her skin as he began kissing his way south.

Yes! was on the tip of her tongue, but he teased her nipple, making her burn with anticipation and shattering her concentration. She arched beneath him, trying to find her voice, but he made her feel too good to give in just yet. "You'll have to convince me better than that."

His dark eyes flicked up to hers, blazing with desire as he lowered his mouth over the taut peak and sucked *hard*.

"Oh God, *yes*…"

He grazed his teeth over her nipple, sending sharp pangs of pleasure rippling beneath her skin. "Is that a yes, you'll come with me?"

She moaned, bowing up beneath him. "If you keep doing that," she panted out, "I'm definitely going to come."

She spread her legs as he angled his hips, teasing her entrance with the broad head of his cock. He continued teasing and sucking, taking her right up to the brink of madness.

"*Graham…*"

"What do you want, sunshine?"

"*You.* Just you," she said breathlessly.

He moved lower, caressing and kissing, slowing to love her most sensitive areas—her ribs, just above her hip bone, and around her sex. His mouth was magnificent, and his big, strong hands...*Lord*, she loved the way he groped and claimed every inch of her. He pushed her legs open wider, kissing her inner thighs until she was trembling with desire.

"Want my mouth on you, sunshine?"

"Yes, so much, *yes*!" She fisted her hands in the sheets as he reached up with one hand, fondling her breast as he lowered his mouth to her sex, teasing so lightly, every slick of his tongue sent a thousand sensations skittering through her.

"Cracker...You're going to make me lose my mind!"

"That's the plan."

He dipped his fingers inside her, expertly finding the magical spot that sent her world spinning. "*Graham!*"

His mouth took over, sending her impossibly higher, until every iota of her being throbbed with need. He intensified his efforts, sending her soaring again in an explosion of sensations. Just when she started to catch her breath, he moved over her, entering her in one hard thrust. He filled her so completely, her entire body stilled with the beauty of their joining. But that was short-lived, because in the next second he was moving, stroking that secret spot again, making her insides sizzle and burn until she shattered in his arms. Her hips shot off the mattress and she clawed at his back, trying to still her dizzying world. She saw a flash of pleasure in his eyes seconds before he captured her mouth in a ravenous kiss. His body stilled for just a second as a throaty groan escaped, and he gave in to his own powerful release. His hips pistoned in one hard thrust after another as he cradled her against him.

When the last shudder of his release rumbled through him, he rolled them onto their sides, keeping her close. "I'm falling so hard for you, sunshine. How am I going to leave Friday when I can't imagine not waking up with you by my side?"

Emotions bubbled up inside her. She was falling hard for him, too, and she was also already mourning the end of their time together. "You'll just have to figure out ways to squeeze in trips to Oak Falls."

"Or get you on a plane..."

Her pulse sped up with the thought of getting on a plane. "Flying scares me a little."

"More than the idea of not being together?" He kissed the tip of her nose.

"No," she whispered.

"More than the excitement of exploring together?"

She shook her head. He moved over her again, and as he lowered his lips to hers he said, "More than the idea of long stretches of time between this...?"

LATER THAT MORNING, as the sun crept into the sky, Morgyn and Graham filled the corn feeders in the deer garden and went for a walk along the railroad tracks.

"I can't stop thinking about the idea of selling my stuff on consignment," Morgyn said excitedly. "Do you think it's good enough that people who don't know me would want to sell it?"

"If I didn't, I wouldn't have suggested it. It's a great option and would give you flexibility to jump on a plane and explore the rest of the world, or take a day trip, visit with your friends."

"There you go again with the whole plane idea."

He pulled her closer and said, "You have to admit, it'd be hard to drive to Bali."

"What if I puke on a plane? I'm sure it's way different from the swings at the county fair." Morgyn gasped and pointed into a meadow. "Your morning gift."

He glanced into the yard and saw deer grazing in the field. Then he brought his attention back to her. "You're my morning gift, sunshine, and if you puked, I'd hold your hair back." He gazed into her beautiful eyes and said, "What you see and what you've experienced here is only a fraction of what the world has to offer. You deserve to see it all."

"What happened to Mr. Risk Assessor?"

"You can be damn sure I'll weigh the risks of our travels, and I'll never take you anywhere unsafe. But I do think we need to get you out and about in lots of different ways. Do you mountain bike?" He took her hand, and they continued walking down the tracks.

"I know how to ride a bike, so I guess I could mountain bike."

"How about rafting?"

"I can hang on real tight to the inner tube when we go down the river, if that's what you mean."

He laughed and gathered her close for a kiss. "I want to teach you to go white-water rafting, mountain biking, and mountain *climbing*. You take such pleasure in the small things in life, it'd be a shame for you to miss out on the bigger things."

"But isn't all that stuff *hard*?"

He laughed. "Not as hard as brain surgery, but harder than walking like we are now. It's all relative, sunshine. How much do you want to experience?"

"A better question might be, is there anything I *don't* want to experience. And the answer would be *yes.* I don't want to wake up at seventy-five years old and feel like my life has passed me by. I want to look back on my life and think, *Boy, that was fun.*"

He slung his arm around her and said, "That makes two of us."

A few minutes later the tracks spilt around an old, dilapidated building, surrounded by graffiti-riddled trains and various rusted train parts lying forgotten on tufts of dead grass. Weeds and ivy climbed up the sides of the building and snarled around the big metal wheels of the trains.

"Looks like the perfect place for a horror movie."

"This is the train graveyard. Come on." Morgyn took his hand and headed for a line of trains. "I've found lots of cool things here."

"You come here *alone*?"

She rolled her eyes. "You've climbed mountains and *this* scares you?"

"Not for myself, but the idea of you here alone? Yeah, I'm not a fan of that."

"Why do people see things like this and instantly think of trouble? I get a warm, fuzzy feeling here because of my grandfather. Don't you have anything like that? Someplace that other people might think is scary but that you love?"

"Sure, but I wouldn't want you going there alone," he said as they walked between the trains. "Aren't you worried about snakes? Vagrants?"

"Snakes are more afraid of us than we are of them, at least that's what my father always says. And we're in Oak Falls. There are no vagrants here."

"There are bad people everywhere," he said as she pulled herself up on the front of a red caboose.

"Well, not here. This is my favorite train. Did you know that cabooses used to be required at the end of every freight train? They provided shelter for the crew, and this is the car they'd use to keep a lookout for trouble with the trains. They were on all trains until the eighties, when they relaxed that requirement because of the developments in monitoring and safety technology. Technology is good, obviously, but when I come here, it really sheds light on how technology can phase people out of jobs."

"Is that what happened to your grandfather?"

She shook her head. "No. They closed the railroad down after he retired. I was just making an observation. Everything changes so fast. I think that's why I love breathing new life into old things. I don't think just because an item is old or used it should be discarded or forgotten. Look at these beautiful trains. They're so big and powerful. They feel regal to me." She ran her hand along the iron railing surrounding the small deck. "Can you imagine standing here on a trip and taking in the sights and smells of the countryside?"

She touched her necklace, and he realized it was the same one she'd worn the day they'd met. She lifted one of the charms and said, "I made this leaf from the copper bonding on the tracks, and I found these glass beads in a metal box that was hidden in one of the cars. They would have been forgotten forever. Look how pretty they are." She held up two rust- and amber-colored beads. "Do you think that makes me a thief?"

"No," he said with a soft laugh. "I think it makes you even more interesting. For a girl who claims to be floaty, you're very deep."

"You were very *deep* this morning." She went up on her toes, meeting his lips for another kiss.

"And I'll get deep again right here if you keep talking like that." He lifted her onto the railing and wedged himself between her legs, holding her so she didn't fall. "You know, this is another option for your store."

"Having sex on the railing? I'm not sure how it correlates." She wound her arms around his neck, grinning with her joke.

"Buying an old train car and making it into a shop. With the right permits you could probably put it up by the road on your property, or you could finagle a deal with Reed and put it on the theater lot up by the main street."

"That's a cool idea, but I bet it would cost a *fortune*. I can't really barter my way into a train."

Graham wasn't so sure about that.

"We should probably get back. I want to get an hour of work in on that necklace I'm designing before heading to the shop."

Two hours later, after Morgyn finished in the barn and left for work, Graham caught up on emails that had been piling up over the last few days, confirmed his plans to meet Knox Friday afternoon at the property outside of Seattle, and then he researched purchasing an old train car. More specifically, purchasing Morgyn's favorite caboose. He left messages for every lead he came across, but by the time they arrived at her parents' house for dinner that evening, he still hadn't heard back.

Her parents lived in a massive old Victorian with a wraparound porch and a gorgeous yard. From the pictures on the walls spanning years of childhoods, to the teasing barbs cast over biscuits and gravy, the love between the Montgomerys was palpable. Graham sat back and took it all in as they ate dinner.

"Have any of you heard from Grace?" their mother asked. Dolly and Reba, two fluffy golden retrievers she was training, sat beside her chair, their tails twitching like it took everything they had not to beg for food.

Brindle grabbed a biscuit from the basket in the middle of the table and said, "Mom, they're on their honeymoon. I hope they're not thinking about anything other than the next position they want to try."

"Brindle!" Amber snapped. "I swear you're as bad as Sable."

"No she's not," Sable said with a laugh.

"Brin's got her own flavor of naughtiness." Their father, Cade, pointed at Brindle and said, "Listen here, little missy. Grace might be an adult, but she's still my daughter, and I'd like to believe she and Reed are enjoying stargazing and theater hopping."

"They're doing something like bunnies, but I'm sure it's not *hopping*," Sable said quietly, making them all laugh, except Cade, who scowled.

"Oh, come on, honey," Marilynn said. "Honeymoons are made for lovin'."

Cade shook his head and looked at Graham. "You should hope you never have daughters." He pointed to his hair and said, "These girls are responsible for every last gray hair on my head."

"Oh, come on," Amber said. "I was always well behaved, and Axsel wasn't exactly the *good* one."

Cade winked at her.

"In my family we have five boys and one girl," Graham said. "I think my mother might say the same thing about me and my brothers."

"How about you bring your sexy single brothers here and we can see how bad they really are," Brindle suggested with a spark of mischief in her eyes.

"As if Trace would allow you near any of them," Morgyn said. "Speaking of your cowboy, what happened with Slutty Suzie?"

"She's back?" Sable glared at Brindle. "Do I need to go kick some skanky butt?"

"Why do you always want to kick someone's butt?" Amber asked as she picked at her salad.

"I don't care what Slutty Suzie or Trace do," Brindle insisted, but something in her eyes told Graham that wasn't exactly true. "I'm done with him."

"Again," Amber said.

"Some addictions are hard to quit," Morgyn said.

Brindle glared at her. "I'm serious. We're *done*."

"Oh, honey," Marilynn said. "Maybe Paris is just what you need to figure out what you want once and for all."

"And to hook up with a hot French guy," Sable added.

"That's the plan," Brindle said under her breath.

"Hey," Cade snapped. "Could we please keep those parts of your plans to yourself? Didn't I just say that I'd like to live under the misguided fantasy that you're all still the virtuous little girls who used to play in the sprinkler?"

"Your father wants to believe you're all innocent little angels."

They all laughed, but Amber's cheeks pinked up.

"Something we should know, Amb?" Brindle said.

"No," Amber said.

"How about you take Amber with you to Paris?" Marilynn suggested.

Amber and Brindle both glowered at her.

"What?" Marilynn said innocently. "Amber's a calming influence on Brindle, and Brindle might help bring Amber out of her shell."

"If they don't kill each other first," Sable said.

"My shell is safe, Mom," Amber said. "I'm not like Brindle, and I never will be."

Her father put his hand over hers and said, "Thank goodness for little favors, honey. You know we adore you just the way you are."

"You remind me of my family," Graham said. "We're always giving each other a hard time about something."

"Oh my gosh." Amber set down her fork and said, "I almost forgot to tell you. I had no idea that Beau Braden was your brother. His fiancée, Charlotte Sterling, is one of my LWW sisters."

"LWW?" Graham asked.

"Ladies Who Write. It's like a sorority, but without all the nonsense," Amber explained. "We went to school together in Port Hudson, New York, and we lived in the same LWW house. She is such a talented writer, and she's been through so much, losing her whole family. I'm glad she and Beau found each other."

"Beau's gone through a lot as well. They're really happy together," he said. "Did you hear about Char's movie deal for her book?" Charlotte had inherited her family's inn, and when Beau had gone there to fix it up, they'd fallen in love.

"Yes," Amber said. "My friend Aubrey runs the film division of LWW. She said they're scouting for locations to film the movie. Charlotte doesn't want the inn to become that kind of tourist attraction. I suggested that they have Grace write the screenplay. Grace has a conference call scheduled with Aubrey when they get back from their honeymoon."

"Wait. Isn't Char the erotic romance writer?" Brindle asked. "No *wonder* Beau's so happy."

Graham chuckled.

"I can't wait to read her newest book," Amber said. "Maybe I should ask her to do a signing at the store. She and Janie Hudson could do it together. They're both erotic romance writers. Which reminds me, have any of you read Janie's new book?"

All eyes turned to her.

"What?" Amber looked innocently around the table. "It was just a thought. Is it a bad idea?"

"No," Sable said. "But who knew our sweetest sister enjoyed erotic romance?"

"It's always the quiet ones," Brindle said. "Maybe Amber likes to be spanked."

"Ohmygosh!" Amber turned bright red. She reached down to pet Reno and said, "You guys are pigs."

"Agreed," Marilynn said.

"Sorry, Mom, but the blush is a dead giveaway that she's not as innocent as you think," Brindle said.

"Hey, leave Amber alone," Morgyn snapped. "I'm sure I blushed, too. If anyone around this table is into that stuff it's Sable and Brindle. Sable probably chains up her guys and, Brindle, I'm sure you whip Trace into shape."

Amber put her hand on Morgyn's and said, "Thanks, but I don't need you to protect me." She sat up a little straighter and said, "What's the matter, Brin? Jealous? Isn't that what every man wants? A lady in the streets and a freak between the sheets? Too bad neither of you can fill the bill. It's a little hard to be considered a lady when you're blowing through men like the wind."

Graham bit back a laugh at the look of shock on her sisters' faces.

"Okay, girls," their father said with a sigh. "Now that you've shown Graham how utterly ridiculous you can be, how about we head over to the sink and see if we can wash out your filthy mouths with soap?"

That earned a round of apologies, and Brindle said, "Daddy, you're such a softie. Remember when you used to threaten to wash our mouths out with soap? You'd end up making us hot chocolate and sitting around the table lecturing us about the difference between appropriate and inappropriate behavior while we fought over marshmallows and whipped cream."

"I see that worked well," Cade said, earning a round of laughter and setting the tone for the rest of dinner.

After eating, they all helped clear the table and wash dishes, and then Graham and the girls took the dogs outside. The dogs took off for the barn, and Graham and Morgyn sat on the porch steps, while Brindle egged her sisters on to do cartwheels. It was easy to imagine them as teenagers raising all sorts of hell. Even Amber. She might be quiet, but she had fire in her belly, and he'd bet Pepper possessed the same hidden fierceness.

"I haven't done a cartwheel in a hundred years," Morgyn said as Brindle pulled her to her feet.

"Can't we do something else?" Amber suggested.

Sable plopped down on Graham's other side and said, "Horseshoes?"

"I'm leaving, and you won't see me again until September third. Anything could happen between now and then," Brindle said. "I want to remember you doing a cartwheel."

"And I want to remember you not being a pain. We can't always get what we want." Morgyn reached for Graham's hand and said, "Come on, cracker. I'll take you down to see my parents' horses, Sonny and Cher."

"Oh no." Brindle grabbed Morgyn's and Amber's hands and pulled them toward the house. "First help me pack; then you can go do the naked-hayloft dance with Mr. Thick Thighs. Come on, Sabe!"

"Pack?" Morgyn and Amber said in unison.

Sable snickered as she followed them toward the door.

"Yes," Brindle said. "It's that thing you help your sister with before she flies a thousand miles away." As Cade and Marilynn stepped onto the porch, Brindle called over her shoulder, "I'll bring them back in a few minutes!"

"Don't take it personally," Cade said as he sat beside Graham on the step. "I've been the odd man out for thirty years."

"Where are they off to?" Marilynn asked.

"To help Brindle pack." Graham took a swig of his beer.

Marilynn smiled. "You know Brindle doesn't live here, right?"

"I figured as much," Graham admitted.

"It's code for stealing away for girl talk," Cade said. "Like I said, don't take it personally." He headed into the yard and whistled so loud it rivaled Graham's brother Nick's whistle, which he swore could be heard from two miles away. The dogs ran up the yard.

"It's fine. I'm sure they're going to miss each other while Brindle's away."

"Speaking of traveling," Marilynn said, "I hear you've been trying to coax my wanderlust girl into traveling far and wide."

He smiled at *wanderlust girl.* "She's got the soul of a traveler and the heart of an artist. She could gain inspiration from other places and use it in the things she makes."

Marilynn looked expectantly at him, brows lifted, head tilted, a small smile tugging at her lips.

"Okay, you caught me. Selfishly, I'd love to be the one to show her the world," he admitted. "What can I say? She's captivated me. But I'm not trying to steal her away from you." The dogs bounded up the steps and licked Graham's face. He loved them up while Marilynn tried to calm them down. "It's okay. I love dogs," he reassured her.

Cade whistled again. He threw two balls into the yard, and the pups sprinted away.

"I'm not worried about you stealing Morgyn away, Graham. Her roots here are deep, but so is her need to be free. I stopped by to see her this afternoon and she told me about your suggestions," Marilynn said. "Putting her things on consignment at different stores? That's brilliant. Her aunt Roxie does that with her soaps and fragrances. Morgyn seemed intrigued by the idea, too."

"I also suggested she think about buying an old train car and running her business out of that. Once it's paid off, she'd have no rent to pay. Her monthly overhead would be solely tied to the items she buys and advertising. It would also be a nice testament of her love for her grandfather."

"She told me that, too. It was a very thoughtful suggestion, although I was surprised to hear she took you to the train graveyard."

"Why is that?"

Marilynn smiled, gazing out at the dogs as Cade tossed the balls for them again. "Because I know Morgyn seems like an open book, but there are certain things she's never shared with a man." She glanced at him and said, "Her love for her grandfather is at the top of that list. When he passed away, he took a piece of Morgyn with him. She was only thirteen, and they were so close. Grandparents aren't supposed to have favorites, but there was a connection between those two, like kindred spirits. He loved all our kids, don't get me wrong, but the two of them saw the world in ways no one else did."

"She speaks of him often." *And now I realize how much of a gift that is.*

"Does she? I'm glad. It's good for her to share that. She cried for two straight weeks after we lost him, and then one day she disappeared. I was frantic, of course, because she'd been so distraught. I thought the worst. She was gone for hours, and we had friends, neighbors, *everyone* looking for her. Sable was sixteen at the time and working at the Stardust Cafe. When she got wind that Morgyn was missing, she knew exactly where to find her. You see, Sable comes across tough, but she has a heart as big as the clouds, just like Morgyn. She's always taken on the protector role for all her siblings. Even Gracie, who's the oldest. Sable has made it her business to know what her siblings were up to. She knew how hard Morgyn had taken the loss, because she'd taken it just as hard, although she hid it well. Thankfully, she'd been following Morgyn down to the train graveyard for weeks. That day, she found Morgyn in an old caboose and texted us to say she was okay. Then she stayed with her until Morgyn was ready to come home. As far as I know, you're the first person she's ever taken there, which means more than you can imagine."

"I think I can imagine exactly how special that is."

Marilynn touched his hand and said, "You're good for her, Graham. I realize this is fast for you kids, but some relationships are written in the stars. They don't need the same time to brew as others. She has so much light in her, and usually people try to tamp it down or bend it to their will. But you let her shine, and I've never seen her happier."

The girls stumbled out of the house in fits of giggles, and Brindle said, "Oh no. Mom's cornered your man."

"She's probably telling him embarrassing baby stories," Amber said.

"Who are you kidding? Look at him all manly and hot," Sable said. "I bet she's begging for grandkids."

Graham rose to his feet and reached for Morgyn, drawing her into an embrace.

"Is my mom scaring you off?"

"If Sable didn't scare me off, do you think anyone else can?" He glanced at Marilynn, who was watching them with love in her eyes, and he said, "I might even be up for grandkids."

"Oh, sweet girl, *please* marry that man!" Marilynn said.

Morgyn's eyes went wide, and he had to laugh at the worry in them. "Have no fear, sunshine. I'm not in a rush for kids. I'm just getting on your mama's good side."

Chapter Eleven

GRAHAM AWOKE WITH a start Wednesday morning, surprised not to be blanketed by Morgyn's sweet, soft body. Over the last several days he'd awoken to find her fast asleep lying on his back, stretched over his stomach, clinging to his legs with *her* leg across his chest, and a handful of other funky positions. She slept like she did everything else, with zest and vigor—just another item to add to the growing list of what he loved about her.

He stepped from the bed, listening for clues of what she was up to, and peered over the railing as he tugged on a pair of jeans. "Morgyn?"

Answered with silence, he went downstairs. The bathroom was empty, and her design notebooks weren't on the coffee table where she'd left them last night. In their place was a note scribbled on a torn piece of paper that read *In the barn!* with a smiley face.

He shoved his feet into his boots and headed outside, thinking about last night. They'd hung around her parents' house for hours talking with her family about Brindle's trip to Paris and Morgyn's business. When Morgyn told them she was worried about whether her merchandise was good enough that other people—strangers in other cities—would want to sell it in their stores, not only had they raved about her work, but they each offered to make a few calls and talk to people they knew who might be interested. They were equally excited about the idea of buying a railroad car from which she could run her business. Graham had seen the prices for old cabooses ranging from two thousand to twenty thousand dollars, and others asking upward of sixty thousand, depending on location and state of wear. If he knew Morgyn as well as he believed he did, then there was only one caboose she'd want, and there was no way that particular one cost more than fifteen or twenty thousand. She was already spending nearly thirty grand a year on rent. In the long run it was a winning concept.

Music streamed out the open barn doors, and just inside, Morgyn bopped to the music in her fuzzy slippers and one of Graham's T-shirts, which barely covered her ass as she leaned over a table working on one of her creations.

"Is this a solo dance party?" he asked as he walked in.

She spun around, with a hilariously adorable mass of tangled hair and a heart-stopping smile. "I couldn't sleep. I kept thinking about all these designs." She waved her hands toward the surrounding tables, which he now realized were covered with fabrics, bags, jewelry boxes, and other items that hadn't been there yesterday morning.

"I'm making fresh stock. The business owners around here will want something new in their stores, and people who don't know me would probably take my existing stock." She moved to the other side of the table and placed a thin line of colorful fabric to the seam of a black bag. "What do you think of this? I thought I'd silk-screen a dream catcher on the front in bright blue, white, and gray." Apparently she didn't expect an answer because she took his hand and led him to another table displaying several necklaces—some with tiny charms and others with interesting shapes of metal and glass. "I made these this morning, and I emailed Magnolia to see if she'd be interested in taking a few. I thought I'd drive them down tomorrow afternoon along with that chair over there."

She pointed across the room to an antique aqua tufted-velvet wing chair. "I adore that chair, and I was never sure what to do with it, but *look*."

He followed her around the table to the back of the chair and was met with an unexpected and gorgeous array of reds, greens, yellows, pinks, and purples embroidered in circular patterns with black accents. Green leaves and small shapes were threaded throughout the design, and it was trimmed in aqua to match the front of the chair. It was magnificent.

"This is hand-embroidered silk Suzani fabric. It's a one-of-a-kind tribal textile from Tajikistan. I found it on eBay a few years ago and, like the chair, I was never sure what to do with it. Then you got me thinking outside the box, and *look*. With the double-welt trim, it's the perfect backing for the chair, isn't it? It takes it from boring to *wow*! See that, cracker? You've inspired greatness!"

He laughed, blown away by everything she'd done. He looked around the barn again. A number of freshly dyed scarves hung on a drying rack. Painted vases and newly embellished picture frames were set up on two other tables. "Sunshine, how long have you been out here? This is *all* stunning."

Beaming with pride, she set her hands on her hips and said, "I don't know. I got up to pee after you fell asleep and decided to see what I could do."

"After I fell asleep? You mean last night?"

"Yup," she said with a sexy smile. "Right after I showed you just how *flexible* I could be." She wrapped her arms around his middle and said, "I wore you out, and you inspired me. Want to know the best part?"

"As I recall that was a pretty mind-blowing part. With an encore."

"Two encores, but who's counting? The best *business* part is that if they don't sell, then I'll have new stock for my shop. This is a test."

He couldn't mask his surprise. "Wait. Is my floaty girl actually *planning*? Strategizing?"

"No," she said with a laugh. "I'm testing a market."

"Which equates to risk assessment and involves both a plan and a strategy."

"I am *not* planning. I don't plan." She grinned up at him and said, "I came out here on a whim."

"And then you came up with a plan to create new inventory and test a market."

She pressed her lips together, her smile pushing at them.

"Admit it. I'm wearing off on you." He lifted her and set her on the edge of the table, stood between her legs, and kissed her neck. "My floaty girl is seeing the value in risk assessment."

"I'm acting on a whim." She pushed her hands into his hair. "God, I love when you kiss my neck."

He sank his teeth into her flesh just hard enough to earn a sinful gasp. He licked over the tender spot, and she moaned greedily, digging her nails into his skin. He bit down again, and she arched against him, pressing all her softness into him. "A *whim*?" he whispered against her skin. He pulled her to the edge of the table, holding her ass as he ground against her. "For someone who's not a planner, it sure looks like you've worked your sexy little ass off preparing. I was going to reward you for planning ahead, but…"

He took a step back, and she grabbed his arms, pulling him close again.

"Do that bite-lick thing again," she said seductively. "Maybe it *was* a plan."

"Oh, *maybe* it was…?"

He lowered his mouth to her neck, earning more needy noises. Her hands moved over his body as he feasted on her neck, her mouth, and then nipped playfully at her lower lip, taunting them both. They'd just made love last night. He should be satiated, but when it came to Morgyn, his desires—and his heart—knew no limits. He didn't just want sex, although their lovemaking was like nothing he'd ever experienced. His desire for her went beyond orgasms and lustful pleasures. He craved their deep connection, the feeling of oneness and completeness that overtook him when they were together.

"What do you think, sunshine?" he asked between kisses. "Am I wearing off on you?"

"Think…? I can't think." She tore her shirt off and dropped it to the floor. "The question is, can *you*?"

A sound somewhere between a growl and a curse escaped as their mouths crashed together, extinguishing all thought. That was how it was with them. Their kisses led to a world of passion where nothing mattered except coming together. They tore at their remaining clothes, and he swept the fabric off the table and laid her down. Perched above her, he gazed deeply into her eyes, wondering again how he'd ever say goodbye for a day, much less a week, a month, or more.

As their bodies became one and her trusting eyes bored into

his, his heart poured out. "I never thought I was missing a damn thing until the day I met you. You soared into my life like a gust of wind or a runaway kite—magical and unstoppable. You make me see and feel so much. I know I'll never look at anything the same way again."

"Neither will I. You're wearing off on me, cracker."

"We're just getting started, sunshine. There's a whole world of possibilities ahead of us. I don't care if you live life on a whim or plan every second as long as I'm by your side for the ride."

"Then ride me, big boy, and I promise not to change."

MORGYN WORKED LIKE the Energizer Bunny, making new inventory and inquiring with stores in Oak Falls, Meadowside, and Whisper Creek, another neighboring town, to see if they'd sell her products. Word spread quickly, and by Thursday afternoon when she and Graham returned from dropping off merchandise at Magnolia's store, nine more store owners had left messages offering to take her products on consignment. They'd spent the day delivering products and making inventory lists using a simple spreadsheet Graham had set up for her. He'd gone to painstaking efforts noting how much each item had originally cost, how much of Morgyn's time she'd put into each enhancement, and the cost of the products she used. It was difficult, given that she couldn't remember what most of the items had originally cost, but she had receipts for some of her more recent purchases, and with Graham's help, it became clear how much she'd underestimated the value of her work. She'd never even thought to calculate the time she put into each item.

She was excited to see if the consignment idea would actually work even though now that she realized she should probably raise her prices, she wasn't sure she'd need to close her shop after all. But the truth was, even with how helpful all of these options were, she was working her fingers to the bone in an effort to distract herself from the obvious.

Graham was leaving tomorrow.

Although they hadn't talked in any detail about what would happen after he left, she knew they'd try to make it work. But every time she thought about bringing it up or talking about how to make a long-distance relationship work, she got an empty feeling in the pit of her stomach. She'd tried to bring it up several times as they cooked dinner and then again as they ate sitting on a blanket by the deer garden, serenaded by music streaming from her phone. She'd never had to *decide* not to think about anything. She naturally didn't worry and assumed situations would work out for the best. But she didn't like the idea of leaving their future up to chance.

He made her want to *plan*. To *strategize* with him about their relationship and figure out their next step.

How scary was it that they were lying on their backs, stargazing under a beautiful night sky, and instead of reveling in their closeness, she was thinking about how this time tomorrow his toothbrush would be gone, his clothes would no longer share the same space as hers, and his coffee cup would no longer be drying by the sink every morning.

Her insides knotted up and she rolled onto her side, putting her arm across his chest and her leg over his legs. His strong arm circled her, and he pressed a kiss to her head.

"How's my girl? You okay?"

"No." She snuggled in closer, clinging to his shirt, her body pressed tightly against him.

"Do you want to burrow beneath my skin?"

She heard the smile in his voice and nodded. "Do you have a problem with that?"

"No, sunshine. I love everything you do, from plastering your body over mine while you're sleeping to changing directions ten times a day."

"Would you still like me as much if I changed?"

"I don't think anything could change how I feel about you." He touched her chin, lifting her face so he could see her eyes. "What's wrong? Talk to me."

She sat up beside him, worrying her hands. "I've never felt this way before, and it's got me all twisted up inside. I *like* living alone. I've never wanted anyone else in my life twenty-four seven, but now..." Her throat thickened with emotion, and he sat up beside her, his serious eyes boring into her. "I don't want to wake up Saturday morning to an empty bed, with all your stuff gone, and leave it up to the universe to bring you back. I've always believed that what was supposed to happen would—but what if this time I'm wrong? What if real life is too busy and this was a fantasy? A week-long break from reality?"

"Is that what you think we are?"

She shook her head. "But I'm not you."

He took her hands in his and pressed a long, tender kiss to the back of each of them. "I'm the planner; you're the floater."

"What does that mean? Does that mean I can't think about it?"

"No, sunshine. Your beautiful brain can think about anything and everything you ever want to. But in this case, you don't have to worry. I've already bought a plane ticket to come back here after my trip to New York. Short of the world coming to an end, *nothing* will keep me from you."

Tears slipped from her eyes. "You did?"

"What did you think I meant when I said you were the only woman I wanted to invest my heart in? Or that I was falling for you? Did you think those were just words?"

She crawled into his lap and said, "No. I believed you, but this whole wanting to think ahead thing is new to me, and it's thrown me for a loop. I *want* to plan with you. I want to *know* you're coming back and that we're real. It's *hard* being a planner."

He chuckled. "Not for me, but that's why we work so well together. I'm learning to float a little more and plan a little less, and you're learning to think ahead when it matters."

"But that's not the girl you were falling for. The girl you were falling for is *floaty* and didn't balk when you said you'd find me and didn't take my number."

"First of all, you're exactly the girl I was—and *am*—falling for." He rubbed his nose along hers, and then he shifted so he could look into her eyes and said, "I'm no expert about relationships, but from what I've seen with my brother, Beau, when you find your soul mate, you can't help but change. The things you've always thought you've known about yourself suddenly seem bigger, smaller, or not at all what you believed. We're written in the stars, babe. Just ask your mother. There's no escaping us."

She laughed, imagining her mother saying that. "My mom's a total romantic."

"Don't fool yourself, crafty girl. You're a romantic, too. How else could you feel so deeply?" He kissed her softly and he said, "Listen. Our song is playing."

He rose to his feet, bringing her with him, and wrapped her

in his arms, slow dancing to Luke Bryan's "Crash My Party."

"This song gives me an open door to call you anytime," she said as she wound her arms around his neck, happiness filling her up inside.

"Day or night, sunshine."

"You might regret that when I miss your voice and call at three in the morning just to hear it."

"I look forward to it. And I'll miss hearing yours, so you can expect lots of calls and FaceTime videos."

"Can I keep a few of your shirts to sleep in?"

"I'll leave everything here if you'd like. My truck is here, remember? I was supposed to drive across country. Have you noticed I haven't made arrangements to get my truck back to Maryland? I'm coming back to be with you, Morgyn. I have to admit, I'm worried about how I'll sleep without you." He smiled and said, "I'm used to being kneed in the groin and waking up to your thigh across my neck, my back, or anywhere else you happen to flop."

She buried her face in his chest. "I have no idea why I do that. I've never spent the night with a guy before you. I guess I'm not very good at it."

"You are impeccable at it. The best bedmate ever. The *queen* of cosleeping. And I'm seriously going to have withdrawals."

Why did that make her heart ache even more?

"Perfect" by Ed Sheeran came on, and he said, "Listen, sunshine. Another song written just for us. We may not have been children when we found each other, but I'm buying into your theory of knowing each other for much longer spiritually than physically, so maybe we aren't far off."

His arms were heavy against her, his heart thumping to the same fast beat as hers. She loved his strength, the way he cherished his family and the environment in equal measure, and most of all, she loved his surety about their relationship.

"Just in case, I'm keeping your hat." She said it teasingly, but she truly didn't want to give it up. It was the first piece of himself he'd ever shared with her.

"I wouldn't want it any other way."

Chapter Twelve

"MORGYN! WHERE ARE you?" Brindle's voice carried in the cool night air. "I know you guys are out here! Cover up the goods and show yourself. I *need* you!"

Graham squinted into the darkness at the flashlight beam sweeping over the yard by the house. Morgyn was fast asleep on top of him, her arms outstretched, her head on his chest, and her legs between his. If she was startled he was sure to get a knee in the groin. He kissed the top of her head. "Sunshine," he whispered. "Baby, Brindle needs you."

She buried her face in his neck with a mewling sound. Thankfully, they were fully dressed. They'd danced and talked until well after midnight, making plans for when he returned and promising to keep in touch. Morgyn had fallen fast asleep holding on to him, like the thought of his leaving had taken everything out of her. It had nearly killed him not to ask her to go to Seattle with him, but with her business up in the air and her excitement over possible new directions in full swing, it would be selfish of him to ask her to leave it all behind.

"Morgyn! Graham! Where are—"

The flashlight beam landed on them.

"Brindle?" Morgyn's head and knee shot up at the same

time, sending searing pain from Graham's groin to his chest.

"Fuuuck!" He rolled to the side, cupping his balls.

"Oh no!" Morgyn reached between his legs, eyes wide and sorrowful. "I'm sorry! I...Oh God! Did I kill them?"

He groaned as Brindle dropped to her knees in hysterics. "I'm sorry," she choked out between laughs. "But you two! Did you *kill* them? They're not *people*."

"Shut up, Brin!" Morgyn snapped. "I'm sorry, cracker."

"I'm fine, sunshine," Graham ground out as he sat up. "What's wrong, Brindle?"

"Wrong?" Confusion washed over Brindle's face. "Oh, you mean why am I here? I need Morgyn. I leave tomorrow—well, technically *today*—and we have to go do something."

"Now?" He glanced at the time on his phone. "It's four in the morning."

Morgyn glared at Brindle. "I'm not leaving Graham."

Brindle knee-walked over to Morgyn, wearing skimpy cut-offs, a halter top, and cowgirl boots. "Please? You have to! It's the last time I can do it all summer. Please, Morg? I need to do this."

"Can't you coerce Sable?" Morgyn pleaded, cuddling up to Graham. "This is our last night, too. Graham leaves tomorrow. I'm *not* leaving him."

"What are you guys talking about?" Graham asked. "Where do you need to go?"

Ignoring his questions, Brindle said, "Sable's not home. I went there first. You know how much this means to me."

"I thought you and Trace were *over*," Morgyn said.

"We *are*, but still...This is tradition. *Please!*"

"Whatever it is, if it's that important, we'll go," Graham offered.

Morgyn bit her lower lip, troubled eyes shifting to him.

"Um…" Brindle looked at Morgyn. "It's…um…"

"You wouldn't like it," Morgyn said quickly. "We've been doing secret adventures since we were kids. It's kind of our thing. They're not very fun, though. You have to climb hills and lie in the grass…"

"Cool." Graham pushed to his feet and stretched. "I'm always up for an adventure. Let's go, sunshine. Your sister needs you. I'm not going to stand in the way of tradition."

A devilish grin appeared on Brindle's face as she stood up. "Have I told you how much I like your guy? Let's go on our *adventure*!" She ran toward the house. "Come on!"

"But—"

Graham silenced Morgyn with a long, slow kiss. "I won't get in the way, promise. It'll be fun to see what you girls do for excitement."

Morgyn fidgeted nervously as they followed Brindle in Graham's truck. "You don't have to go," she said for the tenth time. "I could have told her no."

"There's no way I'm standing in the way of a sisterly tradition." He reached across the seat and squeezed her hand. "I really don't mind, sunshine. I'm excited to go."

They parked on a side road near her parents' house and followed a path up a big hill.

"This is going to be awesome," Brindle said with a giggle.

"Yeah, right," Morgyn mumbled.

When they neared the crest of the hill, Brindle grabbed Graham's arm, speaking in a hushed whisper. "Get down, and speak quietly. If they hear you, they'll catch us."

"They?" Graham asked, ducking like them.

"Shh!" the girls said.

He crawled to the edge of the hill with the girls, and a big barn and riding ring came into view.

"Whose barn is that?" he whispered.

"The Jerichos'," Morgyn said. "She wants to see Trace ride. The guys are breaking in horses. They ride the wildest ones."

"Now?" Graham asked. "Why not during the day?"

"Shh!" Brindle glowered at him. "You can come, but you can't talk."

"Sounds like a bad porn movie," he said with a snicker, earning an eye roll from both of them.

Trace and JJ came around the side of the barn, both of them shirtless. Brindle made an appreciative noise as they pulled open the barn doors and two more shirtless guys sauntered out. The guys were talking, but they were too far away to make out what was being said.

Trace strode into the barn, and Brindle said, "That's right, baby. Get on that horse. Show them who's the baddest guy in Oak Falls."

"So much for it being over between you two," Graham said under his breath.

Brindle glowered. "It's *over*. I'm leaving tomorrow, and trust me, I'm not looking back. My summer is going to rock, and when I come home I'll barely remember who he is."

Morgyn shook her head. "Ignore her. When she comes back, she'll probably go straight to his house for hot miss-you sex."

"Hey, don't knock hot miss-you sex." Graham pressed his lips to hers, knowing just how hot their lovemaking would be when he returned from his trip. *My fucking trip.* He'd never wanted to put off work for a woman before, but the best deal in the world couldn't make him want to leave Morgyn for a day, much less for ten. But he couldn't let Knox down.

A horse burst into the ring, bucking wildly with Trace on its back. The guys hooted and hollered, cheering him on as the horse tried its best to throw him off.

Brindle went up on her elbows, her brow furrowed. "Hold on, baby. Hold on. You've got this. Show him who's boss."

Morgyn clutched Graham's hand, eyes wide—and locked on the shirtless dudes below. Jealousy clutched him, an unfamiliar and fucking awful feeling. He wasn't about to let his girl drool over another guy. Tradition or not.

"I can't believe *this* is what you do on your adventures," he whispered.

"I told you that you wouldn't like it," Morgyn said, eyes still locked on Trace riding that wild horse like a pro. "But you have to admit, it's exciting!"

He scoffed. *You want exciting, I'll give you exciting.* "I'm going to take a piss."

"WHERE'S HE GOING?" Brindle asked, scooting closer to Morgyn.

"To pee. I think he's mad."

Brindle giggled. "No kidding. You should have told him not to come."

"*You* shouldn't have begged. You knew this was our last night together," she whispered harshly.

"It's our last night, too," Brindle said. "Yours and mine. Doesn't that mean something?"

"Yes, but I *love* him, and he's leaving, and now he's mad

and…" She buried her face in her hands.

"You *what*? Wait. You *love* him? After a week?"

Morgyn nodded. "Yes! I know…I don't understand it, either. But I *do*, Brindle. I love who he is, the way we connect, the way he looks at me like I'm everything to him. He's everything to me, Brin. I can't look into my future and not see him right there with me."

Brindle's mouth hung open.

"Stop looking at me like that!" She sat up and wrapped her arms around her knees. "Now he's probably rethinking everything because I was stupid enough to come here with you. I don't care about these guys. They're like brothers to me!"

"Well, Trace is *not* like a brother to me," Brindle said sharply, pulling Morgyn down to her stomach. "Stay down or they'll see you."

"What am I going to do? I swear if this ruins us, I'm going to fly to Paris and kill you."

"You're asking me what to do? What the fuck do I know about wanting to keep a man?" She knocked Morgyn with her shoulder and said, "Maybe *you* should come to Paris with me."

"I don't want to go anywhere with you. This is all your—" She grabbed Brindle's arm. "Holy shit. What is he doing?"

Graham strode toward the riding ring. He tore off his shirt and laid it over the fence beside JJ. JJ hollered something, and then there was a flurry of activity getting Trace's horse back into the barn, and all the guys followed him in.

"If he tells them we're up here, I'll personally kick him in the groin," Brindle said. "We've been doing this for more than a decade and they have yet to find out."

"He won't," Morgyn said, although she had no idea what he was doing. "Do you think this is his way of telling me it's over?

Like *fuck off, I'm hanging with the guys*?"

"Get real. If anything, he's asking for man-up lessons."

Morgyn swatted her. "Shut up. He's ten times the man Trace is. He's not afraid of commitment, he's always got my back, and he doesn't play games."

Brindle's face blanched.

Shouts rang out from below, drawing their attention as a horse charged out of the barn with Graham on its back. The other guys moved outside the ring, waving their cowboy hats, egging Graham on.

"Oh my God!" Morgyn pushed to her feet, watching Graham's strong arms hold the reins, his body moving *with* the horse's bucks, as if he were born riding. She must be seeing things because he'd never said a word about riding horses. "He's going to get killed! We have to stop him."

She ran down the hill with Brindle on her heels, begging her not to go. But Morgyn was *not* slowing down. She barreled forward, waving her hands and hollering, "Trace! JJ! Stop him! He'll get hurt!" She lost her footing, falling to her ass and taking Brindle down with her. They tumbled down the hill, laughing and cursing.

Morgyn popped back up to her feet and saw Graham scaling the fence, eyes trained on her. He sprinted toward her as the other guys ran for the horse.

"What the hell?" JJ hollered.

"Morgyn!" Their bodies collided.

"Where'd you guys come from?" JJ asked.

"Shh!" Brindle waved him off as Graham grabbed Morgyn by the shoulders, stepping back and visually inspecting her for injuries.

"Are you okay?" Graham asked with a voice full of concern.

"Are you hurt?"

"Me? No! What were you doing? You could have gotten killed!" She didn't mean to yell, but her heart was racing. She was out of her mind with worry and out of breath from running.

He wrapped his arms around her, crushing him to her. "Thank God you're okay. I can't leave you alone, baby. What if you got hurt and I wasn't here? I don't want to go a single day without you. Come to Seattle with me. I'll buy everything you have in stock if you just say yes."

She laughed, unable to believe her ears. "That's not a good investment. I think I'm making you dumber."

"Then I want to be as stupid as a man can get." He gazed into her eyes with love and concern written all over his face as he said, "I want to be with you, Morgyn. You haven't traveled to the West Coast, and I know it means closing your shop and that's not ideal right now, but it *still* seems like a no-brainer to me."

Emotions bubbled up inside her, but she was *thinking* again. *Stupid thinking-ahead thoughts.* Why couldn't she stop thinking? Life was easier without thinking ahead. But she didn't want to make a mistake, not with Graham. "You have to work. What if I get in the way?"

"*Never.* You couldn't get in my way if you were with me all day every day. I want you to come with me to see the property after we arrive and meet my business partner, Knox. I have meetings for a few hours Saturday morning, but then I'm all yours until Sunday."

"Sunday..." Her stomach sank. He was going to New York on Sunday and she'd come back to Oak Falls alone.

"Yes, but I'll be back right after I wrap up my meetings in

New York. I want you with me, Morgyn. I know it's selfish with all you're going through with your business, but I can't leave you behind when you belong by my side. Tell me you'll come with me, sunshine."

"Holy crap, Morgyn." Brindle's voice broke through their private bubble, reminding Morgyn they weren't alone. "Since when do you hesitate to do anything? Tell the man you'll go before he breaks out in hives."

"Forget hives," he said vehemently. "If you don't say you'll come with me, I'll get arrested for abduction and then you'll have to visit me in jail. Say *yes*, sunshine. I promise I'll work twice as hard to figure out your business when we get back. I'll help you make jewelry or chairs or whatever you want."

"How could you ever think I'd say *no*? Besides, I can't leave *you* alone. You'll hurt yourself doing stupid things like climbing on that wild horse."

His dimples appeared, warming her from her heart right down to her toes.

"I've been riding wild horses with Nick since we were teenagers. If I'm not everything you've ever wanted in a man, you can bet your sweet ass I will be."

Chapter Thirteen

"I CAN'T BELIEVE I'm on a plane! I thought I'd be nervous, but I'm too excited to be nervous," Morgyn said as passengers settled into their seats around them.

Graham had come armed with antianxiety and antinausea meds and a slew of magazines to distract her, just in case she had a hard time with the almost-six-hour flight to Washington. He was glad she didn't seem to need them.

They'd both been too wired after returning home last night to sleep. *Home.* The word slowed his thoughts. He traveled so often, he had places he stayed, which meant everything from his house to a hotel, his truck, or a tent. But he had the overwhelming feeling that *home* now meant *Morgyn*, not a place to rest his head.

"I'm so happy you asked me to come with you," she said, breaking through his thoughts. "I hated the idea of being apart."

"I know, sunshine. I didn't want to be away from you, either."

He'd gotten another pang of longing last night when he'd arranged her flight back to Oak Falls on Sunday. He had been happy for Beau and Charlotte when they'd gotten engaged, but he hadn't fully understood what true love could do to a man.

Now, as he watched Morgyn's wide-eyed amazement at the people and the plane—things he'd taken for granted for as long as he could remember—he got it. He would rearrange his entire life just for the chance to experience more firsts with Morgyn. To see and feel her excitement and be part of the awakening that came with every new endeavor.

A disturbing thought floated through his mind. Had he suggested the consignment idea for subconsciously *selfish* reasons? There was no doubt that he found himself hoping she'd choose to move in that direction, but he never made business suggestions to others based on his personal feelings. They were always based on hard facts, numbers, smart business decisions. The thought bothered him, and he mentally walked through the landscape of her business again, rethinking the numbers and the strategies he'd suggested. Even if he had subconsciously hoped to have more time with her, short of owning the property where she sold her work so she was free to come and go as she liked, consignment was definitely the next best suggestion.

Feeling more at ease, he reached for her hand. Morgyn had an eclectic style all her own, and she owned it with such confidence, it made her even more beautiful. Today she wore a yellow-and-blue tie-dyed minidress with flared sleeves and a plunging neckline. The dress hung loose around her body, flowing like a wave when she walked. On anyone else it might look like she was wearing someone else's clothes. But on Morgyn? Paired with brown boots she'd embellished with tiny circular mirrors and gold hearts, a wrist full of bracelets, dangling mirror and heart earrings that matched her boots, several long necklaces, and his MIT hat—which she insisted they bring for luck since he and Knox were negotiating a big deal—she looked like she belonged on a runway.

"What are you looking at?" she asked with a sweet smile.

"Everything," he said, causing a blush as he kissed her again. Every kiss seemed to deepen his feelings for her, and that was something he hadn't known was possible. "I went online this morning and found a street market that's walking distance from the hotel. Maybe you can check it out while I'm in my meetings tomorrow and pick up a few things for your shop. I also arranged for the concierge at the hotel to have a list of other attractions—shopping, museums, that kind of thing—and there will be a driver available to take you wherever you want to go."

"You did all that for me?"

He slid his hand to the nape of her neck, drawing her closer. "I'd do anything for you, sunshine."

"Anything?" she asked with a glimmer of heat in her eyes.

That look got to him every time. "Anything your heart desires."

"I was hoping you'd say that." She leaned closer and whispered, "I want to join the mile-high club."

He laughed. "Seriously? Your first flight and you're ready to go there?"

"Hey, make every minute count, right?" She pushed to her feet and said, "I'll go first. Meet me in five minutes."

He tried not to chuckle as he pulled her down beside him. "I think we'd better wait until the plane takes off for that one, sunshine."

SEVERAL HOURS AND two mile-high club initiations later,

they checked into their hotel in Seattle. Morgyn stood by the window looking out at the city streets. Graham wrapped his arms around her from behind and kissed her neck. They were meeting Knox in an hour at the property they were considering purchasing, and Graham was excited to introduce him to Morgyn.

"You've been quiet since we got off the plane. Second thoughts about what we did?"

She turned in his arms, and the love in her eyes was all the answer he needed. "Not even a little. That was so much fun. I never knew airplane bathrooms were so small. Movies make it sound like we'd have all sorts of room." She put her arms around his neck and said, "But we never need much room, do we?"

"We sure don't." He was certain everyone in the surrounding seats had heard them laughing as they'd made love in that confined space. "If it's not that, then why have you been quiet? Worried about closing your shop for the weekend?"

"No. My shop is fine. I'm used to closing it for a few days here and there, and this is so much better than being at home and worrying about whether my things are selling in the other shops. I have to admit that I wasn't sure how I'd feel giving my merchandise to other people to try to sell, but it's *freeing*. You have good ideas, cracker, and I want to be with you. Please don't think I'd question this weekend. If I was quiet, it's just because I was thinking about how big and fast everything is here. Going from the airport to the hotel was like sensation overload."

"Culture shock?" he asked. "Is it too much? Are you worried about getting around when I'm at my meetings tomorrow?"

"No. It's not that. I always knew Oak Falls was small, but

this *really* brings it home, you know? I thought Charlottesville was big, but this city makes that look like a sleepy little town."

"There's a whole wide world out there waiting for you to discover it, Morgyn. We'll explore tonight and make sure you're comfortable before I leave tomorrow. If the city is too much for you, I'll tell Knox to handle the meetings on his own."

"Don't be silly. I'm *road-trip girl,* remember? I'll be fine." She looked around the room and said, "But don't blame me if you come back and find the room livened up a bit."

He imagined her cutting loose with paints and fabrics and bringing the nice, though boring, room to life. "Are you going to get me in trouble?"

"Nope." She went up on her toes and kissed him. "Just wishful thinking. This room could be homier with textures and colors. I never understood why hotels make everything so bland. Honestly, if we'd driven here, I'd ask if we could just go park your truck somewhere and stay in that. This room feels bigger than the first floor of my house."

"Next time we'll look for a cozy B and B, or we'll bring my truck."

"*Next time,*" she said with a sweet hopefulness that made his heart squeeze. "I like the sound of that."

They unpacked and then they headed down to the lobby, where Morgyn checked out pamphlets about the area while Graham touched base with the concierge. Then they hit the street to grab a bite to eat before meeting Knox. The sidewalks were crowded, and Morgyn clung to Graham's hand, taking it all in.

"The buildings are so tall. Why is everyone in such a hurry?" She gasped and made a *tsk* sound. "Did you see that guy throw his cup *toward* the trash can?" She let go of his hand and hollered, "Hey! You can't leave that trash—"

He hauled her against him and said, "Morgyn, you can't just yell at strangers."

"But if everyone does that the whole city will be trashed, and *not* saying something is how that happens."

"I love that you care so much, but this isn't Oak Falls. You don't know who's going to take offense and start a fight or pull a gun."

"A *gun*? Over *trash*?"

"It's a big city. Life is different. Come on, there's a sandwich shop up ahead."

Morgyn picked up the trash the guy had tossed and threw it away. "Every little bit helps. In Oak Falls the high school kids do community service hours, and one of the things they do is clean up the parks. I think it teaches them to take care of their community."

"I agree. That's why I only work with environmentally and community conscious companies."

"That makes you much sexier than a billionaire in an ivory tower," she said as they neared the café.

Graham's phone rang, and he pulled it out to answer as they walked. "Graham Braden."

"Hi. This is Chuck Windsor. You called about a caboose in the Oak Falls railyard."

If the caboose was a feasible option, he wanted to surprise Morgyn with it, so he said, "Yes. Just a moment, please." He lowered the phone and said, "Sunshine, I need to take this. Can you give me two minutes?"

"Sure. I'll peek in the windows of the other shops."

He gave her a quick kiss and stepped aside to talk to Chuck. A few minutes later, as he gathered information about the caboose, his gaze swept over the crowded sidewalk in search of Morgyn. He spotted her a few stores down, crouched in front of a homeless man who was sitting against a building. Graham's pulse accelerated.

"Thanks, Chuck. Let me think about this and get back to you." He shoved his phone in his pocket and hurried down the crowded sidewalk, weaving around people but getting hung up by a family with three small children. His gaze remained trained on Morgyn and the long-haired, scraggly bearded man she was talking with. He wore several layers of clothing, as if he were afraid someone might steal them if they weren't on his body. There was a coffee can at his feet and a cardboard sign with WILLING TO WORK written on it propped up against a ratty backpack. Graham clenched his jaw as he pushed past a couple. He'd heard stories about the number of mentally unstable homeless people, but he'd be an asshole if he hollered for her to get away from the guy.

"There he is," Morgyn said with a cheery smile as he approached. "Graham, this is John."

Morgyn rose to her feet, and Graham pulled her against his side, breathing a little easier. "How's it going?"

John didn't have a second to answer as Morgyn said, "John was a gardener before he fell on hard times. He lost his wife and his job two years ago, and because he's in his sixties, he's had a hard time finding employment. I want to buy him lunch. And I was thinking, maybe you know someone around here who could use his help."

Only my sunshine…

Graham's gut instinct was to buy the guy lunch and tell Morgyn she couldn't save the world, but her mother's voice sailed through his mind—*She has so much light in her, and usually people try to tamp it down or bend it to their will*—and the hope in Morgyn's eyes bored into his heart so deeply, he didn't want to do anything but build it up.

"Sure. Let's get John some lunch and I'll think about who I know." Graham offered his hand to John. "Would you like to come inside?"

"Thank you. Thank you so much," John said as he shook his hand. "I'll wait here, though, if you don't mind. Have to mind my things."

"We'll be right back, John," Morgyn said, and with a bounce in her step, they headed into the café. "He's so nice, and all those people were just walking by him like he didn't exist. I don't understand how they can ignore someone in need like that."

"There are thousands of homeless people, and there are scammers who pose as homeless to get money."

"So what? Even if he were a scammer, which I don't think he is, to stoop to that level he must need money and food more than we do, don't you think? It's got to be embarrassing to sit outside with a sign begging for money." Sadness rose in her eyes. "And, Graham, John is a good man. It's what drew me to him. He resonated goodwill and kindness. And when he told me about his wife, Sylvie, his love for her practically dripped out of his pores. I really want to help him."

He gathered her in his arms and said, "Have I told you lately that I adore your generous heart?"

"And I adore yours, too. But maybe a generous heart isn't enough. It's just not right that in a city this big people can't find jobs."

"That's part of the problem. There are more people than there are jobs. You don't feel it as much in Oak Falls, but it's everywhere. I'd venture a guess that there are a number of people there that are unemployed, too."

"There must be more we can do." Her brows knitted. "I really have been living in a bubble."

"Not anymore, sunshine. We're going to broaden your horizons so you can spread your light far and wide."

AFTER GIVING JOHN a sandwich, some cash, and his phone number, Graham promised to make a few calls and see if any of his local connections needed help. John said he'd call in a few days and thanked them so many times, Morgyn couldn't stop thinking about him as they drove through a quaint small town on the way to the property where they were meeting Knox. Graham pulled off the main drag, winding through narrower back roads, and finally, he followed a dirt road up the mountain and parked at the crest of a hill. She stepped from the rental car, in awe of the breathtaking views. There was so little green in the city, and here, just forty minutes away, they were surrounded by hundreds of sprawling acres, lush pastures, undulating hills, and pockets of forests. She turned as Graham took her hand in his. *He* was the best view of all—tall, sexy, and strikingly handsome in a soft gray shirt, dark jeans, and a pair of brown leather boots. He hadn't shaved, and his scruff made him look even more rugged. Though every inch of him was deliciously captivating, it was his expressive eyes and those adorably hot dimples that made her heart somersault.

"What do you think, sunshine?"

He stepped closer, bringing a whiff of his spicy cologne. The potent scent reminded her of their airplane tryst, and her pulse quickened. She still couldn't believe they'd done that, but she wanted to experience everything with Graham. The thought was as exciting as it was nerve-racking, because in two days they'd be apart again. Every minute apart was too long.

She inhaled a shaky breath, went up in her toes, and touched her lips to his. "I think I'm really glad I'm here with you."

"Me too," he said as a motorcycle roared up the hill and came to a stop beside their car. "There's Knox."

Knox killed the engine and climbed off the bike. He took off his shiny helmet and raked a hand through his thick black hair. "Graham, my man."

He set the helmet on the bike and pulled Graham into a manly embrace. Then he opened his arms to Morgyn. He was tall like Graham, with the quintessential good looks of a movie star—manicured scruff, expensive-looking button-down, and a watch that probably cost more than her entire house. But his eyes were warm and his smile was friendly.

"I never thought I'd see the day a woman wore Graham's MIT hat." He shifted his eyes to Graham and lifted his brows in a this-is-the-real-deal look that would be hard to miss.

"Knox Bentley," Graham said, "Morgyn Montgomery. Morgyn, this is my partner in crime."

"It's a pleasure to meet the woman who's got my buddy's shorts in a knot." He embraced her.

She laughed and said, "It's nice to meet you, too."

"I'm still getting over the idea that you caught him with his pecker in his hand and didn't run the other way." Knox chuckled, and Graham shook his head.

"I took one look at his…" She gazed up at Graham and

said, "*Dimples* and I was done for." The guys laughed and she added, "But that python he's packing is a definite bonus."

Knox choked and coughed out a laugh. "Damn, girl. Hey, Graham, does she have a sister?"

"Yeah," Graham said with a cocky grin. "A bunch of them, but none stupid enough to go out with you. What you really need is to let Taylor be your wingman."

"Who's Taylor?" Morgyn asked.

"His virtual assistant of the past several years. The guy's like a clone of Knox."

"He literally runs my life. I'd be lost without him, but I don't *need* a wingman, thank you very much," Knox said firmly.

"Whatever you say, Knox, but you're looking pretty single over there. Well, other than that chick you hook up with at those charity events." Graham arched a brow. "Something you want to share about her?"

Knox scoffed. "Let's check out the property before you annoy me so much I tell Morgyn all your dirty secrets."

"Oh, I like dirty secrets," Morgyn said. "But I prefer if Graham and I make our own."

"I like her," Knox said.

"Don't even..." The warning in Graham's voice shouldn't have been a turn-on, but it was. He slung an arm over Knox's shoulder and said, "Come on, let's focus on the issue at hand. We can worry about your love life later."

As the guys talked about acreage, zoning laws, and other things, Morgyn's thoughts drifted back to John. She knew about the country's homeless crisis, but it was so far removed from her life, it hadn't felt real. What if her grandfather hadn't left her family that land? What if she'd never been able to negotiate a price she could afford on the retail space she'd had for the past few years? Would her business have taken off at all? Would she have ended up working for someone else and then lost her job and had to live with her parents or siblings? What if they lost their jobs? It was a stretch to take herself there, but what if the universe hadn't guided her down the right path and she'd ended up in a similar situation?

There had to be a better way. She knew she couldn't save the world, but as she looked around at the property, she wondered if Graham and Knox could make it a little easier for a whole lot of people.

"A sustainable community," she said before she had a chance to think it through.

Graham and Knox turned, curiosity brimming in their eyes.

"What, sunshine?"

"You're thinking of putting up an environmentally friendly hotel, right?"

"That's the plan," Graham said.

"What good will that do for the community? The area is full of hotels just forty minutes away, and at the bottom of this hill is an adorable small town. Maybe it'll help with tourism, but what if you could build something the whole community could get behind? There's so much land here, so many possibilities."

"One hundred and sixty acres," Knox said.

"Holy smokes. That's a *lot*. Couldn't you put up a sustainable tiny house community where they grow their own food and work together for solutions that help them as a group rather than one neighbor's goal squashing the other's? And if you're worried about investments or profits, you could make half of it rentable. Green living is on the rise everywhere. More and more people are environmentally conscious. You could build a sustainable community where people could come spend a week at a time, or a month, and they could learn skills to bring back to their hometowns so they could help others do the same. You could employ people like John, with years of gardening experience. He *needs* a community, a goal, an extended family to help and count on. I'm not saying employ every homeless person, but maybe fewer people would find themselves on the streets if there were places like this where they could buy a house cheaply and cut down on utility bills because you could build passive houses and use solar energy, and—"

"I don't know that we can do a total sustainable community," Knox said. "You're talking about schools, jobs..."

"But you don't have to do it *all*. Maybe I used the wrong terminology, but you could offer inexpensive living, with community projects like gardens, a community kitchen for meals, and I don't know...I'm winging it, but it seems like the seeds of a great idea." The more Morgyn talked about it, the more excited she became, but she realized these guys were big-time investors, and she was, as she'd said, *winging it*. "Sorry. I just can't help but think you've got a chance to do something bigger and more meaningful than just a hotel. Not that your environmentally friendly hotel isn't special. It's just..."

"Not doing *enough*." Graham put his arm around her and said to Knox, "Sunshine connected with a homeless man today, and her heart is still trying to recover."

"Sage would get a kick out of her," Knox said.

"Who's Sage?"

"Sage Remington. He's an artist who runs HTC, Hydration Through Creation," Graham explained. "HTC's a nonprofit that holds auctions for artwork, then donates the money toward installing wells in developing nations and villages. We've invested in a number of their projects."

"We're in talks with them now about a project just like what you're suggesting," Knox said. "Bringing tiny homes to a small village in Belize, where Sage and his wife, Kate, first came up with the concept for HTC. They already have gardens and schools, but their housing situation is deplorable."

"Why *wouldn't* you do that?" It seemed like a no-brainer to her.

"There's a lot that goes into making these decisions, sunshine," Graham said tightly.

"You know what?" Knox said. "I bet Kate would love Morgyn, too."

Knox's quick subject change didn't go unnoticed, but their business decisions were way out of Morgyn's league, and she assumed he was saving Graham from getting mired down with explanations.

"They have the cutest little girl, Sadie, with big blue eyes that could make a villain change his ways." Graham reached for Morgyn's hand.

"Oh man, here we go again." Knox hiked a thumb toward Graham. "You know he wants a dozen kids, right?"

"A *dozen*?" she said. "As one of seven, I can tell you that you're crazy."

"He's just giving you a hard time," Graham reassured her. "Three or four is good. But I know where you stand on the whole marriage issue."

"I don't," Knox said, eyeing Morgyn.

"I'm not big on it. I have no issues with commitment, but I don't need a legal document to make it real," she said, wondering why it felt strange to say what she'd believed wholeheartedly for ages.

"Sorry." Knox's smile faded, and he shot a look at Graham.

"I thought you two were serious."

"We *are*," Graham said emphatically, then a little lighter he added, "Someone recently pointed out that you don't need to be married to stay together or to have children."

Knox held his hands up and said, "Whoa. I'm not touching this conversation with a ten-foot pole."

"Good plan. Let's get back to Morgyn's idea of a community that works together *and* teaches others how to do the same. I'd like to do some research on that in general and for this area, check out the profitability, zoning, run the numbers…"

"Really? You guys will consider it?" She looked at Knox, who shrugged one shoulder. She squealed and threw her arms around Graham's neck.

"No promises about our final decision, sunshine, but Knox and I already agreed we're buying this land to keep it out of the hands of the wrong people. We have time to look into it and see if it's a viable solution."

"Remember when I said you couldn't get any hotter? I lied." Filled with hope and happiness, and thankful to have met a man who cared as deeply about others as she did, she touched her lips to his.

"Man," Knox said. "I've got to start hanging out at festivals."

Chapter Fourteen

AS PROMISED, AFTER they met with Knox, Graham and Morgyn explored the streets of Seattle, window-shopping and getting ice cream from a cute little parlor. Street noises sounded magnified against the hustle and bustle of people hurrying along sidewalks like they were on important missions and couldn't afford to slow down. Even in the stores the undercurrent of rushing was palpable. Graham kept a firm hold on Morgyn as they meandered through busy shops, taking it all in. She loved how he pulled her closer when they encountered crowds, and his stolen kisses made their day even more wonderful. She got so swept up in the energy of the city—and in the sparks between *them*—she stopped comparing the area to her quiet hometown. After a while, even the hustle and bustle no longer felt strange.

When they jumped in a cab for what Graham called their *next expedition*, she was still buzzing. "What about our rental car?"

"Time for a change." He lifted his MIT hat from her head and put it on his. She made a pouty face and he laughed. "Trust me, sunshine. You're going to *love* this."

He handed a piece of paper to the driver and then he pulled Morgyn closer. They sat like that for a long while, watching the city pass by. Morgyn couldn't remember a happier time in her life. It didn't matter what they were doing; everything was better with Graham by her side.

"Blindfold or eyes closed," Graham whispered out of the blue.

"Is this a sex game? Because I'm up for just about anything with *you*, but not with an audience." She glanced at the driver.

Graham drew her face toward his with a gentle hand on her chin, but there was nothing gentle about the serious look in his eyes. "If you think I'd let anyone see us do anything more than kiss, you don't know me the way I thought you did." He lowered his face until his lips were a breath away from hers and whispered, "Blindfold or eyes closed, sunshine?"

Her pulse skyrocketed at the heat in his voice. She put her hand on his thigh, feeling his muscles flex, and said, "If it's only us, then blindfold. But if you're talking about being somewhere we might get caught, eyes closed."

He tucked her hair behind her ear as a slow grin brought out his dimples. "I've gotten to you. You're thinking ahead."

"I'm thinking *of* a *head*," she said playfully. "How about you? Blindfold or eyes closed?"

"With you, eyes *open* all the way."

Their mouths came together hungrily, and he threaded his fingers into her hair, holding her possessively. Would she ever get used to the heat their kisses sparked? The desperate longing their happiness stirred? The rest of the world faded away, and soon she wasn't thinking at all. She could only *feel* his body reaching for hers as she straddled his lap, pouring all of herself into their connection. He rocked beneath her, his hard length creating the most exquisite friction. She moaned into their kisses, earning a greedy, masculine noise that drilled into her, making her entire body pulse with desire. She met every rock of his hips with a grind of her own as their kisses intensified. She felt herself go damp and desperately wanted to unzip his pants and take him inside her.

"Morgyn…" he growled against her lips.

He grabbed her thighs, squeezing so tight she knew he was struggling to hold back just as badly as she was. He'd just told her he would never let anyone watch them, but could the driver see anything other than them kissing? They were seated directly behind him. Her heart raced as their mouths crashed together again and Graham's hips began their torturous movements. She didn't want to get caught having sex, but his hand was hot on her skin, his mouth was wreaking havoc with her mind, and she wanted to be dangerous with him.

But not too dangerous.

Oh God! He was making her *think.*

And feel.

And *love.*

She drew back, meeting his lustful gaze, and then she framed his handsome face with her hands. Feeling naughty, excited, and so damn in love with him she ached with it, she whispered, "Eyes open all the way," and then she guided his hand between her legs.

His jaw clenched as his fingers swept over her damp panties. The struggle in his eyes was as real as the love between them. She leaned up and forward, putting her mouth beside his ear, and said, "He can't see us, and I need to feel you touching me."

Graham's eyes shot over her shoulder, and then he put his hand on the base of her neck, drawing her into another passionate kiss as his fingers pushed eagerly into her, expertly finding the place she needed him most. She moaned, and he clutched her hair as he said, "Shh," against her lips.

Her hips bucked and writhed as his thick fingers worked their magic, turning her body into a pulsing, throbbing mess of live wires. His thumb pressed down at the cleft of her neediness, sending the world careening away. He swallowed her lustful sounds, holding her at the peak for so long she thought she'd explode into a million pieces. When he finally relented, she tore her mouth from his, panting through gritted teeth as she buried her face in his neck, her body jerking with aftershocks.

When he withdrew his fingers, she made a needy noise she couldn't have stopped if her life depended on it. "I'll pay you back doubly as good," she promised.

He sucked his fingers clean and then he kissed her slow and deep. She didn't care that he tasted like her because there was no more him and her. There was only *them*.

"No paybacks in this relationship, sunshine." He kissed her softly and said, "What I do for you, I do for us. Your pleasure is *mine*, and when we do more later, which we *will*," he said cockily, "anything you do won't be reciprocation. It'll be pure, unstoppable desire."

The cab slowed at a light, and Graham said, "Blindfold or eyes closed for your surprise? You have about ten seconds to decide."

"My *surprise*? When did you have time to set up a surprise?"

"A gentleman never tells," he said coyly.

She looked around, but it was getting dark, and she had no idea where they were. It wouldn't matter if he took her to a fancy restaurant or to a back road where they could stargaze, she wanted to have her eyes open. But since that would ruin whatever he'd so thoughtfully set up, she said, "Eyes closed."

He kissed her again and said, "Close them, sunshine. I'll

save the blindfold for later."

MORGYN COULD IDENTIFY the sounds of a train idling in her sleep—the constant *whoosh* reminded her of a never-ending compressed air leak, the underlying hum and rumble of a monstrous machine holding still, and the secret whispers of her grandfather's voice reminding her never to play on the tracks following a little train lore. But as Graham guided her up a high step, her eyes closed tightly just as he'd requested, it was the smell of cold steel, oil, and fond memories that brought tears to her eyes.

"That's it. I've got you," Graham said, one arm around her lower back, the other holding her hand. "Don't peek."

"Cracker," she said shakily as he guided her along a vibrating path and helped her sit down. She tried not to let her happy tears fall as he settled in beside her. Eyes still closed, she felt the wall beside her, her fingers trailing along cold glass. "What have you done?"

"Open your eyes, sunshine."

They were alone on a train. "Where are we going? Why are we alone? How did you find this train?"

He laughed. "I will never tire of seeing that excited look in your eyes." He kissed her tenderly and said, "I know you weren't crazy about the hotel or the congestion of the city, so I thought we'd have a little adventure. I rented the train to take us near a waterfall I found, because what fun is a car when you can ride a vintage train like your grandfather used to? When we get there, we'll cook under the stars and sleep serenaded by the sounds of nature. I had our stuff shipped up to a lodge and arranged for camping gear. We aren't allowed to camp in the park near the falls, so we'll be staying on the grounds of the lodge with a view of the falls, and I reserved a room in case it rains—"

"Oh my gosh! Thank you!" She threw her arms around his neck, feeling like she did a lot of that lately, and she had a feeling that being with Graham, who paid attention to the most meaningful things she said, meant she'd be doing it a lot more. "What about the hotel? You already paid for it. I'll pay you back."

"No, you won't. We'll need the hotel room tomorrow when we get back to Seattle in case my meetings run longer than expected and you want a place to chill."

"Graham, you're doing too much. Let me pay for some—"

He kissed her again, slowly and sweetly and so lovingly, she didn't even notice when the train began rolling down the tracks.

THE TRAIN RIDE was just as romantic and fun as Graham had hoped it would be. The scenery wasn't anything special compared to the places he'd seen and he wanted to show Morgyn, but that didn't matter. Being together made the run-down houses, power lines, and trees feel special. They took dozens of pictures and texted them to their families with captions like *Our first adventure!* and *Guess who found a train!* which started a flurry of texts from each of their siblings. Morgyn confiscated his phone to return Jillian's texts, and by the time they arrived at the lodge, the two of them were texting like they'd been friends forever. Nick sent a selfie of him and one of his horses with the caption *Looks fun, but I'll stick with my girl.* Jax said he won the bet despite Jillian cheating, and then he messaged *You know who to see for the wedding dress.* Graham didn't reply, though he did reply to Beau's text, which said, *What's that look I see in your eyes?* He kept his response *Probably the same look you had after meeting Char* on the downlow, sending it after Morgyn returned his phone. But it was Pepper's text that had them both in hysterics. *I knew you two were meant for each other when I heard you met at the festival. You're the poster couple for osmology, the science of smell research. After two sweaty, dirty days of festival life, you're a testament to pheromones at their best!*

He'd never forget their first train ride together, and he hoped Morgyn wouldn't, either.

The lodge had met his every request, providing a tent on the grounds overlooking the falls, complete with a two-person sleeping bag, their suitcases, and a grill, which they used to cook dinner before they returned it to the lodge so they wouldn't have to worry about four-legged creatures snooping around their campsite. He sat beside Morgyn on a blanket listening to the sounds of the falls and trying not to think about Sunday, when they'd go their separate ways.

Moonlight reflected in her eyes. She wore his sweatshirt over her dress and tucked her bare feet beside her. She looked happy and more at ease than she'd been all day, and he found himself daydreaming again about what it would be like to be together in everything they did. She turned, catching him watching her, and leaned closer for a kiss. He loved that about her, too, the way she never tried to hide her emotions.

"You have opened my world so much in such a short period

of time. I can't stop thinking about my business. If selling on consignment works, it might be a great option, but I'm still on the fence about not having my own space."

"What if you could have your favorite caboose?"

She looked at him like he was crazy. "That's a wild idea, but I haven't even had time to think about how to go about it."

"We can do it, Morgyn. The call I got earlier today when you were with John was from the guy who handles the trains. They're willing to sell, and it would only cost eighty-five hundred to buy it."

"Are you kidding?" Her eyes bloomed wide. "They'd sell the red caboose? How did you get the right guy? I couldn't even imagine where to start looking!" Excitement crackled in the air around her.

"I'm good at research, sunshine. Think about it. You'd have it forever. You could pass your memories down to your kids with something substantial that was part of your relationship with your grandfather. We'd have to fix it up, but..."

She bit her lower lip, hope brimming in her eyes. "You said *we*."

"Because we *are* going to stay together. We might have to be apart sometimes, when I travel for work and you're busy with your business, but we're a *we*, and I don't see that changing." He took her hand and said, "I used to wonder if I'd ever find a woman who enjoyed the simple things in life as much as I do. I have no idea what I've done to deserve you, but whatever it was, I'd do it all over again a trillion times if it keeps you by my side."

"You flashed your dimples, you weren't pretentious or fake, and you were kind and funny, and just cocky enough, if you know what I mean." She giggled and leaned in to him as she said, "But just so we're clear, mountain climbing and white-water rafting are hardly *simple.* I want to stay together and to learn to do everything you love, but I might suck at them."

"You won't, but if you don't enjoy them we'll do other things."

"I'd never want to take you away from what you enjoy. I know we're getting way ahead of ourselves, but if we stay together, I'd be happy meeting you at the bottom of the mountain to celebrate your trip. You can send me pictures on the way up, and I can give you motivation to make it to the top and come back down."

"Morgyn," he whispered. "I adore you."

"Even though I have no idea what I want to do with my business? You're so sure of every move you make. The caboose sounds amazing, but I'd have to figure things out, like how to buy it, where to put it..."

"There's no *even though.* I like that you entertain different options and that you're thinking them through and making strides toward figuring out what will make you happiest. I'm not trying to push you toward making any decisions."

"I know you aren't, but my time is running out. I'll see if the items sold through consignment, and now that I know the caboose is an option, I'll put some thought into that, too. But you've spent time in my world, and I feel like I need to know more about yours. You and Knox seem like a great team, and based on the texts you showed me, you obviously love your family, but what's it like to spend a month in Graham Braden's world?"

He gazed out at the falls, watching the trees across the way blowing in the breeze and listening to the constant rush and hum of the water, thinking about how to answer her question.

"That's a pretty big question."

"What I feel for you is pretty big. I want to know."

Her sweet voice brought his eyes back to hers, and he said, "What I feel is huge, too, sunshine. My life changes from week to week. I don't have a set schedule. I go where my work takes me, and when I'm not doing that, I'm traveling with family or friends for fun. I could hear about an opportunity tomorrow that could take me across the country or overseas, or I could decide to go cross-country skiing with a group of friends and be gone for weeks."

"I hope I didn't derail your plans with Knox today. I just got excited."

"You didn't derail us. You gave us something to think about. You opened a door, and we'll check out the data to see if it's worth walking through."

"Good. Can you tell me more about your business? You said you only invest in environmentally friendly companies and endeavors, but as an investor, do you own a piece of the companies? Do you buy properties and then build on them? Do you buy and then flip raw land? Or do you keep it all?"

"It depends on the investment. We own, operate, and finance income-producing real estate of all different types. Sometimes we own a piece of the businesses we invest in, providing a constant income stream, and other times we purchase businesses and then sell them off in pieces. With a project such as the land you saw today, it'll depend on what we end up doing with the property and where the profit lies."

"So, you buy companies and sell them in pieces, like you would sell a used car for parts?"

He chuckled. "Something like that, yes."

"And you can do that without an office?"

"We have offices in Maryland and New York, with a small staff in each, but we don't need to spend the majority of our time there."

"I'll never understand the mechanics of your business, but I find it interesting."

"I'll never understand how you can see things and turn them into beautiful pieces of art and clothing, but I appreciate that you can."

Her expression turned serious, and she said, "But I'm not the kind of smart you are, Graham. That might wear on you."

"That's the second time you've implied that you're not smart *enough*, and that's such crap. We're both smart in different ways, and you proved it today when you came up with an idea that Knox and I hadn't even thought about. It pisses me off to think you don't see your own brilliance."

"I grew up with siblings who aced every test. I was never like that."

"Who gives a fuck? I grew up with a father who could run numbers in his sleep and brothers who have all made their way to success in ways I never could. Pepper might be science smart and Sable can rebuild engines, but could either of them look at a dress and see a pair of flare pants? Could they make a toy train into a necklace?"

"Sable could, if I told her how to make it pretty."

"Oh, baby, don't you see how boring the world would be if we were all the same? Don't ever worry that because our minds work differently, we'll go off in two different directions. Do you think I worry that because I'm not as creative as you are you'll get bored with me? Hell no. What we have goes so far beyond books or boots it's crazy. We complement each other in the best ways. Don't you see that?"

"Yes, and I feel it almost every moment we're together. But when we were with Knox I got the feeling you didn't want to get caught up in explanations and I felt bad."

"That's a reflection on *me*, sunshine, not you." Guilt sliced through him for cutting off that conversation and making her feel that way. "We were talking about Sage and what he's doing in Belize. I didn't want to get into a big discussion about that with Knox. It had nothing to do with you understanding what we were talking about." *And everything to do with how long I'd have to be away from you if we move forward with the opportunity.*

She exhaled, and her smile reached all the way up to her eyes. "Thank goodness. I never want to be someone you can't talk to."

"You never will be. Now, do you have more business-related questions? Because we have tonight and tomorrow night together before we're apart for several days, and I'd really like to just hang with my girl and talk about silly shit, figure out what's written in the stars, or make out like horny teenagers."

"Door number three, please..."

Chapter Fifteen

GRAHAM AND MORGYN watched the most incredible sunrise Saturday morning, and then they headed back to Seattle. The contrast between the serenity of the falls and the congestion of the city gave Morgyn even more appreciation for the trouble Graham had gone to setting up their special night.

"I know you're *road-trip girl* and don't need me to take you around town, but I'll have my phone on in case you need anything." Graham kissed her softly and said, "I'm so glad you're here with me, and I can't wait to see you later."

"Good luck negotiating. I'll throw all sorts of good energy out into the universe for you."

After he left to meet Knox, Morgyn headed straight for the café they'd visited yesterday. She bought breakfast for two and went in search of John. She found him in the same place as yesterday and assumed it was where he spent most of his time. She sat with him as they ate and got to know each other better. John asked her dozens of questions about her family and the work she did. He explained that he had no family left, and he said he'd been devastated when he'd finally accepted that he had to give up his apartment. Morgyn's heart hurt for her new friend.

After they finished eating, as Morgyn gathered the trash, John touched her hand and said, "My Sylvie would have liked you. She always wanted a daughter, but we were never blessed with children. She used to volunteer for the youth programs at the YMCA to get her fill of little ones. Being in this position is embarrassing, and it's tested my faith in many ways. I almost lost hope, Morgyn, but you gave it back to me. I was praying I'd see you today. I think Sylvie sent you to me as a reminder not to give up." He pushed to his feet and said, "I'm going to the shelter to shave and wash up, and then I'm going to use some of that money you and Graham gave me to get a haircut and buy clothes. Then I'm going to hit the streets again and apply for every job I can find. Thank you for caring enough to talk with me. You've made me feel less invisible and a little more human."

Nothing compared to the feeling his words gave her. After an emotional goodbye, Morgyn made her way toward the street market. Something inside her had changed. She was more aware of the homeless people, the sad and stressed expressions of the people hurrying along on the sidewalks, and the way the air seemed heavier here than in Oak Falls, weighed down with big-city problems. Struck by the number of homeless people holding cardboard signs or sitting in front of cans hoping for money, she wanted to help them all. But it wasn't like she could set up a training center that could lead to jobs. Even if she wanted to, she wouldn't know the first thing about it. But maybe she could do *something*...She bought breakfast for two more homeless people and then she bought a box of protein bars and handed them out to other people in need on her way to the market. It wasn't a solution, but it sure felt good to help.

Colorful flags and banners announced the bustling market,

which was lined with white tents. She was so drawn in by the energy of the crowds, it would be easy to push the uncomfortable thoughts about people in need away. She wondered if there were homeless shelters near Oak Falls, and she felt a little guilty for not being aware enough to know the answer. She vowed to stop living in her safe little bubble and to seek out opportunities to help others.

She meandered through the vendor tents, checking out crafts, homemade foods, clothing, and just about everything else under the sun. Her phone vibrated with a text from Brindle. She opened it and found her smoky-eyed sister's smiling face squished between two handsome men. No surprise there. Brindle was a hot-guy magnet. A second later, her phone rang with a call from said hot-guy magnet.

"Hey, Brin. Looks like you're having fun," Morgyn said as she headed for a jewelry vendor. "You've been there for a day and you've already met hot guys?"

"That's Andre and Mathieu. We're on a boat cruising the Seine. I just met them, but they're great. They said you should come to Paris! I told them they'd need a crowbar to pry you away from Graham."

"You can say that again. Please tell me you're being careful."

"I am! You know I can take care of myself. This place is insanely pretty, and there's not a cowboy in sight. It's perfect."

"You love cowboys," Morgyn said, moving with the crowd to the next booth.

"Yeah," Brindle said with a sigh. "I do. They're strong and sexy and never afraid of anything." She was quiet for a second, and then she said, "But they're also bullheaded and annoying as hell. This is a good change. I'm glad I came. This is the perfect distraction."

"What do you need a distraction from? You said you were going because you wanted to see the world."

"I do!" Brindle said *too* strongly. "A distraction from work and home and everything. How's Graham?"

"He's amazing. We're in Seattle."

"I almost forgot! You got on a plane! How was it? Did you freak out?"

"No. It was fun." She was tempted to tell Brindle about their sexcapade in the airplane bathroom, but Brindle wasn't the greatest secret keeper, so she said, "I can't wait to do it again."

"That's great. You're so lucky to have found someone who's as crazy about you as you are about him."

"So you don't think I'm nuts for coming with him this weekend?"

"Hey, you're talking to the queen of nuttiness. I'm in *Paris*. You're not even on the loony spectrum. You're totally grounded, Morg."

"Grounded? You guys are always teasing me about how often I pick up and leave for a day trip. When we were at the festival you said I cared more about the energy flow of the tent than the functionality of it."

"So? You did. All that means is that you see things differently and you like to go on adventures. But you've got a *business*, a *house* that *you* built *and* paid off. You've got a *greenhouse*, for heaven's sake. You grow things and bring life into this world. You knew what you wanted to do years ago."

"So did you," Morgyn reminded her.

"I knew that I wanted to teach, but that's all I know."

A hint of sadness in Brindle's voice caught Morgyn's attention. "Are you sure you're okay?"

"Me? Yes. I'm beyond okay. Tell me about Seattle."

Morgyn wasn't completely buying her sister's exuberance, but she knew Brindle wouldn't talk about anything serious until she was good and ready. She told her about meeting John and Knox, her idea for the tiny house community, and how Graham and Knox were thinking about it. She went on to describe their romantic train excursion and overnight adventure, and then she told her about their morning.

"Guess what else." She was too excited to wait for Brindle to guess. "He found out that I can buy a caboose from the old train graveyard and fix it up to use as a shop."

"Wow. That would be so cool. Can you afford it?"

"I have some money saved. I think I could pay for it, but I'd have to beg Sable to help me fix it up."

"She'll do it in a heartbeat. Are you going for it?"

Morgyn walked into another craft booth and said, "I don't know. I put some of my stuff on consignment with Jeb at his furniture shop and with a few other shops in Oak Falls and the surrounding areas." Jeb Jericho owned the Barn, where he sold the custom furniture he made. "And Graham and I took some stuff to the thrift shop in Romance I told you about. I'm hoping some of it sells, but it's nerve-racking."

"You're thinking of going the consignment route? That would allow you to take off anytime."

"I know, but I don't know what I want. I love the idea of not having a shop to maintain, but that means putting a lot of trust into other shop owners, and I'm not great at keeping track of things."

"What a load of crap that is. Morgyn, you can tell me where every single item is in your barn. Even things you bought years ago. You never lose track of the important things."

"But you know me and finances."

"I know you hate them, but that doesn't mean you can't keep track of them. You're wicked smart. If you stay in your current space, the rent increase will change everything. You'll have to work harder just to stay open, and you'll hate that."

"It's kind of all I have to show my business is real, don't you think?"

"No," Brindle said sharply. "That space doesn't make it real. *You* make it real. The things you create are gorgeous. You could sell them at a street corner and your business would still be real. In fact, maybe that's what you should do. You're always going to flea markets anyway. You could travel all around selling that way."

"*Ugh.* I don't know. That seems like a lot of pressure. The craft shows and festivals wouldn't be as much fun if I *had* to do them."

"Then think about the caboose or the consignment idea. Or do them *all.* Don't let bookkeeping scare you off. You just have to make it a priority, like you did with building your house and starting your business in the first place. Besides, we can all help you. Amber does her books for her store. She can show you anything you need to know. And I'm sure Mr. Smarty Pants Big Cock can help you, too."

Morgyn laughed. "He's really good to me, Brin. I've never met a man who actually listens and understands what makes me tick."

"If you really think about it, there aren't many women who listen and understand, either. Everyone has an opinion on what we need to do, don't they? You're happy, and that's what matters."

"I am happy, but there's more than that. With Graham I'm discovering even more about who I am. I thought I *knew* who I was."

"Maybe you did know who you were, but you're someone else with him or because of him," Brindle suggested.

"Maybe." She wondered if Brindle was really talking about herself and Trace, but again she didn't push. "Graham leaves for New York tomorrow when I go back home. I know he'll come back to see me, and I'm sure I'll go see him in the future, but even those few days apart are going to feel empty."

Brindle was quiet for a long moment, and then Morgyn heard a male voice through the phone. It sounded like he was talking in French. Brindle said, "Give me a sec. My sister needs me," to the guy. Then she sighed into the phone and said, "I think Mathieu understands about every other word I say."

"You took French. Can't you use it?"

"Yes, but I talk slowly in French, and they stare at my mouth the whole time. Have you ever had a hot guy staring at your mouth?"

Morgyn laughed, thinking of the way Graham often looked at hers in the seconds before he kissed her. "It's distracting."

"Exactly. Okay, the hotties are getting restless, so I've got to go in a sec, but here's my best advice. When you told me you loved Graham, you didn't just say it. You *exuded* it. I think Grace is proof that once your heart knows what it wants, nothing will stand in its way. You might feel empty in the days when he's gone, but Mom always says that a little distance can make our hearts see more clearly. He loves you, Morgyn. That night at the Jericho's, everyone saw it. JJ told me that when Graham came down to the riding ring, he didn't ask to ride. He said, 'I need to ride. My girl loves this shit.' I would give anything for a man to say that about me."

Morgyn's insides melted. "He does love me, Brin. I feel it in everything he says and does."

"Then stop worrying about how much you'll miss him and start planning great miss-you seductions. I love you, but I really have to run."

"Hey, Brin? Just tell me this. Are you really there so Trace has a chance to miss you?"

After a few seconds of silence, she said, "I'm here to see the world, remember? Let me know what you decide about your business, and start planning your seduction sex! Love you!" The line went dead.

Seduction sex. That was a much better thought than lonely nights.

Morgyn was surrounded by vendors selling everything from furniture and tapestries to food and antiques. She'd passed a silk screener when she'd first come in. Maybe she could find a cute lingerie booth and silk-screen PROPERTY OF MIT MAN on the butt of a pair of panties. Smiling at the thought, she made her way down to the next booth.

She spotted an eclectic vendor offering a variety of different items, from clothing and shoes to jewelry and paintings, and just beyond, a tattoo booth and a chocolate vendor. She headed directly for the chocolate, took a selfie in front of the booth, and sent it to Graham with the caption, *Benefits of having my own personal cracker. I'm going hunting for marshmallows next. I'm in the mood for s'mores tonight!* She added a winking emoji and then typed, *I'll bring the goodies. You bring the heat! Xxo*

GRAHAM'S MEETINGS RAN much longer than expected,

but at least he and Knox got their offer on the table. They had a team researching Morgyn's ideas, and they were both excited about the prospect of doing something different from their normal investments. As Graham left the meeting, he couldn't wait to tell Morgyn the news about the lead on a job he had for John. He'd hated leaving her alone all day, but she'd texted earlier, and it had sounded like she'd enjoyed the street market even more than he had thought she would. She'd sent selfies with three vendors who were interested in carrying her merchandise, two from Seattle and one guy who went across the country selling at large flea markets. He'd have to remember to show her how to check them out to make sure she didn't end up trusting the wrong people, but the way she'd taken the reins and run with the consignment idea further proved how remarkable she was.

He followed his GPS to the park where she said she was hanging out with friends she'd made at the market. The area was so crowded, he had to leave the car around the corner. He looked at the bag of marshmallows he'd bought on the way and grinned to himself as he locked the doors. When he arrived at the park, he realized the crowds were watching people painting a mural on the side of a building by a basketball court—and there by the wall sat Morgyn, beside a little girl in a sun hat who was busy painting a flower. Morgyn had her cell phone pressed to her ear as she guided the little girl's hand. *The perfect multitasker.* Another woman joined them. Morgyn hugged the little girl and the woman, and then she stepped aside, still talking on the phone and carrying a bag. She was all legs and sun-kissed skin in her cutoffs and tank top, which were both marked with paint, as were her arms.

She looked up toward the sky, took a few steps, and then

stopped. She was looking away from him, but he heard her exclaim, "Yes, definitely!"

As he made his way toward her, he passed a sign that read COMMUNITY ARTS PROJECT, JOIN US! Leave it to his girl to be there for a weekend and still manage to help a homeless man, make business connections, and get involved in a bigger way. It was no wonder he'd fallen in love with her. She wasn't a festival goddess. She was a goddess of all things positive and hopeful.

And she was *his*.

She turned as he approached, and her eyes widened. "Jilly, I have to go. Graham's here!"

Jilly? He laughed under his breath. Of course she'd call Morgyn. The two had become instant best friends.

Morgyn held up her finger and mouthed, *One second.* Then, into the phone she said, "Yes! I'll call my family. They can send it overnight and it'll be there Monday. I can't wait. I'm so excited!" She ended the call and launched herself into his arms. "I'm so glad you're here! I need help changing my flight. I'm going to Pleasant Hill."

"Pleasant Hill? Without me?"

"You're going to New York, so yes, I guess so. I'm going to see Jilly. Oh wait. You don't have a problem with that, do you?" Before he could answer, she said, "She checked out my website and offered to sell some of my merchandise in her store. Isn't that awesome? She said if I get my best pieces there fast enough, she'll put some of it in her fashion show on Tuesday. You didn't tell me she did fashion shows! I'm so excited I can barely see straight. I'm going to call my mom and see if she can pack a few things and send them to Pleasant Hill right away. Will you help me with the flight arrangements? She said she can show me how to do some grassroots marketing, too. I want to be there and see how Jilly does it all. Your sister is *incredible*."

He was excited for her, but he was still processing the idea that she was going to Pleasant Hill and *he* was going to New York. "Of course I'll help you, but I'll change my plans and go with you."

"You can't miss your meeting," she said, stepping out of his arms to shove her phone in her pocket.

"Like hell I can't." His eyes caught on a bandage on the left side of her chest peeking out from beneath her tank top. He pulled her into his arms again. "What happened? You got hurt?"

She looked down at her chest and said, "Oh no. I can't believe I forgot. Look what I did at the street market."

She peeled off the bandage, revealing a small tattoo of a heart-shaped sun. There were three rays on each side of the sun and each had two words. KNOW IT, TRUST IT, and ACCEPT IT. The skin around the tattoo was red and angry, but the sun was gorgeous, and the meaning touched him so deeply, he choked up.

"It's for us," she said proudly. "And I got you something else, too."

Before he could get a word out, she unbuttoned her shorts and pulled them open, revealing pink panties with CRACKER'S written in white letters across the front.

His heart just might explode. "Holy shit, sunshine." He stepped closer, blocking the view from others.

She buttoned her shorts and then reached into her bag and pulled out a pair of black boxer briefs with SUNSHINE'S JUNK written across the front in bright yellow letters. "These are for you. Well, for me as your girlfriend, but for you to wear."

"I'll wear those briefs every damn day if you want me to, but I'm *not* going to New York tomorrow. There's no way you're meeting my family without me by your side." He crushed her to him, both of them laughing as they kissed. "I love you, sunshine. I love you so damn much, I can't think past it."

"That's okay. I'm learning to think, so maybe I can do it for the both of us."

He gazed into her beautiful eyes, finally understanding why people said he'd never forget his first love. She was his first and only love, and she'd become such a big part of him, he could no longer picture a future without her in it.

Chapter Sixteen

"YOUR TOWN IS adorable," Morgyn said as they drove through Pleasant Hill, Maryland, on their way to Graham's house early Sunday evening. "I love the brick-paved sidewalks and all the green space. Can we explore later?"

Graham reached across the console of the rental truck and brought her hand to his lips. She smelled like a warm summer afternoon at the beach, which was also on his list of places he wanted to go with her. He longed to take her to a private beach, far away from eyes and ears. To see her pretty painted toes in the sand and hold her sun-drenched body against him as they made love to the sounds of the sea lapping at the shore.

"I can't wait to explore with you and to introduce you to my family and to see your stuff in Jilly's shop. You'll love her even more when you meet her in person." Jillian had texted earlier to say she and his mother were stocking his refrigerator so his house would be ready for them. But he had a feeling they just wanted to get a glimpse of the woman who had stolen his heart. He'd spoken to Knox and they'd put off their meetings in New York until Wednesday. The last meeting was scheduled for Saturday afternoon. He also rescheduled dinner with his cousin Josh for Thursday evening.

Graham and Morgyn were flying out Tuesday night, and if all went well, he'd return to Virginia and she'd be in his arms again Saturday evening.

Graham drove through town and wound along back roads toward his property. He lived on eight wooded acres just far enough outside town to feel like he was a world away from anyone else. He stole a glance at Morgyn, who looked beautiful in a cute sundress that clung to her breasts and showed off her sexy shoulders and legs. She wore several long necklaces and colorful bracelets. Her hair cascaded over her shoulders, barely covering the edges of her tattoo, which was mostly visible beneath the straps of her dress.

As he pulled onto the narrow dirt road that cut through the woods toward his home, Morgyn said, "This reminds me of where I live."

"I know, sunshine. We really are meant for each other."

The solar lights on the walkway to his house burned bright as his tiny treehouse came into view.

Morgyn's eyes widened and she squealed. "You live in a *treehouse*?"

He'd been dying to see her reaction, and the excitement in her voice was worth every second of holding his secret for the last week and a half.

He was surprised to see Nick's truck and Jax's car alongside Jilly's Jeep and his parents' car.

"Looks like everyone who's around came to meet you, sunshine," he said as he parked. "Beau and Charlotte are in Colorado, and you've already met Zev."

"Cracker, this is amazing! I can't believe you didn't tell me that you live in a treehouse—a *tiny* treehouse!" She climbed from the truck, jaw agape as she took in the long wooden ramp leading up to the house, which was nestled between two enormous red cedars. "Did you build this?"

He draped his arm over her shoulder as they followed the ramp up toward the house and said, "My brother Beau and I built it." He pointed to a covered ramp that led from the back of the house to a small utility building on the ground. "That's where the washer and dryer are. There's no dishwasher, and I've got Internet but no television. Other than that, you've got all the amenities of home, fifty feet above the forest floor."

"This is like something out of a fairy tale."

"That's the same thing Charlotte said. I like to think of it as being something out of a manly adventure, like *Swiss Family Robinson.*"

The front door swung open and Jillian barreled outside. Her burgundy hair flew behind her as she raced toward them wearing a black tank top and shorts. She and Morgyn both squealed as they collided into each other like two long-lost friends.

"I'm so happy you're finally here!" Jillian said. "I can't believe Graham put off his meetings. He never does that."

"He doesn't?" Morgyn gave him a curious look.

"Another first," he said with a wink, which sparked a flurry of conversation between the two women.

They changed subjects so fast Graham didn't even try to keep up. His parents stepped into the doorway, his father's big body dwarfing his mother's tiny frame. Nick appeared behind them, his longish black hair sticking out from beneath his ever-present cowboy hat. He crossed his arms, surveying the girls gabbing on the front porch. Jax stepped beside him. Like Graham, he wore his brown-blond hair short.

All four of them were grinning like fools.

Graham had a feeling he wore the same grin as his father's wise eyes locked on him with an expression he'd seen only once before. He remembered the look fondly, having seen it the day he told his father he'd decided to pursue investing rather than engineering. After spending a lifetime patterning himself after his father, hoping to become half the man he was, and as the only one of his siblings to have followed in his footsteps, Graham had worried about how his father would take the news that he didn't want to be that big a part of the family business after all. But his father had set his wise dark eyes on Graham and said, *I've always known you were destined for greater things, and this world will be a better place because of your decision.*

Graham had never been the kind of man who needed his father's approval, but when his father stepped onto the porch to embrace him and whispered, "Love sure looks good on you, son," it was the best feeling in the world.

"Welcome home, baby." His mother patted his cheek before hugging him too tight. "You look happy."

"Of course he does," Jillian said. "He has Morgyn."

Graham reached for Morgyn's hand, bringing her closer. "Damn right. Mom, Dad, Nick, Jax, *this* is Morgyn Montgomery. Sunshine, this is most of my family."

"It's nice to meet you all," Morgyn said as she hugged his mother.

"You can call me Lily," his mother said. "I can't wait to get to know you."

"I'm Clint. Between Jilly and Zev, I feel like I already know you," his father said as he hugged Morgyn.

"Should I worry?" Morgyn asked with a smile. "We did a lot of joking around with Zev."

"Our family is full of jokesters, and honestly"—amusement

rose in his father's eyes—"*Foreplay* is the perfect name for that boy. He left his heart behind years ago."

"One day he'll find it again," his mother said.

"I can't believe he told you that," Morgyn said, her cheeks flushing.

"Nothing to be embarrassed about, sweetheart," his father assured her. "You gained bonus points for being so clever. And where are my manners? I almost forgot to thank you for the graphometer you and Graham sent me. Thank you," his father said.

"I'm glad you liked it, but that was all Graham—"

Graham gazed at Morgyn and said, "I found it, but it was from both of us." He kissed her cheek and whispered, "I knew even then we'd stay together."

"The universe told you," she said softly.

Nick's eyes drifted appreciatively down Morgyn's sexy little patchwork sundress.

Graham cleared his throat, shooting Nick a dark, warning look.

Nick chuckled and tipped his hat. "Nice to meet you, *sunshine*. I'm Nick. I hear you've got a little gypsy in your blood, just like Graham."

"We do have a lot in common. You're the one who works with Trixie Jericho? Wow, she was spot-on about you," Morgyn said. "She said you were a burly cowboy."

Nick stood up a little taller and rolled his shoulders back, sticking out his chest. "A damn fine one at that."

"He's also arrogant as all get out," Jillian said.

"I might have heard that too," Morgyn said. She turned to Jax and said, "That means you're Jax, the wedding gown designer. That must be so much fun." She embraced Jax.

"He's designed for a lot of famous people," Jillian said.

"Wow, that's exciting," Morgyn said.

"Not half as exciting as the celebrities he's slept with," Nick said.

"Nicholas Braden!" Their mother glared at him.

"What? The guy's a stud." Nick slapped Jax on the back and said, "Don't let his good-boy facade fool you. He's a badass."

Morgyn laughed. "From what I've heard about all of you, it sounds like all Bradens are badasses, including Jilly." She glanced at Jax and said, "You two are twins, right? I never would have guessed. You look nothing alike."

"Thank God for small favors," Jax teased.

"Hey," Jillian protested, making them all laugh.

"Let's go inside. I want to hear all about your trip to Seattle, and your business, and your family." His mother looped her arm into Morgyn's, leading her inside, and Jillian followed them, leaving the men alone.

"Damn, bro," Nick said. "She's hot."

"Show some respect, Nick," his father said.

"It's okay," Graham reassured him. "I know she's hot, Dad. She's also brilliant, adventure-seeking, and the sweetest woman alive."

"Aw, hell. You really are in love," Nick said. "Jillian said you were, but I couldn't imagine it."

Graham glanced inside, where the girls were lifting wineglasses in a toast. He loved that she was already at ease with his family.

"This is how it happened with our cousins," Jax said. "One fell, and then the rest dropped like flies."

"All I know is that I've never experienced anything like what I feel for Morgyn," Graham said. "You and Nick better watch out, because when love comes for you, it'll blow you away."

Nick scoffed.

"He's right," their father said. "There are only three things you can count on in this world. The sun will rise and set, family will always have your back, and when you find your soul mate, who you are will change forever."

"Hell, not me," Nick said. "I need a drink."

"I'm with you." Jax followed him inside.

His father sidled up to Graham and said, "I'm happy for you, son."

"Thanks, Dad."

As they walked inside, his father said, "Tell me about Seattle. Did you make an offer?"

"We did. We should hear back later this week." He told him about Morgyn's ideas for the property.

"Sounds like you found a woman with as big a calling to help others as you have. That sounds a lot like the opportunity in Belize. When do you leave for that?"

Graham glanced across the room at Morgyn sitting with his mother and Jillian by the fireplace, and his gut clenched. "I haven't made a decision about it yet."

"I thought you and Knox decided that getting involved in more international projects was the direction you wanted to take your business."

Graham faced his father and lowered his voice. "It is, but Morgyn's got a life in Virginia, and she's in the midst of making major decisions for her own business. We've spent the last ten days figuring out options—options *I* recommended. I want to be there *with* her to help her through whatever she decides, not disappear for eight to ten weeks and leave her hanging."

His father's lips curled into a knowing smile. "You spent

that last ten days falling in love. The rest is all part and parcel to that. I get it, son, but she doesn't sound like the type of woman who needs you to hold her hand."

"She doesn't," he admitted. "But maybe I'm the type of guy who wants to be there for her every step of the way."

JILLIAN AND GRAHAM'S mother had not only stocked his fridge, but they'd brought a cherry pie as a welcome-home gift, and it was delicious. They spent the last couple hours getting to know one another, joking around, talking about Morgyn's family, her shop, and the things she was considering doing with it. His family asked a million questions and offered interesting input about the different options. They were eager to help and excited about the things she made. Like Graham, there was no pretense. His family was as loud and wonderful as her own, and as she sat beside Graham on the sofa, she felt like she'd been around them for years instead of hours.

"Do you know the story behind this treehouse?" Clint asked from his perch on the window seat beside Lily. They were always touching and passing secret smiles, reminding Morgyn of her own parents.

"Aw, come on." Graham shook his head, like he'd heard the story far too many times. He had his father's strong features and his mother's dimples, and he wore his love for them on his sleeves.

"I want to hear the story," Morgyn urged, looking around the treehouse. It was a lot like her house, but with nicer finishes and a slightly different layout. The front door led them through the kitchen to the living room. A small wooden table sat near a gorgeous fireplace and built-in bookshelves. The shelves were riddled with books and interspersed with photographs of Graham and his family and, she assumed, friends. There were pictures of him leaning over a drawing table beside his father, barbecuing with his siblings, and standing by a Christmas tree arm in arm with his mother as he kissed her cheek. There were various pictures telling the story of his adventurous lifestyle—standing at the top of a mountain with two other men, skiing, rafting, sprinting over a finish line, and many others, showing the strong, determined man he was. The man who had built a tiny house in a tree, with a loft above the kitchen and so many windows it felt like they were part of the forest.

The man who had won her heart without even trying.

"He'll tell you it was because of his love of nature," his father said, bringing her back to their conversation. "Some of that is true. It has to be to live in a one-room treehouse."

"She lives in a tiny house, Dad. She knows what it's like." Graham pulled Morgyn closer and kissed her cheek.

A single deep laugh escaped his father's lips. "Of course she does. You two really are perfect together. Anyway, your boyfriend was enthralled by Tarzan when he was younger. He spent all his time in trees. At ten years old he built a treehouse with Beau and Nick. A kid version, not like this. He spent weeks coming up with a plan using pullies and ropes so he could get supplies into the treehouse, and when that proved an easy task, he went on to steal every sheet in the house and tie them together so he could swing from tree to tree."

Morgyn stifled a laugh. "Tarzan, huh?"

"Go big or go home." Graham smirked. "Who's manlier than Tarzan?"

"I am," Nick said, puffing his chest out.

Jax glared at him. "Dude, don't steal his moment."

"Did you make it?" Morgyn asked. "Did you swing from tree to tree?"

"Damn right I did," Graham said proudly.

"He broke his arm," his father said. "*Twice* in one year. That's when we knew there was no keeping that boy down."

"It's a Braden thing," Jillian said. "When we see something we want, we don't stop until we get it."

"We probably shouldn't have indulged his wild ideas so often," his mother said. "But look at those dimples. How could we tell him no?"

"Those dimples did me in, too." Morgyn touched Graham's cheek. He was looking at her with so much love in his eyes, she was sure everyone else could see it, too.

"Oh boy, it's getting late," his mother said as she rose to her feet, pulling his father up with her. "You guys are probably exhausted after traveling all day. We'd better get out of here and give you some privacy."

"Guess she noticed that look, too," Nick said under his breath, earning a dark stare from Graham.

"I'm so excited you and Jilly have come together for this fashion show. I can't wait to see your merchandise." Lily embraced her.

"Thank you. I'm excited, too. Will I see you all at the show?"

"Of course," Lily said. "Most of the town turns out for it."

His parents were so loving and supportive, it was easy to see how he'd been raised to be the kind, incredible man he was. "I can't wait," Morgyn said. "We'll head over tomorrow as soon as my stuff arrives."

After another round of hugs and lots of teasing taunts between the guys, Graham's father said, "Come on, boys, before you scare Morgyn off."

"Did you see that look?" Jax said on his way out the door. "It'd take a hell of a lot more than us to scare her off."

Nick winked and said, "See ya around, sunshine."

Graham shoved him out the door. "Get out of here, and get that twitch in your eye fixed before I pound it out of you."

After they left, Morgyn and Graham stood on the front porch, moonlight streaming through the trees, the sounds of the woods coming into focus. Crickets chirped, and leaves rustled beneath tiny scurrying feet.

Graham gathered Morgyn in his arms and gazed into her eyes. "You survived the first wave of Bradens."

"With you I could survive a monsoon." She went up on her toes and kissed him. "But I think your mom had the right idea." She feigned a yawn and said, "Maybe we should check out your loft."

Lust sparked in his dark eyes as he lowered his lips to hers, and the rest of the world fell away.

Chapter Seventeen

JILLIAN HAD RENTED out an old warehouse on the outskirts of town for the fashion show, and she'd transformed it into an elaborate showroom, complete with a professional stage, hundreds of chairs, and decorations that gave it a New York City vibe. When Graham and Morgyn arrived with Morgyn's merchandise Monday afternoon, a handful of people, including his brothers, several of their cousins, and some friends, were erecting tables and hanging long, flowing fabrics between the fashion show area and what would become the banquet area. Lights were strung across metal rafters in the open ceiling, and a black banner with MULTIFARIOUS BY JILLIAN BRADEN in gold letters hung above the stage.

Jillian was busy giving directions to a group of men like she was commanding an army. She sent them off and turned her attention to Graham's cousin Sam and proceeded to rattle off instructions.

"This is incredible," Morgyn said. "Is she expecting New York fashionistas? Everything looks so high-end. Why does she want to show my stuff? It won't fit in."

"Because Jillian has an eye for eclectic fashion, and your merchandise is gorgeous and one of a kind, sunshine, just like you."

"There you are!" Jillian strode toward them. "I can't wait to see what you brought."

Sam followed her over. "Hey, Graham, good to see you, man. I thought you were in New York this week." He embraced Graham, giving him a strong slap on the back.

"I was, but—"

"He fell in love," Jillian interrupted. "Sam, this is Morgyn, Graham's other half. She's going to be showing her designs tomorrow, too. Sam's our cousin. He lives in the next town over and owns a river rafting and adventure company." She clapped her hands and said, "Introductions done. Let's get to work."

"Jilly, give me a second to greet Graham's better half. It's nice to meet you, Morgyn," Sam said with a chuckle.

"Graham told me about your company. It sounds like fun."

"I'm going to get her out on the river one day," Graham said.

"Okay, enough small talk. I'm sorry, you guys, but we have *hours* of work to do." Jillian pointed to a wall of fabric panels. "You can put Morgyn's stuff behind there. That's where we're staging the models. Then I'll get started with Morgyn while you help Sam with the lighting."

"You're a little tyrant," Graham said, only half teasing.

Sam took the box from Morgyn and said, "I've got this."

"Thanks, Sam. Can you show Graham the layout?" Jillian took Morgyn's hand, dragging her away. "We'll catch up with you later. I need to show Morgyn how this is going to work."

"Man, it's weird seeing my bossy sister in charge of her kingdom."

"She's fierce," Sam said, "but she's got this business down pat. Wait until you see the layout she's drawn up."

"Who do you think she wrangled into drawing it up? She just about drove me crazy when we were putting the plans together." Graham set the boxes in the designated area, and then they retrieved the others from the truck.

Graham worked throughout the afternoon setting up lights, testing sound equipment, and doing a hundred other things. He'd attended Jillian's shows in the past, but this was the first year she was holding the event outside of her store. She'd spent the last two years expanding her designs into edgier realms, and in doing so she had tripled her income. Graham was glad he'd changed his plans, and he made a mental note not to miss next year's event. She worked hard for her success, and he wanted to support her.

By early evening the work was complete, and everyone but family had cleared out. Graham stepped outside to take a phone call from Knox, and when he returned, the warehouse was quiet. He went in search of Morgyn. Having caught only glimpses of her throughout the day, he was dying to get back to her.

"Hey, bro," Nick said as he came out of the bathroom and fell into stride beside Graham. "Can you believe all this is for Jilly?"

"She's something."

"So is your girl."

Graham narrowed his eyes.

"Don't worry. I'd never hit on your woman. I had a few minutes to talk to her when I was helping move the stairs on the back of the stage. She said you hooked up a homeless guy with a job in Seattle."

"I made the connection. I haven't heard if he got hired or not," he said as they moved past the fabric borders toward the staging area. "But really, that was Morgyn's idea. She befriended a homeless man and figured out how to help him."

"She's a bleeding heart, like you." Nick patted him on the back and said, "That's good, man. But just keep those love germs away from me. The last thing I need is a woman telling me what to do."

"It's not like that," Graham said.

"That's what you and Beau say, but I don't need to test my theory." He nodded toward Jax, Jillian, and Morgyn, who were gathered around a laptop. "They're Skyping with Beau, Char, and Zev. Come on."

"There they are," Beau said through the laptop screen as they approached.

Morgyn stood from the chair where she was sitting and went to Graham.

"Hey, sunshine." The warm press of her lips eased the stress of the day. "I missed you."

"Me too," Morgyn said softly. "Beau reminds me of you. I really like him and Char."

"We can hear you two," Jillian said. "So no dirty talk."

"Wait!" Charlotte leaned closer to the screen and said, "I can always use a little naughty inspiration for my books. Go for it!"

Graham laughed. "I don't think so, Char. Sorry. Good to see you guys. How's life in Colorado?"

"Better than ever," Beau said. "We're digging into the renovations at the inn. Did you decide about Belize yet?"

"Yeah, I need to know if I'm meeting you there or not," Zev said.

Leave it to his brothers to bring up the one thing he *didn't* want to talk about. "Not yet. There's a lot to figure out."

"I thought you were starting next month?" Beau asked. "Did the project get delayed?"

"No, but there's a lot to consider." He glanced at Morgyn, who was watching him curiously.

"I don't understand. I thought that was what you wanted, to expand your business to include more international work, to be more hands-on," Beau said. "You were pumped about it a few weeks ago."

Graham clenched his jaw, wishing they'd shut the hell up. He'd decided earlier in the day that he probably wasn't going to see the project through. "Things have changed."

"What's changed?" Morgyn asked. "You said this project would help hundreds of residents in a village where their homes were deplorable. What could possibly have changed enough to warrant not helping them?"

Christ, you too? "Can we talk about this later?"

"Uh-oh," Zev said. "I think I know what changed."

Graham glared at him.

Morgyn's eyes moved between Zev and Graham. "Wait...is it because of *me*?"

He pulled her closer and said, "No."

Nick coughed to cover his voice as he said, "*Bullshit.*"

"Graham, you can't not go because of me," Morgyn said. "I don't want you to do that. Those people need your help."

"I'll invest," he reassured her. "I don't need to be there to give money."

"No." She shrugged out of his arms. "You can't do that. Beau just said you wanted to be more hands-on. You told me that when we first met, too. Why would you give that up because of me? I don't *ever* want to stand in your way, especially not for something like this."

"Goddamn it, sunshine." He didn't mean to raise his voice, but pressure had been mounting for days as he'd made his decision. "Because you've got all this stuff going on with your business, and I'm not going away for eight to ten weeks and leaving you to figure it out alone. That's not who I am. I love you, and I want to be by your side. I want to be the man you can count on. You come before *everyone* else, and yeah, maybe that's selfish, and maybe it's a shitty thing to do to throw money at a problem instead of getting my ass down to Belize and being part of the solution. But life isn't always fair, and I have a choice to make. Be by your side and help you through this difficult process, or walk away knowing I wasn't the man you thought I was."

"Holy shit," Jillian whispered. "You guys, we shouldn't—"

"Shh!" Jax and Nick said in unison.

"You're *off*, cracker. Your energy is all out of balance. I can feel it. This isn't right."

Morgyn took a shaky step forward with tears in her eyes and reached for his hands. Her hands were sweating, and it killed him knowing he was the cause of her angst.

She swallowed hard and said, "Then *don't* leave me. *Be* the man I know you to be. Keep all your promises. Take me *with* you. There's too much good we can do to walk away or leave the project in someone else's hands. Those people are far more important than where I sell my stuff or if I have a shop of my own. I realized in Seattle that I wanted to do more to help others, too, Graham. We can do this *together*. I can get out of my lease instead of renewing it, and we can figure out what to do with my business after we come back."

"Oh my gosh, that's so sweet," Charlotte whispered.

"I won't ask you to put your life on hold for that long." He squeezed her hands to keep them from trembling. "I can't ask that of you, sunshine."

"If you can't go without me, then you don't have to ask. I'm going. I have savings. I was playing with the idea of buying the caboose, but that's a luxury I don't need. I can afford a plane ticket, and how expensive can it be to stay in a place where they grow and hunt for food? We aren't a conventional couple, Graham. We're meant to float wherever we're needed. We're meant to make a *difference.* I didn't realize that until just now, but don't you see? The universe is testing us, and it's up to us to make the right decisions."

"Sunshine," he said, his throat thick with emotion. "That's asking a lot of you, and it feels selfish."

"It would be more selfish if you walked away from the chance to help those people to be with me. I don't want to be the one who makes them lose out. We have more than we need in this world. We have *two* homes, *two* amazing families. We're so blessed." She shrugged, a smile lifting her lips as she said, "This is who we're meant to be. *Know it. Trust it. Accept it.* Right?"

They reached for each other at the same time, and he said, "Always," as his lips came down over hers.

Applause and cheers rang out, and Jillian threw her arms around them and said, "I love you guys so much. I want what you have."

"Guess that means I'm heading to Belize," Zev said.

"This is definitely going in a book!" Charlotte called out, and they all laughed.

"A bestseller," Graham said, and then he kissed Morgyn again and said, "I couldn't love you more than I do right now."

"That's too bad," Morgyn said. Then she went up on her

toes and whispered, "I was sort of counting on you showing me just how much more you loved me tonight with hot make-up sex."

Chapter Eighteen

MORGYN'S HEAD HADN'T stopped spinning since yesterday. She and Graham had celebrated their decision about Belize with a barbecue at his parents' house. His mother hadn't been surprised that Graham had been ready to give up going to Belize for Morgyn, because, she'd said, *Your happiness has become his happiness.* She'd confided in Morgyn that Graham had always been the peacemaker in the family and that she believed the treehouse he and his brothers had built as kids was one of his peacemaking endeavors. She'd said it had been a tough year, with Beau and Nick both full of teenage testosterone and at each other's throats. The project had given them something to focus on, a reason to work together, and it had done the trick. While working on the project, Beau and Nick had once again become close. From what Morgyn had witnessed earlier that morning, they were clearly still just as close. Beau had called Graham before the fashion show and they had spoken for more than an hour.

Now the fashion show was in full swing. Between lightning-fast clothing changes, models parading on and off the runway, flashes of lights, and blaring music, the warehouse vibrated with beautiful chaos. Friends of Jillian's were modeling the clothes.

They might not have been professionals, but they were sure pretty enough to be. There were two gorgeous brunettes, Gemma Gritt and Chelsea Helms; an adorable blonde named Jewel, who was married to one of Jillian's cousins; Dixie Whiskey, a tall redhead who was all legs and badass attitude; and Dixie's friend Isabel Ryder, who looked just like the lead actress from *Blindspot*, one of Brindle's favorite shows. They strutted down the runway like they'd been modeling their whole lives. Morgyn had never been to a fashion show, and she didn't think her clothes were worthy, but the women made her dresses, jeans, flare-legged hippie pants, and everything else they wore look like a million bucks.

"I saw your cowboy brother out there. Is he still single?" Dixie asked as she shimmied into one of Jillian's sexy corset dresses. Her flame-red hair looked stunning against the black leather, and her tattoos gave off the edgy vibe Jillian had said her new clothing line needed. She glanced at Morgyn and said, "You must have all sorts of hot cowboys where you live."

"Some of the hottest," Morgyn answered.

Jillian buttoned the back of the corset and said, "I didn't know you were into cowboys, Dix. I'd think you'd go biker all the way."

Dixie scoffed. "My family founded the Dark Knights motorcycle club. If I ever want to have a man in my life, he's either got to be *part* of the club or from a whole different world."

"Then you're out of luck." Jillian turned Dixie by the shoulders, giving the outfit a once-over. "Nick's not in a motorcycle club, but he rides."

"Perfect," Dixie said with a smirk. "At least for tonight."

"That's TMI about my brother. Now get out there and shake your gorgeous booty." She gave Dixie a shove toward the stage.

"Morgyn, is this right?" Gemma twirled before her in one of Morgyn's halter tops and flare-legged pants.

"Almost!" Morgyn grabbed a handful of necklaces and slipped them over her head. Then she fashioned a colorful bandeau around Gemma's forehead. "God, you make my clothes look hot. Thank you for doing this."

"Are you kidding? Dress-up is what I do! I own Princess for a Day Boutique in Peaceful Harbor. You should come by and see it. We could use some hippie outfits for the kids to dress up in. Maybe you could make a hippie princess dress."

"I'd love to!"

"Not now!" Jillian nudged Gemma toward the stage. "Can't get off schedule, princess. Go show them how fantastic you look!" She spun around and said, "That's the last one. Then I'll go out and take my bow and introduce you. Are you ready?"

"Ready to pass out, maybe. My heart hasn't stopped racing all day," Morgyn said as they watched the girls strut across the stage. "Thank you for sharing your spotlight with me. It's a once-in-a-lifetime opportunity I never would have gotten if not for you, and I'll never forget it."

"You're crazy. Do you know how rare one-of-a-kind merchandise is? Jax is out there lining up buyers who want to talk to you after the show."

"Buyers? What does that mean?"

"It means they'll want to place orders to carry your stuff in their stores. Jax and I have loads of connections. We'll make you a star! His fashion shows are *huge* affairs that take place all over the country. If you ever design wedding gowns, let him know because he's *the man in the know*. If only you weren't leaving for Belize next month. We have a lot of planning to do to get your consignment business to the right people."

She was overwhelmed by the outpouring of support from Graham's family. "*We?*"

Jillian rolled her eyes. "I told you I'd teach you about grass-roots marketing. You'll need it now more than ever."

Jillian's name was announced over the loudspeaker, and Morgyn's nerves caught fire.

"That's me!" Jillian said. "When they call your name, you *own* that runway. Head up, boobs out, smile pretty. Graham's out there waiting for you. Focus on him and you'll be fine. This is your coming-out party, Morgyn, and I'm proud to share the stage with you!"

Jillian hugged her, then hurried off, leaving Morgyn in a state of panic. She repeated Jillian's instructions in her mind. *Head up, boobs out, smile pretty.* When her name echoed in the warehouse, she froze.

A strong arm slipped around her waist, startling her.

"Come on, sunshine. This is your moment."

Graham's coaxing, comforting voice made her heart swell. "How did you know I needed you?"

"You're part of me. I'll always know."

GRAHAM WATCHED MORGYN from across the room as Jillian introduced her to the people Graham knew were her most influential clients. Morgyn's smile never faltered as she shook hands and blushed at what he was sure were a host of much-deserved compliments. Seeing her creations up onstage had sparked overwhelming emotions in him, but when Morgyn had joined Jillian to take a bow, he'd thought his heart might climb out of his chest.

Jax sidled up to him, looking sharp in an expensive dark suit and purple tie. His hair was brushed back, and perfectly manicured scruff made his chiseled features appear even more defined. "I've got to give it to Morgyn. She knows how to work a room." He handed Graham a drink and said, "How does it feel to see your girlfriend being swept up in the world of retail stardom?"

"Is it weird to feel insanely proud of her? You should have seen her this morning when we heard that John, the homeless man from Seattle, got hired for the job I recommended for him. She lit up so bright, I thought I'd never see that look again. But this? Look at her, Jax. She's in her element and she doesn't even know it."

"I wondered if you would notice that. Even Jilly looks nervous, but Morgyn doesn't. She looks *thankful* or appreciative. That blush she's got going on works in her favor, and it doesn't look like it's from nerves. It'll endear her to them. She's not the cutthroat businessperson they're used to. Do you think she realizes the buyers she's talking to are worth millions?"

Graham chuckled. "I don't think she'd care."

A better question was the one ping-ponging around in Graham's head. Could their timing for the Belize trip be any worse? Now that buyers had *found* her, he couldn't help but wonder if they'd made the wrong decision. This was just the beginning for Morgyn. He knew how rare solid business opportunities were. He turned down five times as many as he took on, and the last thing he wanted was for her to miss out on something that could catapult her career to unheard of levels.

"How about you?" Jax asked. "Do you care?"

It was a good question. Graham mulled it over as he took a drink. Morgyn trusted him completely, just as he trusted her. He needed to be sure they were taking this next step for all the right reasons. She shined brightest when she was helping others or doing what she loved. He'd known she loved everything about her business, but what he hadn't realized was what her enthusiasm might spark in industry professionals.

"Tough question?" Jax said with a raised brow.

"Yes, because I care a hell of a lot about Morgyn's happiness. But I don't give two shits about the prestige or money that could accompany it. The question is, should I? For her sake?"

Jax shrugged. "You're asking an artist. All I know is, even if my gowns never sold, I'd still make them. I'd starve, but then I'd come live with you in that treehouse, hunt squirrels for food, forage the forest for nuts and berries." He glanced at Morgyn and said, "Your girl is hot, but right now? That mix of confidence and bashfulness? I bet every one of those *suits* is sporting a chubby."

Graham ground his teeth together. "How about you keep your nuts and berries at your place—and thoughts like *that* to yourself."

WHEN THEY ARRIVED at the airport several hours later, Graham was still wrestling with the worries that had plagued him all day. Morgyn had been speed-talking ever since the fashion show, raving about how excited everyone was about her designs and how honored she felt to have shared the stage with Jillian. Her goodbyes with his family had been emotional for everyone, most surprisingly *him*. He hadn't realized how seeing his family welcome Morgyn into their close-knit circle would make him feel.

"Is it crazy that I'm tearing up right now?" Morgyn asked as they came to her gate. "When did I turn into such a mushy girl?"

He gathered her in his arms and kissed her salty tears away. "You're my mushy girl, and you've been on an emotional high for days."

"I know, but I'm always on an emotional high," she said adamantly. "It's *everything*. I love your family so much, I want to live in your treehouse as much as I want to live in Oak Falls. And even though we're only going to be apart for a few days, that makes me sadder than anything else, and I'm *not* a sad person. So what's wrong with me?"

He swallowed hard, realizing she hadn't said anything about traveling to Belize. "You're in love, sunshine. I hear it messes with the strongest of people. Myself included."

"Then it's worth it." She wrapped her arms around him, holding him tight. "I might have to sleep on your side of the bed tonight."

"Damn, baby. I'm going to miss the sweet, loving look you're giving me right now, and your octopus-like sleeping habits." He reached into his bag and slipped his lucky hat on her head. A bright smile stretched across her beautiful face, and she sighed.

"Now I feel a little more aligned," she said, adjusting the hat. "I love you, cracker. Good luck with your meetings in New York, and thank you for letting me tag along to Seattle. You know what I'll be thinking about while I'm flying?"

"Our *club* initiation?"

Her fingers curled into his shirt, and her eyes darkened as she whispered, "Well, *now* I will be. I was going to say how incredible it will be to travel to Belize together and help all those people."

Her words eased the tangle of worries inside him. After several steamy kisses, he watched her disappear through the gate, hoping like hell they were doing the right thing.

Chapter Nineteen

WEIRD DIDN'T COME close to describing how it felt to wake up Wednesday morning without Graham by her side. It was almost as strange as coming back to her small, happy town, where there weren't homeless people or millionaires vying for her merchandise. She couldn't stop thinking about the people in that tiny village in Belize Graham had told her about. She'd left a naive, small-town girl, and her limited travels had poked holes in her safe little bubble. The rest of the world was seeping in and puddling around her. She was so busy reacclimating to real life, working in her greenhouse, checking on the deer garden, and working at the shop that all those uneasy feelings were pushed to the side. She'd gotten so swept up in taking care of business she had to get done that when she finally arrived home that evening and saw Graham's truck in front of her house, her heart went crazy. For a second she thought he was *there*, making reality that much harder to accept.

They talked on the phone late into the night. Hearing his voice had soothed her longing, but she'd woken up Thursday morning missing him again. Only this time, as she worked in her shop, trying to figure out how to organize the *closing* of her business, she thought about how much had changed—for her and *within* her—adding to her discomfort.

She had three weeks to move out of her retail space, arrange for her inventory to be sold on consignment, and figure out who would take care of her plants and deer garden while they were in Belize. Could she really close the doors to the retail space where her business had come to life? The space she'd been so proud of? An empty feeling swirled in the pit of her stomach. She sank down to a chair in the back of her shop, thinking about the buyers she'd met at the fashion show. She'd been so caught up in the moment, she hadn't realized the full extent of the opportunity Jillian had given her. Several of the buyers wanted to carry her merchandise. Some had wanted to place large orders. Orders there was no way she could fill—and orders that would suck the enjoyment out of what she did. They didn't want her to make several of the same products. That wasn't the issue. They loved her one-of-a-kind merchandise, but they wanted *so much* of it, she'd have to work fast and furious to meet the demand.

Would it make her ungrateful if she chose not to mass produce?

"I must be crazy," she said as she crossed her arms over the table and rested her forehead on them.

"Nah. I talk to myself all the time."

Morgyn's head popped up at the sound of Beckett's voice. He strode toward her in jeans and a T-shirt. The sound of his boots on the floor was comfortingly familiar—not because they were his, but because it was a sound she had grown up with. Cowboy boots on grass, gravel, linoleum, hardwood…

"Beckett. What are you doing here?"

"Nice to see you, too," he said as he sat down beside her and stretched his long legs out in front of him.

She remembered how he used to make her heart go wild. A teenage crush finally reciprocated as twentysomething new adults. It was funny how quickly that had changed.

"Sorry," she said. "I've got a lot on my mind, and I didn't expect to see you here."

He stretched his neck to either side, the way he used to when he played football for Oak Falls High. His green eyes held hers with a seriousness that reminded her of how disconnected they were in the most important aspects of their relationship. "Neither did I."

"Then why are you here?"

"You look good, Morgyn. Better than good. You look happy."

She rolled her eyes. "What do you want, Beck? I know I don't look that way. I have about a hundred things shooting through my mind."

"You're wrong, Morgyn." He leaned his elbows on his thighs and rubbed his hands together, eyes still locked on her. "You might feel conflicted or have a lot on your plate, but that doesn't change what I see. I came to apologize."

"Why…?"

"Because once upon a time someone told me to give up my ridiculous dreams and get on a better path. Lucky for me, it worked out. But telling you to do the same was wrong. I'm glad you didn't listen to me."

"Beck, are you *dying*? Because this sounds a lot like cleansing yourself of your supposed sins, and you don't need to do that with me. Unless you're dying? Are you sick?"

He laughed and shook his head. "No. I'm healthy as an ox. When I saw you with Graham at the festival, I was a dick." She opened her mouth to protest, but he held his hand up and said,

"Can we just agree to call it what it was? I was jealous. Not that I want you back, or wanted to come between you two or anything like that. It just made me realize that I was wrong."

"Beckett…?"

"It's a pretty awful feeling to realize some things are too ingrained to be changed. You were right to walk away from our relationship, and you were right when you said I didn't trust you. At the time I thought you meant that I didn't trust you as a girlfriend, but I get it now. You *knew* I didn't trust your capabilities as a businessperson, and you were right, because I didn't see all of you, Morgyn. Not the way Graham does. He sees who you've always been and who you were meant to be."

She thought it was in bad taste to admit he was right, so she kept quiet, feeling a little lighter because of his words.

"When I say his name, your eyes light up, like just the thought of him makes your life better. I'm happy for you, Morgyn. I didn't want you to leave town thinking of me as a dick, because, well…Okay, maybe you still will. But our friendship is important to me. I can't change who I am or how I acted, or the things I suggested that were obviously way off base. But I'm man enough to apologize."

"Beckett, you really don't need to, but it means the world to me that you did. Thank you. I have no bad feelings about what happened between us. We had fun. We're just too different on some levels."

"That's what makes you such a good person." He pushed to his feet and said, "You see the good in everyone, and you forgive the not so great parts."

"Your business beliefs don't make you not so great; they just make us not so great for each other. But if a floaty girl like me can find a man as amazing as Graham, there's hope for you yet."

She rose to her feet and hugged him. "Thank you."

"Listen, if you need anything here while you're away, I'm your guy. I can keep your deer fed and haul Twyla's sexy little butt from the flower shop to take care of your herbs and gardens. I'll even make sure no one messes with that toy house you call a home." He laughed with the tease as they made their way toward the front of the store. "Want to tell me about those thoughts that are driving you crazy?"

"Thanks, but I'll figure it out."

It would probably help to talk about them, but Beckett wasn't the person she wanted to discuss them with. While Beckett needed to find forgiveness, she needed to figure out if she was making the biggest mistake of her career by going away when it was just taking off—or the best decision of her life by following her heart.

GRAHAM CLOSED HIS laptop and stepped onto his hotel room balcony. It was a humid, sticky night. The kind of night they'd surely experience many times over in Belize, with oppressive heat that sent most people running for air-conditioning. His gaze swept over the city lights, and his mind drifted to Morgyn, as it had done throughout the last two days of meetings. It was a wonder he'd been able to keep up at all.

She'd never prefer air-conditioning to the heat of the evening, and she'd adore the view. *But she'd hate the room.* He smiled at that. Damn, he missed her. He couldn't shake his worries about taking her away from everything she was being offered. During dinner with Josh and Knox, Knox had offered to take care of Belize without him. Graham had nearly jumped at the offer, but he knew Morgyn too well. She was meant for helping others, for shining her light on the far reaches of the world.

The trouble was, he didn't know if she could ever be happy if these business opportunities slipped through her fingers. He'd asked Josh for his advice, knowing Josh had chosen love over business when he'd fallen for Riley. As a world-renowned fashion designer, he was in a whole different world from Morgyn. But he'd had to start somewhere, and he knew the pitfalls of lost opportunities. Josh's advice had rung true. *Fashion is a fickle business. Today's trends are tomorrow's has-beens. But true love can stand the test of time and distance.*

Graham pulled his phone from his pocket and called Morgyn. He had to give her the chance to jump into business with the buyers with two feet.

She answered on the first ring. "Hey, Cracker Jack. Guess what I'm doing?"

He laughed and sank down to a chair. "Sitting in the moonlight pining for me?"

"Something like that." The cheerfulness of her greeting waned from her voice. "I *am* wearing your hat and your favorite T-shirt, and I *might* be sitting on the roof of your truck."

"I wish I were there with you. Stargazing?"

"Mm-hm. Life's greatest answers are written in the stars."

"What am I hearing in your voice, sunshine? There's a heaviness to it. What's making your think so hard?"

"I'm fine," she said softly. "Just tired. It's been a crazy couple of days, and it's catching up to me, that's all."

Fine wasn't in Morgyn's vocabulary. *Fine* was reserved for people who didn't know the meaning of *amazing*, *excited*, or *floaty*. *Fine* was for people who didn't see auras or feel energies of those around them. Two weeks ago, he hadn't been aware of those things, either, but when it came to Morgyn, he felt everything.

"Are you having second thoughts about closing your shop?"

"A little," she admitted. "But I think that's natural. It's a big change."

Natural or not, it slayed him. "We don't have to go—"

"Cracker, don't. We've been through this. We're doing what we are meant to do. By the way, Beckett came to see me at the shop today."

Even though he knew she wasn't interested in Beckett, his chest constricted.

"He apologized for telling me I should close my business. He was really thoughtful, and happy for us. He offered to help while we're away. It was big of him, and I'm glad he did it, even though he didn't need to. I think he knows that you're the *dream catcher* and I'm the *girl*, and our life is written in the stars."

"If that's a metaphor, I'm ten steps behind."

"It's a song. 'Written in the Stars' by the Girl and the Dreamcatcher. It's *us*, our lives."

"Then why do you sound so down?"

"I'm not down. I'm *adjusting*. Realigning my thoughts and energies."

He remembered what she'd said at the airport about feeling more aligned and said, "I have the remedy for being misaligned." He grinned as he said, "Polly want a cracker?"

Her melodic laughter burst through the phone. "Yes! Polly wants a *big* cracker. With seconds."

"Hot miss-you sex coming up."

"You sure know how to distract a girl."

"It's really good to hear your smile, sunshine."

"Good. Talk dirty to me and you'll hear more than a smile."

And just like that, *she'd* distracted *him*. "Maybe I ought to get off the balcony."

"Get off on the balcony?" she said in a husky voice. "Now, that sounds like a plan. Wish I were there to help you with it."

"Let me call you back." He ended the call and immediately called her back with FaceTime. Her beautiful face lit up the screen. She was lying on her back, her hair fanned out from beneath his hat. He'd never known the sound of someone's voice or the sight of a smile could be the calming force he needed. But there were many things he hadn't known before the universe had guided them into each other's orbits—like the fact that the universe had the power to bring them together at all.

Chapter Twenty

EVEN AFTER TALKING with Graham last night, Morgyn had slept fitfully. She'd gotten so tangled up in the sheets she'd rolled off the mattress and *plunk*ed onto the floor. She'd crawled back into bed and tried falling back to sleep on *his* side of the bed, but it smelled so much like him, it made her miss him even more. She lay staring at the ceiling until the first bit of light snuck in through the window, when she figured it was an acceptable hour to go to the barn. But no matter how hard she tried to concentrate, her mind jumped from one thought to the next—*Am I making the right decisions for my business? What if the consignment idea fails? Can I start over after Belize? How can I get more involved helping people after Belize?*—making it impossible to focus on any one project. She finally decided to take a short walk and try to clear her head.

The sun warmed her as she walked along the railroad ties in her fuzzy slippers, which she hadn't thought to take off before leaving the barn. She tipped her face up toward the sun and breathed deeply, trying to center her thoughts, which were still fluttering around like uncatchable butterflies. She needed to talk things out, but not with Graham. She'd heard worry in his voice last night, and she didn't want him thinking she was unsure about going to Belize. Being with him was the *only* thing she *was* sure of.

She thought about calling her mother, but her mother had stopped by her shop yesterday, and she'd been so excited about all of Morgyn's plans, Morgyn wondered if she'd tell her the truth if she thought she was making a mistake with her business. She trusted her parents, but she knew they wanted her to be happy above all else.

They'd brought her up to trust her instincts and her heart.

Morgyn's instincts told her she needed to talk this out with someone else. She debated calling Sable or Amber. They had their own businesses, but Sable would tell her not to follow any man—ever—and Amber wouldn't want to hurt her feelings by saying the wrong things. She'd err on the side of caution and would probably tell her to do whatever felt right. Pepper would give her a lecture and would probably leave her more confused than she'd started out, and Grace was gone.

She had to call Brindle.

Brindle might not be the best person to give relationship advice, but she was always honest. Right now Morgyn needed honesty more than anything. Someone to cut through the questions and help sort out the answers.

"Hey, Morg," her sister said flatly.

"Brin? What's wrong? Oh crap. Is it the middle of the night there or something? You know I suck at time differences."

"No. We're only six hours ahead of you."

"Good. Are you okay? You sound hungover."

Brindle sighed. "I'm fine. I stayed up all night talking with Andre."

"Talking, *right*. Sorry. I can let you go."

"No, don't hang up. We were talking! I was lonely and

needed someone to talk to, and he's going through a lot right now. He's a doctor, and he's introspective and deep, and—you'll love this—he's an artist, too. If you think *I'm* dramatic, you should see this guy. You'd love him. He's all about the universe doing this and that, and he's also hot as fuck. I'm talking holy smokes hot!"

"Like I said. *Talking?*"

"I *do* know how to have a male friend without sleeping with him," Brindle insisted. "Now, his friend Mathieu is another story. I might have to get drunk on that tall glass of champagne."

Morgyn laughed and balanced on the rail as she made her way down the tracks, like she did when she was a little girl. A warm breeze tickled her skin, and she had the sense that her grandfather was watching over her.

"But Andre is a great guy," Brindle said. "He's really easy to talk to. But he's *still* hurting over a breakup that happened ages ago, and he pours all of his devastation into his artwork. I'm trying to help him move past her. I mean, why cry over spilled milk, right?"

There was a hint of sadness in her voice, but before Morgyn could respond, Brindle started talking again.

"His ex is like us. She has no interest in marriage, but she also has no interest in staying in one place. I *like* Oak Falls. I'm in no hurry to get out of there on a permanent basis."

"I didn't *think* I wanted to, either," Morgyn admitted. "But now that I've traveled farther than a stone's throw, I realize how small and protected Oak Falls is." She told Brindle about her trip to Seattle, meeting John and Knox, her ideas for the property there, and about her time in Pleasant Hill with Graham's family. She didn't spring the news about Belize or closing her store on her sister. She sensed that Brindle was struggling with something, and Brindle was so protective of her, she didn't want to give her more to worry about.

"His family sounds great."

"They are. They harass each other like we do. I love them, and the fashion show was amazing, but I don't know that I fit into that world in the same way Jilly does."

"Well, *duh*. You're not a fashion-show girl. You make things and believe they have one special person they were meant for and that the universe will somehow unite them."

Morgyn arrived at the train graveyard, and her spirits lifted. "You know what, you're right. I do. But the buyers Jilly connected me with are making huge offers for my merchandise. Wouldn't it make me ungrateful or *stupid* if I turn some of them down?"

"No. That's what makes you *you*, Morg. You're not like everyone else, and you're the most grateful person I know. You're thankful for the sun and the moon and everything pretty and floaty. You're grateful for what other people take for granted. Now, *me*, on the other hand. I have serious gratitude issues. But I'm working on that."

"No, you don't," Morgyn said as she made her way through the long grass to the red caboose. "What's really going on? You can talk to me."

"I know," she said softly.

Silence stretched between them, and just when Morgyn was ready to break it, Brindle said, "I'm not coming back at the end of the summer. I need time to figure out my life."

"What about your job?" Morgyn was beyond shocked. "School starts at the beginning of September. Brindle, don't put your job in jeopardy."

"I already handled it. They're getting a substitute. As long as I'm back by the first of November, my job is safe."

"Holy crap. *November?* Brindle, please tell me what's going on. That's a *really* long time."

"Some things can't be put off. I need this time away to figure out who I am and who I want to be."

"Just tell me this. Should I worry? I'm supposed to go to Belize with Graham, but I can cancel and come to Paris."

"Whoa! *Belize?* When did this come up? What about *your* work?"

Morgyn told her about the project in Belize and that even before that opportunity arose, she'd been considering closing her shop and putting her merchandise on consignment. "Helping those people is way more important than my shop, and even though I can make the rent with the increase, as you pointed out the last time we talked, it would mean working a lot more. Am I doing the right thing? Giving up my shop? Selling my stuff on consignment? What if it doesn't work and I have to start over? What should I do about the offers from the buyers? I want to keep selling my stuff, but I don't want to become money-driven. I want to help people, but how can I do that if I'm stuck here? And I don't even *fit* in Oak Falls anymore, Brin! Do you think I'm crazy? Going to Belize? Do you want me to come to Paris?"

"Whoa, chick. That's a *lot* of worries. Do *not* come to Paris, and you're not crazy. I think you're brave. You're staying true to your heart, and that's not always easy to do. I hope I can learn to do the same."

"I wish there were a sign, you know? Something to show me I'm following the right path."

LONG-DISTANCE RELATIONSHIPS are for the birds, Graham thought as he paid the cab driver in front of Morgyn's house at eleven o'clock Friday morning. He threw open the door as the driver retrieved his bags from the trunk. When the cab drove away he called out Morgyn's name and ran to the front door. Last night had sucked, and Morgyn's admission about her shop had bothered him all night. He'd tried calling her before he got on his flight—and after he landed—but she wasn't answering her phone. He'd stopped at her shop, which was closed, and was hoping to catch her before she put any plans into motion.

He flew through the front door and called out, "Morgyn?"

Silence.

Damn it.

He bolted out the front door and around the house. There were new herbs drying in the sun outside the greenhouse, but no sign of Morgyn.

"Sunshine?" he called as he headed for the barn.

He pulled open the doors, and although the tables were in their normal state of chaos, his girl wasn't there. He headed to the deer garden and called Sable on the way.

"What's up, *jetsetter*?" Sable said when she answered.

"Hey. I'm at Sunsh—*Morgyn's*—and I can't find her. Have you seen her?" He cursed under his breath when the deer garden came into view and she wasn't there, either.

"I thought you weren't coming back into town until tomorrow night."

"I wasn't. But I'm here. Do you know where she is?"

"Uh-oh. Trouble in Lovers Land?"

"No. I just—" He spotted the train tracks. "Never mind. I think I know where she is. Thanks anyway."

He ended the call and sprinted down the tracks with his heart in his throat. If she was still at the train graveyard, she was probably even more upset that he'd anticipated. When the trains came into view, he sprinted for the caboose.

"Morgyn?" he hollered as he ran, his gut clenching at the sight of the empty deck.

He climbed up and peered inside. Morgyn lay on her stomach on a bench, one leg and one arm hanging off. Her chin rested precariously upright on the edge of the bench. His favorite T-shirt was bunched around her waist, exposing her beautiful butt in a pair of bright yellow underwear with KISS MY ASS written in black across them.

She was sleeping like the dead.

Just as that thought registered, Morgyn rolled onto her side and off the edge of the bench. Graham dove to break her fall, and she landed on top of him with a fierce hip to his groin. He choked out a groan.

She lifted her head, blinking several times. "Am I dreaming? Or is it Saturday?"

"Friday," he eked out, pushing at her body. "*Hip.*"

"Sorry!" She scampered off him as he sat up. "Did you say *Friday*?"

She squealed and rose up to climb into his lap. His hands shot protectively over his groin, and she stopped in midair.

"Oops," she said, and she sat beside him.

Drawn in by her sweet smile, he pressed his lips to her.

"Missed you," he said, and then he rubbed his nose over hers.

Her breathless sigh brought his lips to hers again. He slipped his hand to the nape of her neck, savoring the taste of her and the sexy, needful sounds she made. There on the cold and dirty floor of the caboose, with the summer heat pressing in on them and his girl in his arms, his worries began to fade. She had that effect on him, calming his overactive mind and then making him unable to think at all. But when their lips parted and he gazed into her eyes, he remembered why he'd had Knox handle the rest of the meetings and jumped on a plane from New York. He remembered the heartache he'd felt at the thought of doing anything that might cause Morgyn discomfort or unhappiness.

"I'm sorry," he said. "We're moving way too fast. You don't need to make all those decisions right now. We can skip Belize. I can help you pay your rent until you decide what's best for your business. I can do anything you need, sunshine, but I won't be the cause of your headaches."

She blinked several times, like she was either confused or still stuck in a lusty haze. "What are you talking about?"

"Last night you said you were having second thoughts about closing your business."

"About what to *do* with it, not if I wanted to go with you to Belize. And if you think I'd let you pay my rent, you're out of your mind. It's a thoughtful offer, especially since you don't like to mix business and pleasure, but no way, cracker." She shook her head and said, "I've always paid my own way, and I've always done what I think is right. Going with you to Belize is one trillion percent the right thing to do."

"It is?" *Thank fucking God.*

"Yes! Don't you think so? What I was having trouble with was the *rest* of my life. I love Jilly, and I'm so grateful for everything she's done—and is doing—for me. I want to sell my stuff in her stores, and I want to work with some of her buyers, but I can't accept all of their offers. And I *don't* want to keep my shop in the same location. From the second I came back to Oak Falls I realized that I'm not the same person I was when I left. I can't sit in this little town pretending there aren't millions of people who need help out there. It would be a frivolous expense to pay more rent when I can use that money toward helping others or traveling to help them. I don't need much, and together we have more than most people—two houses, two vehicles, two amazing families."

She looked at his lap and said, "Can I sit there now if I'm careful?"

He lifted her onto his lap. "You're sure, sunshine, about all of this?"

"Surer than anything in my life. I had a dream right before you woke me up. My grandfather and I were standing on the tracks looking down them into the distance. He didn't say anything in the dream, but I remembered how he used to tell me that one of the things he loved most about the railroad was that when he looked down the tracks it felt *limitless.* He was showing me the way in my dream, Graham. The universe has been guiding me toward this forever, only I never realized it." Her eyes lit up and she said, "*Life Reimagined!* The name of my shop! It makes total sense, doesn't it? My desire to repurpose things, to make used things special for the next person? It all stems from a bigger desire to help. I don't know how it'll all play out, but I know two things for sure: Helping others is what I was born to do, and doing it by your side is where I was meant to be. This is my life—*our life*—reimagined."

"God, I love you, sunshine, and I can't wait to float around this world with you."

"Good," she said, grinding her butt against him. "Then show me how much. We have to make sure I didn't break *the goods.*"

As their mouths came together and they tore at each other's clothes, Graham's wish from the fountain in Romance, Virginia, came true—*I hope our adventures together never end.*

Epilogue

"IT FEELS STRANGE to be wearing so many clothes," Morgyn said as she and Graham walked across the grass toward the Jerichos' barn.

It was Halloween night, and the barn was lit up with strings of black and orange lights and decorated with scarecrows, ghouls, witches, ghosts, and gauzy fake spiderwebs for their annual Halloween barn bash. Morgyn couldn't wait to hug her parents and see her siblings. She and Graham had arrived home from Belize last night after ten wonderful, life-changing weeks, during which they'd worn as little as possible to combat the heat. They'd worked morning until night alongside the residents of the village, volunteers, and a host of professionals. Knox was as cocky as could be, although he was also warm and funny. He'd decided to stay in Belize for a while longer to try and *figure out his personal life*. Apparently the woman he hooked up after charity events was more important to him than he'd initially let on. The poor guy was all tangled up in knots over her. Sage and Kate Remington were staying as well, and they were just as wonderful as Graham had said, and Sadie was beyond adorable. Morgyn had gotten food poisoning at the beginning of their trip, and as Graham had long ago promised, he'd held her hair back while she puked. It hadn't been pretty, but she'd do it all over again to help such a gracious and interesting community.

"I promise to get you out of that costume the second we get home," Graham said, and then he kissed her, alighting sparks beneath her skin.

She was waiting for the electricity between them to wane the way couples often said it did, but their connection had become even stronger. Helping others had not only brought them closer together, but it had sparked bigger dreams of helping even more people. Knox, Sage, and Kate also wanted to do more to help others, and they'd spent a lot of time brainstorming ways to make that happen. It was a great feeling to be in love with a man who cared as much about others as she did, and knowing he was partners with people who were equally generous made the work they were doing that much sweeter.

"Welcome back!" Beckett hollered as he cut through the crowd dressed in jeans, a white T-shirt, and a leather jacket, his hair slicked back in a fifties style. He embraced each of them, and then he eyed their costumes and laughed. "Graham, you look sharp as a groom, but I gotta admit, I never thought I'd see the day Morgyn Montgomery wore a wedding dress. Y'all look great." He pointed to the entrance of the barn. "Your family's all here, standing just inside the doors, except Brindle. I heard her plane was delayed."

"Thanks," Graham said. "I'll catch up with you later."

Beckett held up his beer, then headed across the yard, dodging excited children who were running around under the watchful eyes of their parents. It reminded her of the nights in Belize, when the community gathered around a fire telling stories. Some nights she and Graham played guitar and the residents danced, and other times they stargazed or talked. Morgyn had learned so much about their culture, and in doing so she'd gained an even bigger appreciation for the things she possessed and for the things she wanted in life. Graham was right. Seeing other cultures was inspiring in ways she never could have imagined.

"You'll catch up with him *later*?" Morgyn looked at him curiously.

"We exchanged a few texts while we were gone. Business stuff. You were right. He's a good guy. Come on, *floaty*. All you've talked about for the last week was seeing your family. Let's go before you burst."

Music blared from the makeshift stage where everyone and anyone who wanted to join in was playing. There must have been fifteen people strumming guitars, banjos, playing drums, flutes, and saxophones. Sable was dressed as Catwoman. She spotted them and nudged Axsel, who was dressed as a pirate. They set their instruments on a table and jumped off the stage, heading in their direction.

"There's my sweet baby girl!" Her mother grabbed her father's hand and rushed toward them. They looked adorable in their Sonny and Cher costumes. Her mother rocked the long black wig as awesomely as her father pulled off the fake mustache. "I got all the pictures you sent and shared them with everyone. I'm so proud of both of you. I can't wait to hear all about the trip."

Her mother hugged her so tight, she could hardly breathe, and then she did the same to Graham.

"Welcome home, sweetheart," her father said. "You're glowing. Helping others suits you." He hugged her again. "We missed you both."

"We missed you guys, too," Morgyn said as Reed, Grace, and her other siblings joined them, each one pushing for a hug from her as well as Graham.

Reno wagged his tail beside Amber, who was dressed as a fairy with bright blue and silver wings and cowgirl boots. Morgyn hugged Amber, and then she loved up Reno. They all spoke at once. She was so happy to see them, she wanted to cry, and yet even though she'd missed them like crazy, she was excited about her and Graham's future plans. After spending two weeks with her family and two weeks with his, they would leave for their next adventure—a ski trip with his cousin Ty and Ty's wife, Aiyla, where they'd discuss creating tiny houses in one of Aiyla's favorite villages overseas. They had several work-related trips scheduled with Knox, and they'd already penciled in the Junk in the Trunk event for next spring, hoping to find a few cool things for Morgyn's business. She continued making new items from treasures she picked up on their travels and sold them on consignment. She was also selling her goods through Jillian's shop and had accepted only two offers from the buyers she'd met at the fashion show, a pace she could keep up with and still enjoy her life.

"You look sexy as hell, Pep," Morgyn said as she embraced Pepper. She was carrying a stuffed monkey and wearing tan shorts and a shirt, hiking boots, and a safari hat.

"Sexy? I'm supposed to look like I'm Jane Goodall," Pepper said.

Graham hugged her and said, "Best costume here besides Morgyn's."

Sable and Axsel pushed their way into the group.

"Belize looks good on you," Axsel said, hugging Morgyn.

Sable scoffed. "Belize? That's Mr. All Nighter's doing. Get

in here, jetsetter." She pulled Graham into a hug, and Morgyn warmed all over.

Reed and Grace were dressed as a sexy cop and a prisoner, handcuffed together. Hugging was awkward, but they were kick-ass costumes.

"How was your honeymoon?" Morgyn asked.

"It was beyond perfect," Grace said. "Reed is the best trip planner ever."

"I'd argue that point." Morgyn slipped her arm around Graham.

"What are we arguing about?" Brindle pushed through the crowd with a wide smile, bundled up in a peacoat.

"You're home!" Morgyn threw her arms around her. They'd talked twice a week while they were traveling, and little by little Brindle had started sounding like her peppy self again.

There was another round of hugs and *welcome homes*. The sounds of her youth surrounded her—chaos and love. The best sounds *ever*.

"How was your flight?" Pepper asked. "You must be exhausted."

Brindle groaned. "My flight was awful. Sorry I couldn't dress for the party, but I came straight from the airport. You guys look great in your costumes."

Reed lifted their handcuffed wrists and said, "Forget the ball and chain. This works much better." He pointed to Graham's and Morgyn's costumes and said, "Bride and groom? Guess you guys are next?"

Everyone laughed.

"You'd have to drag Morgyn kicking and screaming to the altar," Sable said. "Didn't you know that about her?"

"No. Really?" Reed asked.

"I bet Aunt Roxie could fix up a marriage potion for you, Morgyn," Grace said.

Pepper scoffed. "It doesn't work that way."

Their mother put her arm around Pepper and said, "One day your protected heart will want to climb out of your chest for a man, and when that happens, you'll realize anything is possible."

"This is probably the *only* time you'll see that particular sister of mine in a wedding gown," Axsel said. "So take pictures while you can."

"Well, actually..." Morgyn's heart raced as her gaze collided with Graham's. There wasn't just love in his eyes. There was hope and trust and everything she could have ever dreamed of. She thrust her left hand out in front of her, showing everyone the gold band with the cardinal directions carved into a little round disk on her ring finger and said, "I wore it once before! We eloped!"

Amber squealed and hugged her. "Oh, Morgyn!"

"What?" Sable snapped. "No way!"

"Holy cow. You're really *married*?" Grace said as congratulations and sounds of disbelief came at them from all sides.

"What the...?" Brindle looked from Graham to Morgyn. "Married?"

Axsel embraced Graham and said, "Leave it to Morgyn to freak everyone out. Congrats, bro!"

"Did you say...?" Her mother's eyes filled with tears as she pulled both Morgyn and Graham into her arms. "My baby girl is married! I love you both so much. Welcome to the family, Graham."

When her mother released them, her father's eyes narrowed like he wasn't sure he believed her. He lifted her left hand and looked down at the ring.

"Graham made it in Belize," Morgyn said, feeling more in love with her husband than ever. "He twisted the band, engraved it, and everything."

Her father's eyes shifted to Graham.

"I know it's not diamonds, but it's special to us," Graham said.

"Morgyn would hate diamonds," her father said, and then he put an arm around each of them and said, "True love doesn't need diamonds. Have you seen Marilynn's ring?"

Marilynn lifted her left hand, showing them the simple braided gold band on her left finger.

Everyone hugged them again amid many "*Married?*" comments. Morgyn wasn't surprised at their shock. She and Graham had been shocked at first, too.

Brindle sidled up to Morgyn and said, "You're *married*?"

Morgyn nodded, still teary eyed. "I'm married."

"And you're so *happy*."

Morgyn leaned closer and said, "Happier than I ever imagined."

"What changed?" Brindle asked.

Morgyn glanced at Graham and said, "*Everything*." Every moment they shared filled her with joy. She couldn't imagine a life without him. "I've been his from the day we met, and I wanted the world to know it." She looked thoughtfully at her sister and said, "Are you happy, Brin?"

"Yes." Her brows knitted, and she said, "I guess this summer was good for both us."

"*Married*," Sable said. "I can't freaking believe it. How on earth did you manage that, Miracle Man?"

Graham looked at Morgyn the way he had the night he'd

told her that one day he hoped to marry her. *Not because we need the paper to make it real, but because one day I want to have a family of our own—creative and risk-assessing little boys and girls—and I worry it might be hard on the children to have to explain to their friends why their parents weren't married.*

"I didn't," Graham said. "She got me to marry her."

All eyes turned to Morgyn, but she was too choked up with emotion to speak, recalling the moment she'd known she wanted to marry him. How could she ever forget? He'd been holding Sadie in one arm while talking with Javier, a tall, skinny boy who wanted to be an artist when he grew up, and she'd been hit with an image of Graham as a father to their children. It hit so hard and so real, she felt it in her bones. *Know it. Trust it. Accept it.*

"Were you drunk?" Sable asked.

"Yes," Morgyn said, earning a confused look from Graham. "Drunk on *love.*"

As Graham pulled her into a kiss, Brindle shrugged off her coat. "All this hugging and mushy talk is making me hot."

Amber gasped. "That's a great costume! Where did you find such a tiny baby bump?"

Morgyn spun around and felt her eyes widen. Brindle wore leggings and a tunic, which clung to her normally flat, now slightly rounded belly. She quickly tried to school her expression.

"Please tell me that's too many French pastries," Grace said.

"Are you…?" Pepper reached over and touched Brindle's belly.

Brindle turned away. "Stop!"

"Brindle," Morgyn whispered, too shocked to say anything more. *No wonder you were having a hard time in Paris.*

"Honey," their mother said, wide-eyed. "Are you...?"

Brindle's eyes teared up as she nodded. Their mother opened her arms and pulled her into them, whispering something Morgyn couldn't hear.

"Holy crap, Brindle," Axsel said.

"Whose French ass do I need to kick?" Sable crossed her arms, staring at Brindle.

Trace appeared beside Sable and draped an arm over her shoulder. "I'm in for some French ass kicking!" His smiling eyes met Brindle's. "Mustang, you're back!" He stepped forward, arms open. His gaze dropped to her belly, and he stopped cold.

Brindle put her hand on her stomach and took a step backward, biting her lower lip. "I can't do this right now," she said shakily. "I'm exhausted. I'm going home. We can talk about this tomorrow." She pushed past Morgyn and hurried away with Trace on her heels.

"I'm going after her," Morgyn said.

Her mother grabbed her arm and said, "Let her be."

"Like hell we will," Sable said, heading in Brindle's direction.

"Mom, she needs me," Morgyn pleaded.

Their father stepped in front of Sable and shook his head. "I know you all want to be there for her, but she needs space. And from the look on Trace's face, she isn't going to get it anytime soon. I'm sure she'll be at breakfast tomorrow, and we can talk with her then."

Morgyn grabbed Graham's hand, and he squeezed it.

"Aren't you mad, Dad?" Pepper asked. "Your daughter just came home from Paris *pregnant*."

Their parents exchanged a glance that spoke of years of experience navigating their children's surprises and challenges.

"Mad? Why, because my daughter has hormones? Or because she might have fallen in love or made a mistake or a hundred other possibilities, some of which I'd rather not think about just yet? Brindle doesn't need a father who's angry because she got pregnant," he said evenly. "She needs a family who realizes that not all pregnancies are planned and who will be there for her no matter what."

"She obviously made her decision to keep this baby," their mother said. "Now it's up to us to welcome it into our family and to make sure Brindle knows how much we love her regardless of whatever is going through y'all's minds right now. You think she's full of piss and vinegar, but she's *human*, like the rest of us, and beneath that tough exterior is a sensitive, loving girl. And right now I'd bet my bottom dollar she's scared."

"I'm still going to kick some French ass." Sable strode away.

Axsel hugged Morgyn and said, "I'm not blowing you off. I'm glad you're here and want to hear all about your elopement, but I think I'd better follow Sable so she doesn't kill anyone wearing a beret."

BRINDLE'S PREGNANCY AND Graham and Morgyn's nuptials were the topics of conversation for the rest of the evening. By the time Graham and Morgyn headed home, Morgyn had snuck in a few texts to Brindle, who promised to talk with her tomorrow.

"Feel better knowing she'll talk to you?" Graham asked as he pulled out of the parking lot.

"Much. But you know what? Now that the shock has worn off, I think my dad is right. Brin needs us to support her decision." She sighed and leaned her head back against the headrest, closing her eyes. "Tonight was a night of surprises, wasn't it?"

"Sure was, sunshine."

Morgyn opened her eyes as they came to the light at the intersection by the theater. "You're going the wrong way. Have you already forgotten how to get home?"

He grinned as he drove through the light and pulled over on the side of the road. Morgyn turned to look out the window and gasped. "What…?"

She fumbled with the door and ran out of the truck and down the hill.

Graham followed her, laughing as she stood before the caboose, which had been moved to the property beside the theater. It was freshly painted red with black railings. LIFE REIMAGINED was written on the side above the windows in bright yellow, with colorful flowers and stars around it. LOVINGLY ENHANCED TREASURES was written in white below the windows.

He put his arm around Morgyn and said, "Surprise, sunshine. This is your wedding present."

"You *bought* it?" Tears streamed down her cheeks.

He unlocked the door, and as he followed her inside he said, "*We* bought it. We're married. What's mine is yours."

"Oh my gosh. How did you get it here?"

"I couldn't trust your sisters not to spill the beans, so I had Reed and Beckett give me a hand." He'd made a deal with Reed to lease the property for the next ten years. Reed refused to take his money because they were family now, so Graham had made a hefty donation to the community theater project Grace was setting up.

"Graham," Morgyn said through tears as she admired the newly renovated interior. "I don't know what to say. This is so unexpected and unbelievably *perfect*."

"Even though your consignment deals are doing well, I knew you still wished you had a space of your own. What better place than one that means so much to you? To *us*. I figured you could run it when we're in town, making it extra special."

"Like a grand opening between our travels?"

"Exactly."

She was shivering with excitement. "Can you feel it? How *right* this is?" she asked as she swiped at her tears. She threw her arms around him and said, "I love you so much. Thank you." She pressed her lips to his in a sweet kiss, and then she said, "I'm not great with words, but I'll show you how thankful I am when we get home."

He laced his left hand with hers and lifted it so the moonlight streaming through the window reflected off their newly cemented union and the charm bracelet he'd given her that she'd never taken off and said, "I'm already there, sunshine. You are my home."

New to the Love in Bloom series?

I hope you have enjoyed getting to know the Bradens and Montgomerys. If this is your first Love in Bloom book, you have many more love stories featuring loyal, sassy, and sexy heroes and heroines waiting for you. The Bradens & Montgomerys (Pleasant Hill – Oak Falls) is just one of the series in the Love in Bloom big-family romance collection. Each Love in Bloom book is written to be enjoyed as a stand-alone novel or as part of the larger series. There are no cliffhangers and no unresolved issues. Characters from each series make appearances in future books, so you never miss an engagement, wedding, or birth. Visit my website for more information on Love in Bloom titles.

www.MelissaFoster.com

Ready for more Bradens & Montgomerys?

Fall in love with Brindle Montgomery and Trace Jericho in
Wild, Crazy Hearts

Brindle Montgomery and Trace Jericho have been close friends forever and on-again off-again lovers for years. As rebellious as they are stubborn, they're both perfectly happy with their no-strings-attached hookups. But when Brindle returns from a trip to Paris with a baby bump, it sends Trace's wild, crazy heart into a frenzy—and Brindle is left wondering if she's made the biggest mistake of her life.

Buy WILD, CRAZY HEARTS

Ready for a great beach read?

Fall in love at Bayside, where sandy beaches, good friends, and true love come together in the sweet small towns of Cape Cod.

Hold on to your hat for Violet's wildly hot love story! Lizza is up to her old tricks again, and Violet is in for the surprise of a lifetime!

Buy **BAYSIDE ESCAPE**

Have you met the Bradens?

Fall in love all over again with Treat Braden and Max Armstrong in their *new* beginning.

Treat and Max have a very special place in my heart. Their love story is the beginning of my beloved Braden series, and it introduces you to some of my favorite characters and to a family that has become so real to me, they're always by my side.

One of the greatest things about being a writer is the ability to reimagine worlds and create new stories. For the past several years, I have had the nagging feeling that there was more to Treat and Max's story than I had originally thought. I wanted to give two of my favorite characters a more mature story without losing the essence of who they are. **This is Treat and Max's story, *reimagined*, and I hope you adore it as much as I do.**

Buy **LOVERS AT HEART, REIMAGINED**

More Books By Melissa Foster

Love in Bloom Romance Collection

Love in Bloom books may be read as stand alones. For more enjoyment, read them in series order. Characters from each series carry forward to the next.

SNOW SISTERS

Sisters in Love
Sisters in Bloom
Sisters in White

THE BRADENS (Weston, CO)

Lovers at Heart, Reimagined
Destined for Love
Friendship on Fire
Sea of Love
Bursting with Love
Hearts at Play

THE BRADENS (Trusty, CO)

Taken by Love
Fated for Love
Romancing My Love
Flirting with Love
Dreaming of Love
Crashing into Love

THE BRADENS (Peaceful Harbor, MD)

Healed by Love
Surrender My Love
River of Love
Crushing on Love
Whisper of Love
Thrill of Love

THE BRADENS & MONTGOMERYS (Pleasant Hill – Oak Falls)

Embracing Her Heart
Anything for Love
Trails of Love
Wild, Crazy Hearts

BRADEN WORLD NOVELLAS

Daring Her Love
Promise My Love
Our New Love
Story of Love
Love at Last

THE REMINGTONS

Game of Love
Stroke of Love
Flames of Love
Slope of Love
Read, Write, Love
Touched by Love

SEASIDE SUMMERS

Seaside Dreams
Seaside Hearts
Seaside Sunsets
Seaside Secrets
Seaside Nights
Seaside Embrace
Seaside Lovers
Seaside Whispers

BAYSIDE SUMMERS

Bayside Desires
Bayside Passions
Bayside Heat
Bayside Escape

THE RYDERS

Seized by Love
Claimed by Love
Chased by Love
Rescued by Love
Swept Into Love

SEXY STAND-ALONE ROMANCE NOVELS

Tru Blue (Set in Peaceful Harbor)
Truly, Madly, Whiskey
Driving Whiskey Wild
Wicked Whiskey Love
Mad About Moon

BILLIONAIRES AFTER DARK

WILD BOYS

Logan
Heath
Jackson
Cooper

BAD BOYS

Mick
Dylan
Carson
Brett

HARBORSIDE NIGHTS

Includes characters from the Love in Bloom series
Catching Cassidy
Discovering Delilah
Tempting Tristan

Standalone Books by Melissa

Chasing Amanda (mystery/suspense)
Come Back to Me (mystery/suspense)
Have No Shame (historical fiction/romance)
Love, Lies & Mystery (3-book bundle)
Megan's Way (literary fiction)
Traces of Kara (psychological thriller)
Where Petals Fall (suspense)

Acknowledgments

I hope you enjoyed Graham and Morgyn's story and are looking forward to reading about the rest of their siblings. If you haven't yet joined my fan club on Facebook, please do. We have a great time chatting about our hunky heroes and sassy heroines. You never know when you'll inspire a story or a character and end up in one of my books, as several fan club members have already discovered.
www.Facebook.com/groups/MelissaFosterFans

Remember to like and follow my Facebook fan page to stay abreast of what's going on in our fictional boyfriends' worlds.
www.Facebook.com/MelissaFosterAuthor

Sign up for my newsletter to keep up to date with new releases and special promotions and events and to receive an exclusive short story featuring Jack Remington and Savannah Braden.
www.MelissaFoster.com/Newsletter

And don't forget to download your free reader goodies! For free family trees, publication schedules, series checklists, and more, please visit the special Reader Goodies page that I've set up for you!
www.MelissaFoster.com/Reader-Goodies

As always, loads of gratitude to my amazing team of editors and proofreaders: Kristen Weber, Penina Lopez, Elaini Caruso, Juliette Hill, Marlene Engel, Lynn Mullan, and Justinn Harrison. And, of course, I am forever grateful to my husband, Les, and the rest of my family, who allow me to talk about my fictional worlds as if we live in them.

Meet Melissa

www.MelissaFoster.com

Melissa Foster is a *New York Times* and *USA Today* bestselling and award-winning author. Her books have been recommended by *USA Today's* book blog, *Hagerstown* magazine, *The Patriot*, and several other print venues. Melissa has painted and donated several murals to the Hospital for Sick Children in Washington, DC.

Visit Melissa on her website or chat with her on social media. Melissa enjoys discussing her books with book clubs and reader groups and welcomes an invitation to your event. Melissa's books are available through most online retailers in paperback, digital, and audio formats.